MARRIED TO A
PHILLY KING

YONA

Marie,
thank you!
Hope you
enjoy!

Beyond our
"Beyond"
Pearson

Mailing List

To stay up to date on new releases, plus get information on contests, sneak peeks, and more,

Go To The Website Below...

www.colehartsignature.com

TEXT TO JOIN

To stay up to date on new releases, plus get exclusive information on contests, sneak peeks, and more...

Text ColeHartSig to (855)231-5230

CHAPTER 1

 ailah

BOOM! BOOM! BOOM!

The loud thunderous sounds of someone banging woke me. Startled I sat up in a panic, and the clashing sounds of windows breaking caused me to jump out of bed. Not sure if we were being invaded by robbers or the damn police y eyes searched the darkness only to land on Kyrie, hurrying into his basketball shorts and Tee. He had the same look of panic on his face as I had when we both realized it was the fuckin' cops.

"Listen to me, baby, okay. Whatever happens at this point is just going to happen. I don't want you going down with me, so just tell them that I held you here against your will, and you were too afraid to leave. Don't argue or show any emotions when they storm in here okay, just do what the officers tell you, baby. Now hurry and get dress and remember that I love you so much baby, and whatever time they give me won't change that shit," he whispered and planted a soft kiss on my lips. I knew that would be our last kiss, but I hurried into my shorts and tank, right before they kicked in our bedroom door.

"Philadelphia Police!" an officer yelled before flashing a bright ass light into my face.

"Get the fuck down!" another ordered with his gun drawn. It was only two of us, so I wonder why so many cops piled in with their weapons drawn on us like we were a damn army.

My heart was beating so damn fast, I thought I would go into cardiac arrest, but I did as they ordered and got my ass on the floor with my hands over my head. I wasn't at all surprised what was going down, because I knew that dealing with a street hustler trying to make a name for himself could lead to a raid or even fucking jail time, but I just had no clue that it would happen so soon. I was on my knees trembling as I witness these motherfuckers slam Kyrie to the ground, and one officer placed his knee in his back t that moment it became too much for me to watch since my man wasn't resisting.

"You thought we wouldn't catch your black ass, didn't you?" One officer smirked as he eyed Kyrie like he wanted to kick in his face.

"Where are the drugs son, we know you got shit, so do try play us," he said with a deep voice of authority, but Kyrie didn't say shit.

must have angered him, so he slapped the cuffs on his wrist and snatched him up by the arms then shoved him against the wall. Then he turned to me, but when he didn't get a word from my lips, he slammed Kyrie back to the floor and proceed to fuck him up, while he yelled out fake ass terms that made it seem as if Kyrie was resisting.

Even though Kyrie told me to pretend that I knew nothing or wasn't in on shit, the sight of them doing that shit to him made me break my silence. "Please, stop it, he is already handcuffed. You're going to hurt him; he's not resisting," I cried, and a second after those words an officer walked in with his stash of weed.

It was a few pounds, not a lot, but enough to sum up, it was for the intent to distribute, and not smoke. My insides quickened when I saw what they found, and my eyes landed on Kyrie, but he smirked. I knew that look meant that he was relieved that was all they found. He had crack and other shit that would get him put away for a long time, but they hadn't discovered it.

I had a feeling our one-bedroom place was all fucked-up. Still, I was relieved that the cops only found the weed. "Look at what we have here, nigga," the officer chuckled. "This will at least get your black ass five years," he said, putting the plastic-wrapped pound close to his nose. It was like he inhaled my man's arrest, and I just wanted them to leave.

"And yo' lil ride or die chick," he said, moving over closer to me. "She is going down with your ass," he said and rubbed a hand down the side of my face.

"She ain't got shit to do with this man, she doesn't shit about shit. All of that shit is mine, so can we go now. Y'all came for me and my shit, so let's get this arrest over with," he blasted.

When the officer didn't cuff me, I knew they didn't want shit with me, and when I thought about my plans to say that I was being held against my will, that shit would have worked. I had tons of clothes and personal items in our place.

After they snatched Kyrie up from the floor and put their findings in a black duffle bag. Before they walked out the door with my heart, the officer knocked over a photo of me and Kyrie that sat on our dresser. I guess that was for dramatics, and I only imagine what the rest of our place resemble after they came through wrecking shop.

Even after I heard the door slam shut, I couldn't move. I fell over and stayed in that same spot on the floor hours as I cried my eyes out and let my mind race trying to figure out any possible solution that I could to keep Kyrie out of prison, but not one damn solution came to my mind. The only thing I could do is hold him down while he was away and lift up his spirits as much as I could, considering. I loved that man, and no way I wasn't going to wait for him to return to me after whatever time he had to serve.

That was ten long years ago and a hard lesson to learn. After that, we knew not to keep anything illegal where we laid our heads. Kyrie got a plea and only ended up serving a little over a year for the weed, and I was so grateful for that. While he was away, I managed to move what was left of his product, and it earned us a nice little stash because I still worked to cover up the fact that I was selling. Yes, I lived off the few ends I made working hard as fuck, usually pulling double shifts. I put away the revenue generated from the sale of the drugs, all except for the money I used to put on his books every week.

By the time Kyrie was home, we had a two-bedroom place, and although I thought he'd chill for a minute and stay the fuck out of trouble, he went right back to handling street business, causing his self to catch another fucking case and there I was holding it all down again. After that time served, he got his shit together and made smarter moves that lead us to where we are now, rolling in the dough. Kyrie was banking so much money, that we had any and whatever we wanted and all of what we needed. I remembered I'd use to pray for that day to come, but now that it was here, I wished it wasn't. I was twenty-eight years old and shook my head at some of the evil deeds I had done, but that came along with the territory of being married to the King of Philly. Yes, my husband had become a big man in the biz, and although I knew deep down inside that he loved me, he sometimes had a fucked-up way of showing it.

I was carrying our very first kid, and at seven months, when I needed Kyrie the most, somehow, the baby and I started to be on the bottom of his list of things to do. Like today, we were supposed to go shopping together for the baby, and somehow, he had found a way to get out of it. I was so pissed at his sister's words when she came through the door to inform me that she was going with me and not Kyrie, I wanted to scream, but that shit wouldn't do any good.

"Zailah, I'm telling you, we still gon' have fun," my sister-in-law Maliyah said, smiling brightly, interrupting my thoughts. She always had a way of making me smile no matter what mood I was in. She was two years younger than me, and from the first day I met her at Kyrie's place, we had an instant bond. Quickly we were like sisters, and since Kyrie was always so damn strict on the girl, I would cover for her to go to parties and dates just so the poor child could have some damn fun. Shit, she was my baby sis-in-law, so I always had her back, just like she always had mine.

"No, it won't be fun, sitting my big ass in the car for close to three hours just to get to the city. New York traffic is horrific, and to do all that just for baby shopping won't be fun."

"It will girl, for one you got me, your lil sis-in-law to keep you company and this long ass trip does not have to be all about the baby. I mean, when this kid pops out, you will not have the baby weight forever, or at least we can hope," she teased, and I swatted her arm with a playful tap. "I'm just playing, girl, but on a serious note, if you keep that ass and them new big ass titties, that would be a positive, however that wide ass nose of yours, must shrink back to normal," she teased more as she laughed too hard at her own jokes.

"Okay, go ahead and just crack all the jokes on you want on me," I said to her. I wanted to just be cool and not let Kyrie upset me, but I needed to know what was the real deal for him not showing up for something so important to me, so I asked, "Why did Kyrie send you to go with me and be honest with me. What is he up to, what does he got going on now that's more important than me and this baby?"

She paused and shook her head. "Wait, now you know I stay out of y'all business, so whatever it is sis, I have no clue or idea," she said with a shrug of her shoulders.

I knew she was looking me dead in my face and lying, but I had to respect her loyalty to her brother. Plus, it had to be bad, for her to not tell me. She had to know that it would devastate me or break my heart, especially since I was pregnant, so I didn't push, and my damn gut was telling me that I didn't even want to know. I just let it go and then went for my phone and ignored the alerts I had from social media. I had too much on my mind to even deal with that, so I decided to check that shit later. "Fine, I will let it go, for now," I said.

"Good, now come on sis, smile, and let's go shopping for you and the baby. I've been dying to go to that baby store on Hudson street, and now that I am getting a new niece or nephew, I have an excuse to go."

"You didn't have to have to wait for the new baby to go, I mean you are already an auntie Maliyah."

"Well, I don't have the luxury of being close to their moms, like I am with you, so this is different. I mean, I love them, but this new bundle has me so damn excited, and I cannot wait until the gender reveal, and if for some damn reason you told that damn Tierra before telling me, I am going to be pissed."

I laughed as I got up and wobbled over to get my purse and made sure I grabbed my smoothie from the table. "No worries, Maliyah, okay. I know you have made it very clear that you are doing the shower, and I'll let you have that, even though Tierra and I have been best friends longer, but you are family, so this one is on you," I assured her and made my way to the door. Maliyah was so damn jealous and didn't like anybody I called friend other than her. In her mind, only our friendship existed, and even though that madness drove me insane and got on my damn nerves, I loved her ass to death and cherished our friendship the most.

"It better be," she joked. I shook my head at her as I locked the door.

"You are such a brat," I joked back with her as we made our way to her car. We rode in silence for a few moments, and then she broke the silence.

"I never told you, but when you first came over, I really didn't like you much," she revealed.

I took a sip of my smoothie and then looked at her. "Is that right?"

"Yes, at first, because you were like the first girl that Kyrie really liked, and I thought you'd take him away from me."

"Well, I am glad I proved your spoiled ass wrong."

"You did and turned out to be cool as hell. When y'all got your place, and you used to cover for me to go out with my friends and how you'd shop for me, let me know that my brother had chosen the right one," she beamed.

I nodded and sipped more of my drink. I turned to look out the window, and my mind began to wonder what Kyrie was up to and why so many of my texts and phone calls were going unanswered. I looked at my screen for the hundredth time only to see there was still nothing from him. I hated that money seemed to be all that mattered to him, and me and our baby took a back seat to whatever the fuck he had going on. I hated that I cared so damn much. Family meant so much to me, and all I wanted was for us to stay together and be as happy as we were before the money, the big house, and material shit that I could care less about. We had enough money at that point that our kids, kids would be okay, but he was addicted to that life, and I was starting to feel that, that would be the end of us. I sighed at that thought and pulled out my phone again.

My phone was dinging with so many damn alerts that day, and I had to see just what all the alerts were for. When I opened my phone and went to the notifications, my heart dropped into the pit of my stomach, and my smoothie slipped out of my trembling hand and went everywhere.

"What's wrong, sis," Maliyah bellowed when she saw the mess.

"Get off and turn around. Take me home," I cried. My eyes immediately welled with tears.

"No, tell me what's going on?" she questioned, still moving forward.

At that point, I had trouble controlling my breathing, and the tears streamed down my cheeks. How could he do this to me, to us, I questioned myself as I tried to focus on the pictures through the fog of my tears.

"No, Zailah, you are fucking scaring me. What in the hell is going on?" she demanded.

"This," I said shoving my phone in her direction. I knew she was driving, but she had to see her damn brother, smiling in the photo with another woman, with his hands resting on her baby bump. "Did you know about this?" I roared at her. "Did you know your brother had another bitch pregnant, while I am carrying his kid!" I continued to yell at her.

She handed me my phone and kept her eyes locked on the road with no words. Her silence said everything, and I knew at that moment that this was why he had her taking me to a store so far away.

I had to remind myself that I was indeed with child and could not go out and put my hands on anyone, nor did I want to be in jail for shooting up the entire baby shower. The picture that hurt me the most was that he even had some of his family there like they were this one big happy family.

But before I go any further into this, let me take y'all back. Show y'all how all this shit got started and how being Married to the KING OF PHILLY, might not be all that everyone thought it was. I have been through hell and back, so maybe it's best to show y'all why this shit hurt so much.

CHAPTER 2

 **ailah**

THE BEGINNING...

"Girl, I'm telling you this party is going to be fucking crazy, real rap." Tierra popped her gum.

She was waving her arms in the air and clapping like this was going to be her best party yet. It had me excited just by how she was acting.

"Like every year? I'm not even sure who I'm bringing this year. I mess around and have to be in pink again because ain't nobody trying to be with my ass. My bitch about to be legal as hell now though, and that's something I can't wait for." I danced in my seat.

Tierra was my best friend, and every year for her birthday she threw a big Valentine's Day party. If you were a single female you wore black, with pink and males wore black with red. If you had somebody, you wore white and whichever color y'all picked between red and pink. She always overdid it, and now that she was turning twenty-one, I knew she was going to go all out. Grabbing my bag, I got up off her couch so that I could go home to do my homework. I had to complete my assignment before class, and I was determined to finish before the morning.

Being a sophomore in college was nothing like I expected it to be. Of course I enjoyed the late nights of partying and just being able to do what I wanted. However, those tests and homework assignments kicked my ass on the daily.

"Girl, you know that nigga he be with Maurice and them from up North? I know he from South West, but he never be around his way. He brown skinned, fine as hell. He real laid back. I think he was in one of your classes." Tierra questioned, snapping me from my thoughts.

"You know I don't pay none of them boys no mind. They all act like they ain't got no sense, plus they don't want nothing more than to be a bunch of corner boys for the rest of they life." I shrugged, heading to the door.

"Well, Ima show you him. I'm trying to get him to be my date for the party. He one of them but he real different I can tell. He a corner boy now, but he definitely ain't trying to be one forever. You can just tell by how he is. I wish I knew his fucking name." She smiled.

I waved her off before walking out. It was cold as hell tonight. I pulled on my coat as if holding onto it would make me any warmer. My body shivered the entire time my feet padded against the light snow as I quickly made it to my car. Starting my car, I sat inside of it until it warmed up. The same boys Tierra was just talking about were standing on the corner, some in hoodies and some in puffer coats, smoking and laughing.

"Aye, get the fuck on. You out here yelling and shit making my block hot." Maurice snapped on a guy that was walking by.

The guy was loud as hell and yelling on the phone, causing a lot of people to look his way. Yet, I didn't see how he figured he was going to gain the attention of the police. I looked around, and there were none in sight. This was one of the many reasons I stayed away from corner boys; they acted as if they had to be in control of everything. Going against my better judgment to leave, I stayed and watched how it would unfold. I was hoping the guy on the phone beat Maurice's ass.

Maurice was probably the main reason I didn't like boys who worked on the corner. He came from a loving home, with a family who worked their asses off and spoiled him. However, he acted as if he'd struggled his whole life and had to put in the work to become the person he was. He also always started problems for no reason. Maurice would never fight for himself. Most times; he got his squad to do it, and to me, that was corny.

"Look man, I'm talking to my girl, I ain't trying to fuck your shit up." The guy apologized.

"Go the fuck head dawg, just chill with all that yelling shit. You in the way, for no reason." One of the other boys said.

"Look, I spoke my peace. I ain't one of these little ass boys y'all be fucking without here. I'm not gone be disrespected." The guy spoke.

Maurice and his crew went to surround the guy. I noticed one was sitting back, not saying anything at all. He was just watching as intently as I was. He had his hands in his pockets with his hood over his head. I could see the fire on the blunt every time he took a pull from it. Just as they started to jump the guy, he stopped them.

"Y'all talking about making the block hot. What y'all doing right now." He snapped.

The way his voice caused them all to stop had me wanting to know who he was and how much power he really had. No, it didn't send chills through my body, but it did get me excited.

"Look, shit ain't even that deep fam, let him be great, he ain't bothering nobody. This some nut shit, if somebody wants to fight hand him a fair one. Y'all know I don't even condone that jumping shit. Fuck is the point." He growled.

"Ky, you always on that civilized shit. How you expect to keep ya respect out here." Maurice yelled.

"You think jumping niggas gone get you respect? That ain't gone do shit but bring some unwanted attention to the block. I ain't letting nothing stop my money. Do that shit on your own time, bro." Who I now know was Ky replied, walking back to his spot on the wall.

Putting my car in drive, I pulled off. For some reason, that action alone had me wondering who he really was, and where he had been all my life. He might have just made my outlook on all boys who worked on the corner a little different. Most people would have just watched. Yet he did the complete opposite. I headed home with the mystery guy on my mind. Shit, I wanted to know him, and see if his face matched his voice. And if it did, I knew his ass was beautiful.

Pulling up to my house, I sighed. Here was when reality hit me. Slowly climbing out of my car, I walked across the driveway and up the steps. Opening the door, I heard my mother on the phone fussing. Instead of stopping to say hello, I went up to my room. I knew she was either cursing my daddy out for choosing his job over her or one of the many women he slept with, while he was gone for work.

Sometimes I wondered how my mom put up with him always being gone due to him driving trucks all around the country. What made it worse was he seemed to start a family in each state he stopped at. Over time, his actions caused a small drift in our family and left me being the shoulder my mother needed to cry on. So while I was once daddy's little girl, it all came to an end the moment I figured my daddy wasn't so innocent.

"Zailah" My mom knocked on my door.

"Yes, Ma?" I answered.

She opened the door and peeked her head in. I looked over at her and could tell how stressed she was just by the look on her face. Back in the day, that look would have me running over to her and hugging her. It used to hurt me, to see her like that. Hell, I used to want to pick up the phone and give my daddy, and his mistress's a piece of my mind. Now it made me sick, had me looking at my mom like that's what she wanted, so there was no point in feeling bad.

"Don't forget you have to turn in that paper for your class. I also prepared dinner if you are hungry, your father told me to tell you he loved you and sent you something." She sighed.

"Cool, thank you, mom. I appreciate everything you are doing." I tried to reassure her.

One thing about my mom, she tried very hard not to wear her feelings on her sleeve. I knew her just like she knew me, so I could almost sense how she was feeling. In my mind, everyone needed to hear thank you and that they were appreciated every once in a while. So I made it a daily habit to make her feel appreciated.

"I love you so much Zailah." She replied, backing up out of my room.

Once she closed my door, I grabbed my phone and listened to the speech my professor gave today. Each class, I would record his lectures, so when it was time for homework, I would have everything I needed from him with my books. I outlined everything I would need for this week's assignment. At the age of eighteen, I was a freshman in college and wasn't ready to face the world. I partied like the average teenager, yet I focused on school a whole lot more. I even had a little job working at Foot-locker. I went down into the kitchen and made me a plate of spaghetti. Sitting at the counter alone, I watched my mother sip on a glass of wine. She had the entire bottle in front of her, and she stared at the blank television screen.

"Ma, everything gone be good. You been handling things so

far. Don't let it stress you out, all you need is right here well besides your knucklehead son." I told her.

She didn't respond to me; instead she lifted her drink in the air as if she was toasting to what I had said. Hearing the front door close, I looked over to see my brother Bentley coming in the house. His eyes were low as hell. Letting me know he was out getting high.

"What's good sis? Ma straight, or ya pops got her in one of them moods again? I don't know why she won't let me beat his ass one good time." He snarled.

Bentley was sixteen, yet he swore he was thirty. He even acted like it. He called himself the man of the house and often challenged our father. Bentley was one of those uncontrollable kids, yet his heart was so kind.

"He is still your father Bent and always will be. That's why regardless of what he and I go through, it doesn't change the fact that he always have and will be a great father to you both. There's nothing any of us have ever asked that man for that he didn't provide us with." She took up for him like always.

"Yeah, it is mom. We asked him for loyalty, the thing that means the most to us. And he couldn't deliver it. Yeah, material-wise he has done his part, but it ain't always the things money could buy that makes a family. Ain't that what you always told us mom? So why that nigga get a pass?" Bentley snapped.

"Don't make this harder on her Bent. If you hurting about this, imagine what she feels." I reasoned with him.

He looked at me with a look that said you know I'm right, and had he asked, I would have agreed with him. However, this was not about us, and even if it were I would never try and make my mother feel any worse than she did. It wasn't her fault that she loved that man, hell she had married him and bore his kids. Nobody could tell a person in love when they had enough; only she could be the judge of that.

"Man, I'm bout to go smoke, this shit is almost self-destructing. Got my dukes all stressed the fuck out for nothing." Bentley walked to his room without uttering another word.

"You know he may be right. Zailah, just don't ever let a man dog you until you don't even have enough strength to love yourself. Never love a man to the point you drag yourself through depression. As much as I tell myself it's over, I can't seem to let go. It's been too many years with that man, hell he's all I know. That man plays a major role in my family. Why the hell would I give that up now." My mother stressed.

Nodding my head, I finished my food then went back to my room. I thought about calling it a night but decided to go sit outside on the porch. Even though it was cold, that did nothing to stop people from being out especially the local drug dealers. I watched as people came and went and even spoke to a few neighbors.

My mind slowly drifted off to my father, he was an outstanding father. Yet, he was a horrible husband. While he should have taught me how a man should treat his wife, he did the opposite. His job had him on the road most days, so he was never really home, besides the holidays. Even those days had to be split in half sometimes due to him having hidden families or so he thought. Everyone knew he had a wife, yet that didn't stop them from wanting to be with him. I was silently praying that God would allow me to have a man that loved me and only me.

CHAPTER 3

*K*yrie

"Come on, Maliyah. My ass ain't trying to be in nobody sneaker store all day. Grab the shoes you want and head back over with mommy. I love you but I got shit to do, and money waits for no man." I told my little sister.

I just had to run into her overly spoiled ass while her and my mom were having their weekly girl's day at the mall. Since it was winter, she felt it was only right she had a pair of Timberlands and who was I to deny her of a pair. I didn't have all the money in the world, nor did I have as much as I wanted. However, I did have enough to splurge a bit, and if getting my sister some boots would put a smile on her face, I was willing to buy them.

"How may I help you?" This little fine ass girl asked.

I was stuck looking at her, I never saw someone so small look so good. If it wasn't for the uniform, I wouldn't even think her ass could work here. Her baby face and deep dimples did something to my heart. I wanted to pull her in for a kiss. However I just stood there looking at her.

"You deaf or something?" She questioned with a frown on

her face.

"Nah, I ain't deaf I heard you." I stuttered over my words.

Shit her ass had me nervous for no reason. I looked over at Jermaine because he had to see what I saw. His ass was over in the corner laughing at me. If I had to explain the definition of beautiful, I would have to just show a picture of her. She had me willing to do things I never done before just so I could call her mines.

"Soooo, are you getting anything or we just gone stand here in a staring contest." She rubbed her ponytail.

"My bad, look, my sister wanted these in a size four." I handed her the boots.

Maliyah ass had snuck off to look for some other shoes, that she wasn't going to get unless she asked her mother. Looking over at the wall, I decided to grab me a pair of shoes too since this Valentine's Day party was coming up, and I wanted to go looking fresh.

"Here are the boots, Let me guess you want these too?" She laughed.

"The shoes ain't the only thing I want." I flirted with her.

I knew I had caught her off guard because she smiled really hard, grabbed the shoes, and turned walking away with the quickness. She came back with the shoe and went to the register. If young had me feeling this nervous, I had to have her. As soon as I was about to ask for her number, my sister came over with two more pairs of shoes and a smile. The girl whose name tag read Zailah, asked if she should get them as well, and I nodded.

"Okay, your total is 432.99." She stated, not looking up.

I pulled my card out of my wallet and paid. I caught her looking me over, and I shot her a wink. The courage I had to ask her for her number was gone, and I was back to feeling like a damn school boy with a crush on the prettiest girl in the entire school.

I wasn't even thinking about the fact that I had dipped into my savings just too impress her like I had the money. I really only had two hundred and fifty dollars in cash that I was supposed to be spending today. Now I would have to put in a little extra work to put that shit back.

"Come on, Ky. Take me to get those earrings you promised." My sister pulled me away.

Her little ass wasn't even supposed to be with me, and now she was blocking. I was gone put my baby sister on a "no spending my money" punishment. As we walk through the mall, I looked at some of the families that were walking hand in hand with each other smiling.

"Taking care of your sister is something you have to always do. There should never be a second thought about it. If ever something should happen to me, it's you that's gone have to cover for me and be the man that needs to raise her." My pop's voice replayed in my head.

I guess he knew that something was going to happen to him because that same night, he was killed in a shootout. That's where my stepfather came in at, he came around weeks after my pops died and that just gave me more reason to believe that my suspicions about my moms and pops relationship was right. I knew for a long time that it had to be over, but they held onto it for the sake of their kids.

My pops wasn't a bad dude either, he was like the typical man, he just couldn't be faithful. My mom must have had enough of his ass because I remember when he use to stay nights away, she would have my step pop over talking about he was fixing shit. I can't lie and say Quincy was bad either, he reminded me of that Melvin dude off of the movie *Baby Boy*. Of course I didn't take a liking to him when he first moved in with us, I felt like he thought he was the king in my father's castle. Shit like that ain't sit well with me, my father had worked day in and out to get that house for my mother, and for her to just move the next man in it right after he died was the ultimate disrespect to me.

Of course, she hit me with the "This is my house and my rules," shit, and if I didn't like it, I could bounce. Me being me, I took that as my opportunity to stay out later at night working just so I could get out of her house. My sister was my heart, and I didn't think I could love a female outside of her. I mean, unless one day God blessed me with a daughter. However, I'm sure God knew I wasn't ready for no kid.

"Man, I know your ass ain't already thinking about that broad from the damn shoe store like that, if she got your head gone now, you don't need her ass. You wouldn't be able to function right if y'all got together." Jermaine laughed.

'Fuck naw, I mean don't get me wrong she was looking good as shit. She wasn't that fine. I was just thinking about life, that's all. I'm really trying to make it out, well you know get me a crib out the hood, but I'm gone always run these streets, and in the future, my name gone ring bells. I'm gone be the man to see." I boasted.

I wasn't sure where I knew ole girl from, but I knew her face was familiar to me. I had seen her around more than once, just couldn't put a name to her face. Baby girl had it going on, and if I had a girlfriend, she would look something like her. She was short, with just the right amount of curves. Her lips looked real kissable, and her ass was something I could see myself holding on to and never wanting to let go. Somehow my mind just kept drifting back to thoughts of her.

"You damn right, and I'm gonna be right there. These streets are ours, we just got to put the work in to take over, plus ya god dad gone hand you the key once you get right with his old ass." Maine jokes.

"We can discuss that later, right now I just need to know if you got them pills like I asked. I need to head back to school so I can give Asian his prescription. I got to keep him happy, that nigga pop more pills then a little bit, he's my number one customer right now. Since I ain't been home like that I'm gone need your ass to bring them up there or at least meet me half-way. I'm trying to see if niggas up here on that juice or not. Cause if so, we gone put this college on lock." I rubbed my hands together.

I knew in due time if we kept moving the way we were moving we would be in a position to be great for the rest of our lives. The only thing I couldn't get from my god pop was the pill connect, and that's cause he didn't know exactly who he was himself after a while I didn't even give a fuck who he was long as it was a guarantee that he would supply me with whatever I needed.

"You're right, I planned on taking a trip up there anyway. Member them triplets I got to know the last time I was up there. Well, they some freaky bitches, and since they all down to let me fuck I might as well see what all the bitches bout. So with this drop, I may bring a little extra and see what you can do with it. Plus, I heard they been looking for that gas them bitches alone need me to bring them a quarter. On the real, I might switch from community and just come up here. It's only an hour's drive, so it ain't like it's that much of a ride whenever I have classes. I could benefit a whole lot from that shit." Maine said.

I looked at him and nodded if that's what he chose to do, I wouldn't go against him. However, I thought it was good that we were in two separate schools because that only meant more money for the both of us. It wasn't no leader when it came down to our team, shit we all were making the same amount but however you spent ya shit was on you. I was more of a saver and wasn't trying to be flashy until I was legit. Maine ass was something else, he came from a home where he never had shit, so everything he ever wanted he went and got. The other people on our team like Maurice just blew money on bitches and the same shit they were selling. I never saw a person smoke so much weed that they didn't see a profit from it.

Now I did keep myself in the latest clothes and sneakers, but when I hit the block, it was the same outfit for a few days in a row, every time. Not that I ain't wash my ass cause I did, it just wasn't nothing to be dressed about. I was strictly out there for the money, and that was it. A lot of them stayed in the flyest gear and chose to be noticed. I'd rather play the back and collect all the money without drawing in too much attention.

"What do you think?" He asked.

"If you ask me, I say stay at your school, we got two schools on lock, and that's money from two different places. On top of that, we hit the block late nights when everybody is sleeping. We keeping business booming in different areas. It should stay that way, at the same time you are my brother, so whatever you feel you really want to do, I'm gone stand behind you, and we gone make shit work." I replied, honestly.

"That's why I fuck with you how I fuck with you. Community do be bringing in a lot of paper though. Especially since all them bitches live in the area and be wanting the shit outside of school too. I ain't gone lie I was just trying to escape the hood." He joked.

"You know your ass ain't leaving the hood, might take a break away from it, but you'll be back." I reminded him.

"Damn straight. I'm gone be a hood celebrity, and I ain't doing shit the legal way. If this mechanic shit don't work out, I'm gone use my street business degree and get the cash the only way I know." He stated.

"Real shit, I'm getting mine however it comes, and I'm bringing you with me," I promised.

And that was a promise I would never break. When my daddy died, and I felt like I was losing myself, my boy was there, and I would forever be in debt to him for that.

CHAPTER 4

*Z*ailah

"Ms. Harris, class is over." My professor said, tapping my shoulder.

I looked up from my paper and let my eyes travel around the empty classroom. My mind was everywhere but on what it should have been. Grabbing my bag, I quickly got up, placed my homework assignment on the teacher's desk, and walked out. Work was draining me, and so were all these classes. It was like I never had a day off since my boss fired one of the workers. Money wasn't tight, but I loved to have extra, plus I knew my parents were paying for my classes and taking care of my brother, and I didn't want to put any extra stress on them.

On top of that my mom was having her moments because my father was fathering yet another child outside of their twenty-three-year marriage. Stepping outside, I cursed myself for not wearing my coat today. The sun was out when I came out this morning, giving off a little heat, but now it was freezing.

I gazed around and saw a group of guys standing off to the side like they were waiting for somebody or something to pop off. This was the usual, and one of the main reasons I only took a two-year course. For this to be a college campus; it didn't seem like it. There was always a group of guys hanging around selling whatever they could sell and a flock of females trying to give them whatever they had to offer. Each day I was leaning closer to taking online classes. However, this was the only thing I had to do besides work. Most of the time, I stayed in the house other than the times I hung with Tierra wild ass.

Being with Tierra was always fun and a lot of partying. Often times guys swore up and down I would let them hit just off of who she was and my association with her. Not knowing I was nothing like her and the other people we hung with from time to time.

"Yo, what you not gone do is try and bitch me, pussy this my spot. I sell whatever the fuck I want when I want. I don't give a fuck who you are, or what you think you are. Nor do I give a fuck about what spot is supposedly yours." I heard a deep raspy voice.

"I don't give a fuck what you talking bout, my guy. You outnumbered right now, and you cutting dick. This my trap, so for you to sell anything to them is dead wrong. Now cut me a percentage or rumble dick head." The other guy snapped.

I could see from here how mad the guy was about who I learned was Kyrie, busting his trap. He had spit flying from his mouth, and his hands were moving every time he spoke. He even punched his hand a few times. Kyrie was standing with his back against the wall, looking unbothered. For all of the guys to be in front of him, he was calm as hell.

"Percentage? Oh, you tripping, I'm not cutting you shit. And cutting dick, how? She said my shit better you out here selling them little ass nick bags, my shit husky and get you way higher. We can do whatever you want to do about this,' but you ain't getting nada from me pussy." Kyrie barked.

My mind was telling me to get in my car and pull off, to get myself as far away from there as I possibly could. Yet, something was telling me to stay. I watched as a group of guys surrounded Kyrie. The times Maurice no good ass should have been out here with Kyrie ready to go to war with people he wasn't nowhere to be found.

"My man, you sure you want it to be like this? Yous a bitch without Maine and Rome. You think you can take us." The guy questioned.

For some strange reason, I wanted to go over and help him, why would they try and jump him. But when he was out there with his friends, they wouldn't even budge and allowed him to do the same shit. Kyrie looked around, and as quickly as my heart started racing, he swung. Kyrie's fist connected with the guy's jaw, and he stumbled backward. If his friend wasn't there to catch him, he would have for sure fell. The guy rubbed his jaw, then spit on the ground. Kyrie was in a fighting stance while the guy laughed. Before I could blink, they all were jumping him. For Kyrie to be by himself, he was holding his own.

I thought they would have got him on the ground by now, but they didn't. Kyrie's back was against the wall, and he was swinging on whoever was close enough to him.

"Argh fuck," Kyrie yelled out and doubled over.

At the point, I couldn't watch no more, especially since he sounded so hurt. Something in my head was telling me to run over and help. After contemplating with myself for a while I grabbed my mace, ran over to them, and sprayed the entire crowd. I kept on spraying until they all were holding their faces and trying to see. Kyrie was on the ground, and I could see blood seeping through his hands. He held onto his stomach with his eyes squeezed shut.

"Hey, come on." I tried to pull him up but failed.

I wanted to cry because I didn't want him to die, and I did nothing. I felt weak because I couldn't get him off the ground.

And I almost felt obligated to help him, like it was my duty to save him. Everything was moving in slow motion, and I almost wanted to throw up from all the blood that was coming from him.

"Come on, Kyrie, your heavy. You got to help me, I know it hurts but you have to try and get up." I was damn near begging him.

"Yo, let's go, for his boys come." One of the guys yelled.

They all ran off as I struggled to get Kyrie off the ground. I gave up, pulling him up and took off the white hoodie I had on under my leather jacket. Lifting his hands and unzipping his coat. I placed my hoodie over the cut on his stomach. I noticed that it wasn't that big, but I couldn't tell how deep it was.

"Okay, hold this until I go get my car we just gone have to try and drag you into the car so we can get you some help."

Running to my car, I jumped in and started it, I pulled off without even closing my door. Once I reached him, I threw the car in park, jumped out and ran over to the passenger side, opened the door, and then went to get Kyrie. It took a minute, but with his help, he was in the car, and I was flying to the nearest hospital.

"Kyrie, can you hear me? " I asked him because he was too quiet for me.

Even though I was helping him, I didn't want to have a dead body in the passenger seat of my car. I didn't know how I would explain that to the cops, my parents, his parents, or his friends. I also knew that I didn't want to have to watch my back from a bunch of people he associated with just to tell a story.

"I'm straight." He groaned.

I loved how he was playing tough like he wasn't hurting like a bitch. Looking over at him, I saw his chest rising and falling rapidly. I didn't know what to do, so I just drove faster while praying to God that he would be okay and that I made it to the hospital safely. As soon as I pulled up to the front entrance I hopped out of the car and waved frantically at the security guard who was taking his sweet old time walking over to me.

"Excuse me I need help, my friend is in the car he was stabbed," I told the security at the front desk.

They did something on the walkie and a bunch of nurses came running out with a stretcher. I pointed to my car so they knew where he was. From the way he looked as they pulled him out of the car, I was thinking the worst.

"Hey do you know his name?" One of the ladies asked me.

I watched as the others rushed him to the back. I was hesitating to tell them because I didn't know his situation nor did I know if he was on the run or anything like that.

"I just know him as Ky," I replied.

"Okay, well, maybe he has an I.D or something on him." The nurse said.

"Since this was a stabbing, the cops will be notified and will want to question you to get the people who did this. Did you see anything?" She pulled a notepad from her pocket.

I knew the code to the streets, and even though I wasn't from the actual hood I lived by those rules. If he wanted them to know what happened or to get those people locked up he would have to do so himself.

"No, I was driving by and just so happened to see him. I offered help that's all. I barely even know him." I told half the truth.

Nodding her head, she showed me where I could wait, and I took a seat. As I sat there, I said a quick prayer for him asking God to protect him and to just let it be something small that just so happened to bleed a lot. Time seemed to be flying by and I still had no word on him. Getting up, I headed back to my car. As much as I wanted to wait I had to be to work.

"Excuse me, did you hear anything about my friend, is he okay?" I asked.

"No, he's still in surgery. He should be done soon though." She replied.

"Okay, what time are your visiting hours over?"

I wanted to slap her phone out her hand for not answering me. She was so focused on the little game she was playing or whatever she was doing that she must have forgot I was standing there. I had to tap on the desk to get her attention. Once she answered my question, I headed out with plans to return.

First, I needed to go home and change into my work uniform and then do my five-hour shift. Hopefully I will be able to leave early so that I could make it back before visiting hours were over just to check on him and make sure he was okay. On my way home, my mind kept drifting back to Kyrie and the events that took place. I wonder if there was something I could have done different or if I should have stepped in with my mace sooner would things have changed.

"God, please let that boy make it out and through this okay. I know you don't give people more than what they can handle but, I'm trying to get to know him a little more and maybe just see where things can go with him. So if you can just keep him here for longer so I can be happy with him, I would really appreciate it." I prayed out loud.

Starting my car, I headed to handle my business. I was hoping like hell he didn't tell, there was no way I could make him mines if he turned out to be a rat. There was no way I could fuck with a snitch. My man had to be as real as me or realer.

CHAPTER 5

Kyrie

"Boy, you scared the shit out of me. I swear Kyrie this the shit I didn't want to be part of your future. They could have killed you." My mom cried.

She sat her purse down and rubbed my face before slapping spit from my mouth. I wanted to wipe her tears, but I was in so much pain I didn't want to move.

"Son, I keep telling you that you need to either keep somebody with you or stay with your hammer. I ain't telling you to stay off the streets no more cause yo ass ain't trying to hear that. I can only advise you of the next best thing," my stepfather said. He was staring at me intently, every once in a while, he would bite the inside of his jaw.

"I will, thanks for stopping by, I know that took a lot out of you," I replied.

"I'll always make sure you and your sister cool. It's another person I would rather not bother with. On that note, I'm going to go before shit gets hectic here." He touched my good side and walked out without a glance or word to my mother.

She had fucked up their relationship when her little habit

became something she couldn't control, and no matter how much he tried to help her, he couldn't. He placed her in rehab only for her to sign herself out. His last straw was when she stole his money from him.

"Lord, that man is still fine, but I hate his ass with a passion." My mom stated, looking at the door.

"Look, I'm cool. If it was my time, then hey, it was just that, my time. But, look, I'm still here, and that's what comes with the life I chose to live. And before you say anything, I know I could live a different life, but I love this one. In the future, I'll maybe do some shit that's legal, like opening up a cleaning company. How I'm gone do that though, if I don't even have my business degree or license yet. I watched you struggle every day to make ends meet. Your little waitress job is barely enough to cover yours and Liyah's habits. I love how you still keep up that shopping trip you started with her when she was younger too. On top of that, you know you struggle every day with dad dying, and the little money he left you, you done blew on whatever undercover shit you been doing." I pointed out.

My mind kept wondering if Zailah was still here or did she just up and leave. I was thinking if she stayed long enough to find out if I was okay, or was she sitting in the waiting room wondering what was going on. I was thankful for her, and her actions only caused me to like her that much more. I swear she had a perfect life and would never understand how it felt to walk in my shoes.

"Kyrie, you remember I asked you for that help with the mortgage this month right? Now I wouldn't ask you, but I slipped up and gambled a little too much at the casino and ain't win a dime back this time." My mother sighed.

"Ma, I got rent that's due too, and if I give you that money, how am I supposed to pay mines? You ready for me to move back in, you telling me you gone let me do what I do, to make my money and get to where I want to be in life?" I questioned.

"Yes, Kyrie damn. It's not like you gone give up that life anyway, so if you can help me with half the mortgage each month, I won't utter a word about what you are doing. Just don't bust any sales from my house or bring the police there, and we'll be fine." She smirked.

Knowing my mom, I knew she was only doing this for her own selfish reasons, but I didn't really care. Giving her three hundred dollars a month was much easier than paying the seven something a month I was doing by myself. On top of that, that gave me more leeway to save money and think of a master plan on how to flip it. Plus, I could start copping pills and syrup and make even more money. Eventually, I could meet the Connect or become him. Either way, my dreams were to become the King of this shit by any means.

"Listen, baby, Maliyah is on her way home from school. I'm going to go make sure the door is unlocked for her. Also, ya stepfather sends his love." She smiled before kissing the side of my head.

"Alright mom, love you," I told her.

I watched her leave before drowning myself in my own thoughts. Here I was thinking I was getting some money, and within a week all my shit seemed to fall apart. First, my car was taken because I was driving without a license. Then I get stabbed, and the doctors talking about being here a few days, and that's a lot of money I missing out on. Now my mom needed money for her mortgage. This was a small set back, but I had to make a major come back. I couldn't stay down, being a broke ass young bull was not the plan I had.

My door opened, and I guess the nurse knew it was time for my pain meds. I know soon as they let me out of here I was going on a paper chase, and I was gone find Bull that stabbed me and have him taking a long nap. Looking over to see who had come in so quietly, since the nurses always made themselves known when they walked in. I smiled at the sight of my little baby.

"Are you okay?" Zailah asked.

"Shit, I ain't dead." I shrugged.

Honestly, I felt like shit, my body was hurting, and I was praying that the doctors came and doped me up with the best drugs they had. However, I wouldn't admit that to her.

"Boy, you ain't even got to play tough for me. If you hurting, let me know ya nurse just walked by." She laughed.

"You know you can sit down right." I pointed to the bed and chairs.

She was in her work uniform but was looking good as hell. I wanted to pull her close to me and thank her for saving me. She slowly walked towards the chair next to my bed and sat down. Baby girl was even smelling good. I knew the smell of cucumber melon from bath and body works from anywhere. It was one of my mother's favorite smells.

"How was work?" I asked.

"It was cool; my fucking feet hurt though. However, I can't complain. How are you really feeling, you saying you cool but ya face keeps scrunching up." She smirked.

"I'm straight. Aye, I wanted to thank you. You ain't have to do what you did, you could have left me there, but you came through for me. I'm gone forever owe you, so if you ever need me for anything, I'm gone be there." I spoke honestly.

"It's whatever." She blushed.

She kicked her shoes off and propped her feet up on the side of the bed. For a second, I looked at her like she was crazy.

"What? My feet are really killing me. I'm ready to go get them done just so I can have somebody rub them." She stated.

I tried to sit up but failed at it, my stomach was on fire, and it was hurting a whole lot at this point. Zailah stood up and pressed the nurse button.

"We not about to keep sitting here acting like you not hurting. So let's just get the nurse and tell her you need some pain medicine." She smiled over at me.

I wanted to argue with her about it. On the other hand, I was glad she did because I doubt if I could have waited for her to leave to get my meds. Unlike my mom, she seemed to be getting comfortable so she could stay awhile.

"Hey, do you need anything?" My nurse peeked her head inside the room.

"Yes, he is in pain and wants to act like he's not. Do you mind getting him his medicine? Thank you." Zailah spoke up.

My nurse nodded her head and walked out. Zailah sat down in her seat and kicked her feet back up. I watched her reaching in her bag and pull her books out.

"So you bout to do some work instead of talk to me?" I questioned her.

"I can do both, plus I'm pretty sure once that medicine gets in your system, you gone be knocked out. This assignment is due tomorrow and is a major part of my grade." She said, not looking up.

The nurse came back in and gave me my medicine, checked all my vitals, and then left. Since I was sitting up a little more, I grabbed Zailah's feet and began to massage them while she worked. It was crazy how I could really sit quietly and just stare at her. She was so pretty in my eyes, in fact, she was beyond pretty; she was beautiful. Her small frame and round plump ass got my attention the most. However, her hazel eyes and small pouty lips caught my eyes. Her hair was a little past her shoulders, and she smelled so good.

"Stop staring at me." She broke me from my thoughts of her.

"My bad, you're just really beautiful, that's all," I told her.

"Thank you." She blushed.

I leaned over as much as I could and pulled her books away from her. I wasn't against her learning, but I wanted to get to know her. I saw her a few times in school, but I just thought she was one of those prissy girls that thought they were better than everybody.

"Boy, I told you I'm trying to get that done." She groaned.

"Okay, you can do it later from the looks of it you on the last question anyway. I just want to get to know you better. So can you do it later, please." I begged.

"Alright." She gave in.

We both sat there quietly just staring at each other. I wanted to pull her in for a kiss just to see if she was a great kisser. Or even if she thought I was a great kisser. I watched her as she tucked a piece of her hair behind her ear.

"I mean, you can continue my foot rub while we talk right?" She stated.

"Yeah, I got you. What's ya birthday, ya favorite things. Tell me anything, what makes you cry, or laugh." I said.

"My Birthday is July ninth. I love to read, watch movies, and make money. Sad movies or anything sad makes me cry; a lot of stuff makes me laugh because I'm goofy. I've had two boyfriends my entire life. People always take me for some kind of stuck up hoe because of my choice in friends. However, I'm not stuck up, hell I'm as humble as life could make me. I am also far from a hoe. Now tell me about you." She replied.

"Ain't much to tell, I'm just trying to make it to see forty. Shit, I'd be cool if I make it to twenty-five out here in these streets."

That was all I could come up with. It wasn't nothing that spectacular or worth knowing about me.

"Come on, it got to be more to you. You are not the average street dude." She doubted.

"Okay, well, I like money, and I'm gone get it. My baby sister means everything to me, and my moms is just that my moms. I love her, but sometimes I feel like I could do without her. My pops was a good dude, but shit, he was the definition of the streets, and we all know the streets don't love nobody. I'm in school because it's not just about the fast money to me. I want it anyway I can get it. I don't really do the whole girlfriend thing, not because I don't want to, but I don't have to. That's me, and I ain't got too many favorite things. I'm just thankful for the shit I can have; that's all." I announced.

"I mean everybody goes through some shit in life. It's not about what you go through that makes you; it's how you come out of it. I can see the determination in your eyes. You gone win, I'm rooting for you to win, and I barely even know you, just don't forget about me cause I need them foot rubs on the daily." She sang.

"I got you," I promised.

The medicine had to kick in at some point because I no longer felt the pain and I was starting to feel a little drowsy. I was mad as hell it decided to kick in now. I wasn't done talking to her nor did I want to fall asleep on her. I was trying to continue our conversation. For some odd reason I was not ready for her to pack up her things and leave me yet.

"I see you over there trying to keep your eyes open. You need that rest Ky, that's gone help you heal faster and get back to that money you keep talking about. I'll try to stop by tomorrow either after class or after work. Do you need me to bring you anything? I'll leave my number on the table. Call or text me if you do. And if you need a ride home let me know, I'll come get you." she calmly stated while getting up.

"My cousin is coming to get me." I lied.

She had helped me enough I didn't need her doing any more than she had already done. Whatever she said fell on death ears because my eyes quickly closed and I fell into a deep sleep

CHAPTER 6

 **ailah**

FOR THE FIRST time in my life, I was really interested in a person. Kyrie was everything I never saw myself liking in a guy. Yet, I was completely drawn to him. It was something about his humble, ready for whatever attitude that got to me. He wasn't loud or always in the spotlight. His persona alone made me want to get to know him even more. I could tell that he wasn't sure about me and the type of girl I was.

I didn't even think I came off as the stuck up type. However, everyone thought I was. What Kyrie didn't know was my life wasn't as good as he thought it was. Granted it looked like it to others, but it wasn't. I made sure I left my phone number on a piece of paper on his bedside table hoping he would use it.

Grabbing my bags out of my car, I walked into the house. Seeing my mom on the couch with a bottle of liquor in front of her was normal. I grabbed the cup from her hand and sat it on the table. She was out cold; however, I knew not to pour that cup out, or she would flip the fuck out on me.

"Zailah, I'm out. I'll catch you later." Bentley told me as he walked passed.

Stopping him at the front door, I asked him where he was going. Once he told me that he was going to chill next door with his little friend I let him go. Heading into the kitchen I looked through the fridge for something to eat. When I came up with nothing I decided just to make a pack of chicken noodles.

"Zailah, where my drink?" My mother asked.

"I don't know I don't drink," I told her.

She smacked her teeth then began to check the cabinets. She began to slam the cabinet doors shut, and each time she searched and didn't find her bottle she got madder.

"I know you poured my shit out again, like what the fuck I ever do to you, Zailah. I don't bother you; all I want is a drink to ease my mind and help me fall asleep. Damn." She whined.

Seeing my mother search for her alcoholic beverage like a crackhead searching for their next fix made me disgusted. My mother was really a functional drunk. Her hair was pulled into a back ponytail, and she was still in her scrubs. Her light skin and Amber colored eyes stood out. She was about five foot five inches, and her hair was a little past shoulder length.

"Baby, mommy just needs a drink. I had a long night of work at that damn hospital last night. And I could use another drink." She begged.

"I left your bottle on the table. If it's not there, I don't know what happened or what to tell you. Mom, you know you better than that bottle right? I've seen you overcome shit worse than daddy stepping out." I reminded her.

See, when I was around ten years old, my mom was diagnosed with cancer, and she beat it. I felt like if she could beat the devil of diseases and not turn to the bottle then she could overcome anything.

"When you fall in love, then you can tell me about something being hard. Just don't be like your mother okay. Your dad and my kids are the only family I have, so I can't turn or walk away from y'all. Your daddy was there for me through everything, and I will never forget that. I work but keep all my money because your daddy pays for everything. So yes, he may step out, and he may have babies. However he doesn't love them or ever choose them over us. He even paid my hospital bills, and I'm forever thankful and in debt to him." She explained.

Instead of responding to her, I nodded my head. Maybe she had a point, and maybe she didn't. I would respect her decisions and stick by her because she was my mother. Instead of finishing my homework, I grabbed my bag and dumped the noodles in the trash. Walking to the door I slid my feet in my slides and grabbed my keys. I had about a few hours left to visit Kyrie, so instead of staying and listen to my mom begging for a bottle I knew my brother took with him I decided to leave.

I damn near ran to my car just so that I could see Kyrie faster as well as so I could make it out the rain before my hair curled up. Getting in my car I headed to Wendy's to grab us both something to eat. I wasn't sure what he liked, but you could never go wrong with chicken nuggets or a spicy chicken sand-wich, so I got both with fries. Driving to the hospital I ate a few out the bag. My mind was on Kyrie, and that beautiful smile he had. Just thinking about him caused me to press the gas a little harder. My heart rate sped up once the hospital was in full view. I parked my car in the parking garage and headed inside the hospital. I was struggling carrying bags of food along with the cup holder and my backpack.

"Hi, I'm here for Kyrie Wilison," I stated to the lady at the desk.

"You know what room he in already don't ya." The older lady who had been here every time I came asked.

I nodded, and she buzzed the doors for me with a smile. I

headed to the elevators and pressed the button repeatedly hoping it would make them come faster. As soon as I heard the ding I rushed to get on. Pressing the button for the fourth floor I watched the numbers wishing for them to go faster.

"Hello, honey." The lady I held the door for the other day spoke.

I smiled and waved at her making my way off the elevator as she got on. Walking the short distance to Kyrie's room seemed like it took forever before I made it to his door. I peeked inside and smiled, he was laid on his bed with one hand behind his head, and the other rested in the top of his boxers. His bottom lip was pulled into his mouth, and he looked as if he was in deep thought. I wished I was his lip, and he could suck on me like that. He must have felt me staring at him because he looked over and we locked eyes through the door. Grabbing the handle to the door I twisted it and slowly walked in.

"What's good with you, Zailah?" He smirked, rubbing his waves.

"Nothing; I brought you some food, so I hope you're hungry," I replied.

I had read a lot of books, and unlike them I wasn't nervous or felt like I had shivers or anything when I was in his presence. Instead I just felt comfortable like I could be myself. I was just happy to be around him.

"I'm a little hungry. I know I need to get the hell out of here. I need to get high, so I can really bust a grub. You missed me or some shit? You just popped up on a nigga, what if I had someone in here." He spoke.

"My bad." I frowned.

Him saying what if he had someone in there had me feeling a bit jealous and angry. I should be the only girl he wants in there because I'm pretty sure I was the best choice for him.

He looked me over once more and then let out a little

chuckle. I was ready to throw the whole bag of food at his head; instead, I sat it on the tray next to him and sat down. I had to take a seat and think about what he just said completely. He had me fucked up like all the way.

"I'm just fucking with ya ass. You all mad for no reason, and aint nobody been too visit me but my step pop once, you, one of my boys,and my mom."He told me.

"Oh, what kind of friends do you have? If my friends hadn't come and visited me by now to make sure I was okay, I wouldn't call them friends anymore. That's not how it goes." I stated matter of factly.

"How you know how shit go? Mufuckas got other things to live for and do. We ain't all come from a happy home and parents that spoil us." He said.

I don't know why, but I felt like he was throwing salt my way. I always heard how I was stuck up or little miss perfect. People swore up and down I had the best life and was wrong as hell.

"What the fuck is that supposed to mean? Just because I have a two-parent home don't mean shit is all good. Just because I don't reside in the hood don't mean I'm stuck up." I spat.

"Watch ya tone, and I'm just saying you don't know how hard it gets out here. So I can't just cancel people out because they ain't come. You ain't ever have to sleep in ya car or sit out on the block watching ya body all for some little bit of money. You've had shit handed to you, and so do ya friends. Y'all act like y'all better than everybody too." He sighed.

"If that's the case, why you talk to me? You figure because I have a car and I have nice clothes that my parents gave it to me, right? I get this big allowance and just get whatever I want. You tell me what it's like to have people loyal to you for just being you and not what you have. Because most people who fuck with me are only there for what they think I have. Yeah, my mother and father are married, but my life is far from perfect. No it's not the worse, but who the fuck cares. We all have problems mines just seem not to be as bad as the next. Yet to me they're big. You're so judgmental, you and your whack ass friends, and to be honest from the outside looking in, you only have about two loyal friends on your team anyway. At least I know my uppity ass friends willing to stick by me through whatever. They may be hoes as you and your friends like to call them, but let me had been laid up in this muthafucka them same hoes would have been here every day giving me the scoop and bringing me get well cards, balloons, and bears." I hissed.

I was pissed off, and if it were possible for steam to come from my head the room would be smoky.

"Because your hoe ass, uppity ass friends ain't got shit to worry about but the next dick they gone swallow. And to be honest them bitches ain't really your friends either. You make them look good. Everybody is a hoe except for you. They know everybody in the hood and school checking for you, so they keep you close so the niggas can be closer. Come on let's not go for friends because I'll chew your friends the fuck up. At least mine are not here just because of who I am. Your friends would miss seeing you to jump on the next dick that's coming up. I bet you, you could tell them you, and I have been kicking it, and I'd be able to fuck the one closest to you by the time I get out this hospital. However, if I told my niggas that, they would automatically put you in the do not touch category. Now whose friends are realer mines or yours?" Kyrie chuckled like he just won the conversation.

"Since when did this become a competition? On top of that, I'm glad to know that, that's how you really feel. So fuck you and your friends." I snapped.

I quickly stood up and grabbed my bags, storming out. This wasn't the first time I heard that about my friends, but it didn't mean that it didn't hurt the same every time I heard it. I had yet to experience my friends do any of the things people said; however, they are always discussing how people always ask about me, and the moment I tell them I'm not interested, they end up being the same ones they slept with. Maybe I needed to keep a closer eye on them. How can I get mad when I said I wasn't trying to mess with the people.

CHAPTER 7

*K*yrie

Zailah had me pissed off in more ways than one. I wasn't sure if it was the fact that I had missed three days of getting money or the fact that I really liked her and felt that she just couldn't relate to my lifestyle. In my eyes she had everything a young nigga could wish for, perfect grades in college, the older friends with money, shit she even came from money and the mere fact that she stayed in the northeast with the uppity people just made me believe she was one of them herself. She didn't understand how hard I had busted my ass and still didn't have a car, one was just handed to her. I was close to buying one, but now that I was out, I had to take the money I have been saving and probably pay my dealer.

On another note, I was happy to be outside, getting fresh air. The hospital had released me, and Maine came to pick me up just like he said he would. I was still sore, but when I had the Tylenol threes in my body I was feeling less of the pain and pushing myself.

"Bro, shit gone be straight. We gone get at them niggas, and they gone pay for what they did to you. Monty's ass better understand too. We make him the most money out of all the young bulls he put on. " Maine tried to reassure me.

"I hear what you are saying, but you know it's not gone play out like that. He gone want his money and shit I can only respect that because if I was in his position I would too. Good thing I been saving cause I would be fucked up." I sighed rubbing my hand over my face.

"You wouldn't, you know I would have put up some bread for you. Look, I have an extra five hundred on me right now. If you can match that, we can go in there pay him whatever and grab some extra work and not no weed either. I ain't trying to step in the line of no crack, but we can grab some syrup and pills or something. Whatever we grab now when we come back to re-up we grab that and some extra shit. We might as well go all the way in now and not look back." Maine smirked.

"Bet." I smiled

Jumping out of the car, I ran back inside the house and grabbed my sneaker box out of my closet. Grabbing an extra thousand dollars, I headed back to the car. We pulled off and went to Monty's trap. His fat ass was crazy enough to have the Africans run it, so it looked like a regular store on Woodland Ave, but when you got to the back of it, shit was different.

"Yo, Mont. We need to re-up, and we need something on top." I smiled tossing the money on his desk.

"Look who it is, my favorite two kids on the block. Where's Rome? Y'all missing y'all third guy." He spoke.

"Rome on the block, ain't no need to discuss him right now. We talking business and what we need. So can we get that?" Maine questioned.

"Same attitude as always. Yall want to get fronted as well or just the usual and what y'all can afford on top." He laughed while counting the money.

"It's all there. Fronted? Nah, we ain't the same boys we were when we first walked through this door. We want what we paid

43

for, that's all. We are not trying to owe you no more than we already do. On top of that we are ready to move up or out on our own. I remember we first came to you like five months ago; you said to get out, we had to pay five thousand a piece. If the offer still stands, we willing to do that." I honestly stated.

Rome wanted to work for him as long as he could. Maine and I just wasn't on that. We wanted our own money, and Rome was cool with whatever he got. Speaking of Rome he walked through the door with a big smile on his face.

"Pops, I just made that last drop for you. Now can I get my cut? What y'all two doing here without me?" He questioned.

"You know you be on your own shit now. You figure we gone keep breaking bread with you when you doing higher up shit and ain't even bringing your team. Shit we left the friendship and the money we made with you." Maine shrugged.

Instead of speaking to him, I sent him a mean glare. Rome wasn't one for the team which was why he was never around. He would rather sit on the block and fuck with bitches then make money. In the beginning we used to always come up short. To fix that problem when we came we would all get the package, split into three and bring back our own profit. Rome constantly fucked up money and since Monty was his father he got away with it most times, which is why he probably had him doing shipments and getting his money that way. However, I think it was pretty fucked up. Maine and I were grinding from sun up to sun down. I even got stabbed behind the shit and still was just on the block. We ain't get promoted to a higher level, not once.

"Shit, like that's why we are trying to go out on our own Monty. We ain't here to count the next man's pocket, but you know like we know, you keep us on the blocks cause we your hardest workers. You don't really want to see us win." Maine said.

"Don't nobody tell me how to run my shit. The only reason

why you two are even here is because Gus asked me to look out for y'all when he stepped down. Other than that y'all could have been started on your own. Now take this package and kick fucking rocks." He tossed the packages at us.

We got our shit and walked out the door. While in the car, we looked at each other knowing our way out was going to be harder than we thought.

"You peep that pussy ain't even tell us if the offer was still on the table. We gone have to call Gus and see what he can do or shit what we can do because this ain't it. I'm gone end up killing that old bitch." Maine snapped.

I sat back in my seat quiet, when my god dad told me that Rome could take me to his father and he would give me whatever I needed, I thought shit would be easier. The mere fact that I felt like he was taking advantage of my situation had me heated. He knew like everybody else around the way that Maine and I were the people to see. Anybody who needed something came to us first, and as of now we were even staying under the radar. Grabbing my phone from my pocket, I flipped it open and sent Zailah a message. She responded quicker than I thought causing me to smile.

"Yo, drop me by Zailah's spot. I'm about to see what's up with her ass and make a few moves."

I had to lay back and close my eyes for a second, rubbing my forehead. My head was pounding from this bullshit I was in, and I needed to find a way out. Calling her phone she picked up on the first ring.

"Hey Boo." She spoke softly.

I had too look at the phone twice, she was acting as if when had not previously had a falling out, if she wanted it like that I would be that I would act the same.

"Straight, can I borrow your car? I need to go see my god dad about some shit." I sighed.

"Yeah, whatever you need. You just have to drop me by the

library. I need to be there for a few hours to study for this test coming up. I know your ass ain't studied, so I'm gone take notes for the both of us." She smiled.

One thing I was starting to love about Zailah was the fact that she was willing to give me things and do whatever she needed to help me get ahead with this business. Maine rolled through the hood, and we made a few stops before pulling up to Zailah's house.

"Damn, she's living good. I wish I could have had a house like this shit growing up. Instead a nigga got to use his flashlight to make it through the house at night cause my peoples won't even pay the damn light bill. I ain't giving up no more money either cause that shit going right back in my pocket or the next nigga." Maine said after a moment's reflection.

"I try to tell her that shit, but she doesn't get it. She gone have to live like us to understand that her problems can't be that bad." I said.

Zailah couldn't tell me that she faced the same problems or anything similar to us. We had to grow up fast and be in survival mode. While she had it made and was living lavishly.

Minutes later she walked out with a big smile plastered across her face. I dapped Maine up before sliding out the car.

"Hey, boo, what's up Maine?" Zailah spoke.

"Yo, Sis. I'm straight, and you?" Maine responded.

"I'm great." Zailah smiles.

I pulled her into a hug and placed a small kiss on her cheek. I could smell the cucumber melon bath and body works shit she always used. That shit smelled so good to me too.

"You always smelling me dirty. Now come on I need to hurry up and get to the library." She smirked.

Sucking my teeth, I grabbed her car keys out her hand and opened her door for her. She climbed in, and I closed the door. Her ass looked so soft in her sweatpants that I wanted to grab it. However, that would have to wait until another time. Walking around the car I climbed in and started it. While we waited for it to heat up I looked over at her. She was so busy looking at her notebook she hadn't even noticed me staring.

I took the time to study her features. I found the dent on the top of her lip sexy and even the wrinkles on her forehead as she looked over a math problem. I wanted to twirl her hair around my finger and see if it was as soft as it looks.

"Damn, you gone burn a hole in the side of my face, the way you staring." She laughed popping her gum.

"Stop doing that shit." I frowned.

I hated when a person continuously popped their gum the way she was doing. It irritated the fuck out of me and fucked with my concentration. She stopped but looked at me like I was crazy.

"Has anybody ever told you, your attitude sucks, and you can't just talk to anybody any kind of way?" She questioned.

"My mom's tell me almost every day, but I personally don't give a fuck. Either you take me as I am or you don't. Plus, I'm nice as hell to you with your fine ass boo." I licked my lips at her.

"Well, unless you want me to leave your ass alone, you better watch how you talk to me. Now you could have asked me to stop differently. Like damn boo could you stop? You know any kind of way was better than the one you said." She looked over at me.

The way she looked at me had me ready to kiss her little ass, but I didn't. Instead I put the car in drive and drove off heading to the library so I could drop her ass off. It only took me about ten minutes to get her there, and within those ten minutes, she called me all kinds of speed demons and placed her seatbelt on.

"Be safe, and make sure you keep the money on your mind right after me," Zailah told me as she got out of the car.

"I got you baby girl, now go study for that test and call me when you done," I stated before pulling off.

Paying my god dad a visit was a must, and the good thing

was that the library was right around his way. I made the drive as quick as I could because he had to hear from me what was about to happen and hopefully he was cool with me stepping out on my own. If not, he would have to get used to it because, as I saw it, his man wasn't to be trusted and didn't want me to expand beyond the little bit he was willing to supply me with. There was no way I was going to be the King of the Streets working under him so it was either they allowed my team and I to take over or we were gone force their hands and do it the hard way. Either way it happened I planned to come out on top.

CHAPTER 8

 ailah

TONIGHT WAS the night of Tierra's party, and I was excited. I hadn't seen her in a few days, and we needed to catch up on everything. Walking through the mall I searched high and low for something to wear. When I finally saw a dress that caught my eye, it was white with long sleeves, and it hung from the shoulders. It wasn't too much, but it was cute, and I knew it would make my body pop. This dress was definitely an eye-catcher yet so simple. Going inside the store I went straight to the dress and grabbed my size. I had a pair of gold heels at home, so I didn't need to get any shoes. Even though I was spending money I was thinking of ways to save too. Instead of going to the nail salon I grabbed some white polish and a wet and wavy weave ponytail from the hair store I left before I could do any more damage to my pockets and headed home to get ready.

"Ma, I'm going over Tierra's for the weekend," I said soon as I closed the front door.

"Alright, just make sure you call me when you get there." My mom responded.

I knew just by her voice that she was sober, and that made me smile. I loved this part of my mom and lord knows I missed it even more. Back in the day my mother was a school teacher by day and a nurse by night, and then my father turned her into a drunken housewife. Sometimes she did her nurse job covering the Emergency room when people took off or did vacations just so she could pass the time.

"You look so beautiful baby." My mother said from behind me.

"Thanks," I told her, looking through my mirror.

"Do you need any money while you're out? I know you have your own, but just in case. You know I don't like you to go out and not have any money on you." She tried making conversation.

"I know, and I have enough money to hold me over until I get paid. Thank you though." I responded.

She nodded, gave me a small smile before she stepped out closing my door. My mother was beautiful in every sense of the word. Even with drinking all the time she still looked good. I looked so much like her it was scary.

Checking my phone, I noticed I had about two hours to get ready. I placed my shower cap on and took a quick shower then got out. I sat in front of my mirror wrapped in a towel and did my lip gloss and eyeliner.

"Put some fucking clothes on," Bentley yelled from my door.

"You in my room, plus I'm trying to get dressed for this damn party," I told him.

"I know, let me get thirty dollars just until I see my nigga Ky, he said if I came to him with a hundred he'd put me on. And I'm tired of asking mommy and dad for money." Bentley pleaded.

"Bent, I'm not helping you with that. You already know I don't want you out there on the block." I declined.

"You're my sister though so you might as well give it to me. If you don't I'm gone get it on my own, so either way I'm gone get it. I am almost a grown-ass man, so I need to get ready to start fending for myself. I'm not about to go get no damn nine to five when I can make more on the block." He stressed.

"Bentley, I swear to God if you get hurt out there it's gone be all my fault, and if you are willing to let me live with that then take the thirty out my bag if not leave it." I spat, hoping like hell he wouldn't take it.

"You be drawlin', you worry too much. Ain't shit gone happen to me out there. I'm good; my peoples gone have my back, and that's all to it. If anything I'm ready for war, I'm a grown-ass man." He boosted.

Bentley being Bentley happily went inside of my bag and took the money. Sighing, I continued to get ready for the party.

"I'll see you at the party baby." Bentley kissed my cheek before leaving out.

I didn't even want to ask how he was going when he wasn't even old enough to go. That was one of the many things I hated, my little brother had pull in the streets and it allowed him to do things I hadn't even done yet. I swore he was growing up too fast, and I didn't like it. I tried my hardest to shield him and give him what he wanted so he wouldn't have to go out in them streets, however, that ain't work, and he ran right to them. My father used to always tell us the streets ain't love nobody, and that's what got his big brother killed.

My mind flashed back to that day, and I instantly wanted to cry. My uncle was throwing his annual block party on 55th and Baltimore, and he swore up and down this one was going to top all the others. He had the moon bouncers and face painting. I remember running up and down the block having a ball. Night time came fast, and just as they began to unblock the block a car pulled up and let off shots that ripple through my uncle's body. He caught every bullet that was sent his way. My father ran to him and cradled his body. He died right in his arms. The image of my dad holding his brother who was killed by his right-hand man was one that will forever be imbedded in my head. I didn't want that to be my baby brother and me.

My phone rang, bringing me out of my thoughts. I quickly grabbed it and picked it up.

"I'm on my way," I told Tierra before hanging up on her.

I didn't wait for her to respond because I knew what she wanted. Getting up, I quickly slipped into my outfit, and shoes grabbed my bag and headed out the door. I got in my car and drove to the party, it was packed and just like I expected Bentley was hanging out front with Maurice and his boys.

Parking my car, I made my way over to the party. People were already stumbling drunk and on cars smoking or hugged up. I saw Kyrie, and he sent me a wink causing me to smile. I could feel his eyes on me, so I put an extra sway in my hips, hoping to keep his attention. Walking into the party I looked around for Tierra. I found her on top of her counter, chugging on a liquor bottle.

"Hey, best friend." She slurred, passing me the bottle of grey goose she was sipping on.

"You gone hurt yourself." I smiled.

"Shut up and drink." She giggled.

Lifting the bottle up to my lips, I took a swig. I instantly put it down and frowned. How she was drinking straight from the bottle was beyond me. It burned my throat so bad. I grabbed a plastic cup and filled it halfway with cranberry juice, then the rest of the way with the liquor. Placing a straw inside I sipped until I felt the liquor take over my body.

I swayed my hips to the music as I watched people dance. The girls even began to have a dance battle in the middle of the floor.

"Girl, there go the fine ass boy I was telling you about." Tierra tapped my shoulder.

"Damn, break my shoulder while you at it." I pushed her hand.

I looked up to see who she was talking about. Low and behold Kyrie, Maurice, and Bentley were walking our way. I hoped like hell it wasn't Ky because I didn't want to be stepping on her shoes, but in my head he was mine already.

"Who Ky?" I questioned.

"That's his name? If so, then yeah, he fine as hell." She smirked.

"Damn, why you ain't tell me?" I asked, facing her.

Just as she went to respond, I felt arms wrap around my waist. I tried to pry his hands off of me, but he wasn't letting go. I knew who it was because of the look on Tierra's face letting me know she was pissed.

"Really, I fucking told you." She snapped at me.

"Woah, I ain't even know who you were talking about," I yelled back to her.

Kyrie was still holding on to me, and I was still trying to move away from him. I didn't want her to be mad at me over some shit I really didn't know. Maurice and Kyrie hung with multiple boys and had she told me it was him, I wouldn't have given him the time of day.

"Damn, why your friend so mad?" Ky whispered in my ear.

His voice did something to me, it was like all the emotions I was just feeling disappeared, and I just wanted to be with him.

"Yo, get off my sister like that." Bentley went into big brother mode.

"Relax, I got her Bent. Plus, didn't you want to come over here cause ole girl." He spoke.

"I can't believe this shit." Tierra frowned.

"I would have never talked to him if you would have let me

know who he was. I promise Tee, and if you really want him you can have him." I spoke honestly.

Our friendship meant more to me then some nigga I had just really started talking to. And even though I liked him I would allow her to have him since she wanted him first.

"Fuck you mean boo? You ain't giving me to nobody. I don't want her; my young bull do, I'm all yours baby." Kyrie smiled down at me.

He turned me to him and pulled me away from the group. We headed over to the wall, where he pulled me against his chest and danced on me. I relaxed against his chest, but my mind was on Tierra.

"Look boo, just that fast she ain't even worried about me. So why you still on that. Even if she had told you who I was that shit wouldn't matter. I don't even like her. Honestly, I would have smashed and passed her to the team. She already fucked Reese, so that would be a no for me as far as making her my girl." He pointed out.

I looked up, and she was smiling in Bentley's face without a care in the world. Saying fuck it, I danced on Kyrie and just enjoyed being up under him.

"So, I'm your girl now?" I wondered.

"Yeah, real talk. Now give me a kiss." He smiled, showing all thirty-two teeth.

He placed his finger under my chin and tilted my head back. His head slowly moved toward mine, and I closed my eyes. The moment his lips touched mine I felt like the world stopped spinning. He bit my lip, and I opened my mouth for him allowing his tongue to slide into my mouth. We tongue wrestled until we were both out of breath. He kept his arms locked around me, and I knew at that moment I would be his forever.

CHAPTER 9

yrie

ZAILAH HAD MY MIND GONE, and after last night at that party she was gone forever be mine. It was just something about her that kept me wanting more from her. I hadn't even fucked her yet, but the way she kissed me let me know that she was the one for me. I was willing to give anything I could to make her mines and keep it that way. I know she agreed to be my girl, yet I felt like it was all because she was drunk. As much as I didn't want her to see my spot because my living conditions weren't what she probably as used to, I said fuck it and invited her over. Before she came over I was gone clean up as much as I could to make it look presentable and spray enough Raid to keep my newly found cousins in their hiding spots. Them roaches in the house are so comfortable that I started calling them my cousins. They were everywhere, and it was nothing we could do. The Raid only kept them hiding for a while, and then they were back invading anyone they could privacy.

My phone rang and I picked up allowing Maine's voice too

"Bruh, that shit Monty gave us was bad. All the fiends are coming back to me like we was on some bullshit." Maine growled, interrupting my thoughts.

"He what? Fuck you mean bad? Like bad, bad? like we ain't gone be able to move that shit and get our money back bad?" I questioned.

Now, normally, I didn't get mad and was as humble as possible. However, I was heated, messing with my money was something completely different. There were a lot of things I didn't play about, and my money was at the top of the list. Monty was on some shit, and I was going to find out exactly what that was. I made sure that I gave him his money on time and kept shit correct without no customers complaining or no money coming up short. Why he decided to play with me was a question I needed to be answered.

"Did you hear me? Ky? Fuck is we gone do? I can't be out here pushing this shit at all. Shit gone give us a bad rep. Now that I know I done smelled the shit and it smells like he cut up some soap and added it to this shit or something. I'm telling you I ain't with this shit, so either he gone refund us or we got to get a new connect like ASAP."

I could tell he was on one because he never spoke about shit over the phone, and for him to be discussing it meant that he was pissed. Looking at my phone I closed it ending the call. Grabbing my jacket and sliding it on, I walked out the door. Walking as fast as I could to Maine's house was the only thing on my mind. Had I not been so pissed off, I would have waited for Zailah to arrive and then drove over, but I needed to make sure that what he said was correct.

"K, man, y'all on some bullshit. Tell Maine, I want my money back. Y'all out here selling chopped up soap." Dot seethed.

Dot was a local customer and was always around. Even though he did more crack than a little bit, the whole hood respected him. He did work for anybody that could pay him and been in the hood through his ups and downs. Crack was a drug he turned to when his whole family was murdered right in front of him. He did twenty years for killing one of the dudes, and when he came home he turned to that white girl to solve all his problems.

"Dot, you know we ain't even on that. I'm gone get you some better shit, and I'm gone make sure we throw you some extra. Let me just handle this shit first." I explained.

He nodded his head before going back inside of the Deli on the corner. Taking the alley to shorten my walk I skipped up the steps and walked right into Maine's little studio apartment.

"Yo, what's that shit you was saying?" I grabbed the pack off the table and smelled it.

Off top you couldn't tell it was soap, but being as though I knew by now what it should look and smell like I knew that it wasn't right. I wracked my brain on why he would do that and came up with nothing. As much as my anger grew I had to somewhat fault us for not checking the package before we walked off with it. That was a mistake that would never happen again.

"For one, we need to take this as a lesson learned. There's no way we should have left without getting a fiend to test this shit in front of him and us before we gave up our money for it. So from here on out, anything we buy gone have to be tested weed and all. I can't afford to take no more fucking loses." taking a seat I pulled out a chocolate dutch splitting it down the middle with my pocket knife.

"You got a point, yet, that shit still doesn't explain why he on bullshit with us. He thinks we some real young bulls and that he just gone get one over on us." Maine fumed.

"So again, what you want to do about it? Like where you trying to take this? Let me know now, so I know what angles to take. Cause at the end of the day, we partners and brothers before anything." I started taking a pull from the blunt after lighting it.

"Real shit, I'm gone either off bull, or get my bread back and some better shit. How the fuck he gone have us out here selling soap?" Maine demanded an answer that I didn't have.

"Are you asking me? How the hell I'm 'posed to know. We gone have to map some shit out. Then go holla at him. Either we gone go at him full blast or give him a chance to explain this shit, but either way, we rocking together." I shrugged.

For one, I wasn't trying to be mad over some shit we had no control over. Who the fuck was I lying to? I was mad as hell. However, I wanted to deal with Monty, and until then I was gone have to do what I could to get by. We had extra work in the stash in case of a rainy day, and I guess today was the day it decided to pour. In a way the pills we had would come in handy too. This was another reason I didn't really want to fuck with this crack shit. It came with too much, and at least I knew what I was getting with pills. Nobody was directly making them or was chopping it up or cooking it to make more of it. However, Maine wanted to get money, and all of the ways we could crack was the fastest-selling drug.

So when he came to me with the plan to get it so we could bring in a larger income quicker, I was down. With all the money we were making, most of mines was going into a savings account, so I could get everything I needed and fast.

"I'm gone call that nigga and set up a meeting. Zailah is on her way over, and I'm bout to see what's up with her. I'm gone play the block tonight, and as of now I would suggest you set that shit aside somewhere until he willing to see us. I know his ass ain't gone be at the spot today because it's Sunday, and you know he be on that family shit on Sundays. If he doesn't respond by tonight we gone walk up in that muthafucka bright and early tomorrow. Hit the stash, and just grab the shit we put up in case this rainstorm hit us, and it's looking like a hurricane for us." I said.

Maine nodded his head and dapped me up. I knew his ass was still mad, but it wasn't shit we could do until we saw him or as we would be searching for a damn ghost. Monty didn't live in Philly and was sure to keep his family and location a secret.

"Make sure you let him know I ain't feeling him, matter of fact I'm gone let the nigga know myself. He better hope I don't find another connect. Fuck it; we might as well become the connect. We just need to find out who he gets his shit from." Maine

CHAPTER 10

 ailah

KYRIE INVITED me to his house, and I was very hesitant about going on top of that Tierra ass was mad at me because I was messing with him. It wasn't my fault that by the time she told me he was the guy she was feeling I had already made him mines, well in my head anyway. Grabbing my jeans, I pulled them on and got ready to make my way to his house. I was surprised he invited me over because he was acting like I didn't know what it was like to be on the west side of Philly.

Getting inside of my car, I drove to the address he had texted me. Before I could even get out of my car, my nerves kicked in. I was so scared that I was ready to turn my ass back around and head home. Not that I was scared of the neighborhood I was in or the looks I was getting from the men that were leaned against the wall.

"Who you here for?" One of them asked.

I ignored him and continued up the steps of the address

Kyrie had sent me. From the outside of the house, you couldn't tell whether it was in the family for a long time, or his parents didn't keep up with it. Either way, I didn't care as long as I got to spend time with him. I rang the doorbell a few times when I got no answer, I called his phone and told him I was outside. He came to the door a short while after in some sweats and a white tee shirt. His Du-Rag was tied to the back. He looked so good even though he wasn't dressed.

"What's good?" He said, stepping to the side.

"Hey." I smiled.

I walked in and looked around, the smell of cigarettes and weed hit me all at once. I frowned up my face but quickly turned it into a smile. The place wasn't messy; however, it was very cluttered. I saw a few pictures on the tables. Kyrie grabbed my hand and led me up the steps and into the back room. This room was clean as hell, and everything was put away neatly. He closed the door and locked it, then pulled his sweats off, leaving him in his basketball shorts. I watched him grab the shoebox that was on the bed with weed, baggies, and a scale in it. He closed it and sat it on his dresser.

"You can finish up if you want too," I stated.

"Nah, it's good. Come sit down, my bed clean." He patted the bed.

Sitting in my bag down on the chair, I slid my shoes off and climbed in the bed next to him. He grabbed his controller and played a movie from his game.

"So what's up? What have you been doing? How's work?" He questioned.

"I've been good, and work is work. What about you? I see you back on the block." I looked over to the box.

"When you come from this, it's usually only one fast way out. I ain't no rapper nor a singer, so I gotta do the next best thing. Shit, the only deals I'm getting is from the plug." He shrugged.

"I understand, I like you any way you come. On the real, you can finish up. I like to watch you when we talking over the computer anyway." I said, handing him the shoe box.

Honestly, I didn't want to stop him from working I knew how much he needed the money or at least from what he told me how much he needed it anyway. I wasn't lying when I said I liked to watch him either. We often video chatted on the computer, and he would be doing his thing. I loved the focus look he would have on his face and how he would bite his lip as he counted or whatever.

"You could still kick it with me and get ya shit together for when you hit the block later. If you want, you can teach me so I can start helping you. I just want you to be at the top of whatever you do, and I'll help you as much as I can." I stated truthfully.

I remember he had been complaining to his mother about getting a car and how he was about two hundred dollars short. Even though I had it I didn't want to offer it, I was going to find a way to leave it or give it to him without him knowing it was me. I was scared of him snapping on me about me being so privileged like he had done at the hospital that one time when I was only trying to help. It was like I only wanted the best for him, and I wish he could see that.

"Bet, but I ain't teaching you shit. If you want to learn, then you gone have to watch and learn. My future girl ain't getting her hands dirty, she just needs to continue to sell sneakers at Footlocker." He stated.

Kyrie grabbed the box and began to bag up his stuff, he didn't agree on teaching me, but I could learn from watching like he said. While he worked, I played his game system and was losing badly. Before tossing the joystick, I went to his music and turned some on. I laid back across his bed and just stared at him. Kyrie looked so good as he bit his lip and concentrated on the scale. He frowned his face up then looked up at me.

"Fuck is you staring at?." He questioned.

"Hmm, I'm sorry." I turned my attention to the colors that flashed across the tv.

"Come give me a kiss." Kyrie licked his lips.

"What?" I asked, uncertain of what he had just said.

"Give me a fucking kiss and stop playing." He pulled me to him.

My heart was pounding as we got closer to each other. I had kissed boys before, but I was never this nervous. I swore I was about to pass out until our lips finally touched. In that moment, I never wanted to pull away. Like if he sucked all the breath out of me, I would be just fine as long as I was with him. Kyrie licked my bottom lip, causing me to gasp. His tongue invade my mouth, and I was fine with it. We tongue wrestled until we were both out of breath. He pulled away first and looked at me.

"Now you're my girl, and you are stuck with me. It's gonna be us against anybody no matter what." He promised.

"I like how that sound." smiling at him, I licked my lips.

Kyrie had just made my night and didn't even know it. For the moment, I didn't have a care in the world, and being with him was all that mattered.

"Hey, let's go to the buffet. I'm starving, and I just got paid." I stated.

Kyrie looked over at me like he wanted to object, but I pouted. He was staring at me for a minute, and I could tell he was contemplating his next words. I didn't want to mess up our first night as boyfriend and girlfriend. However, I saw nothing wrong with me paying for a date.

"Nah, I'm supposed to be paying for shit like that. Not the other way around. Give a nigga some time, and I swear we gone do everything." He sighed.

"Listen, if we gone do this, then you gone accept the fact that sometimes I can step up and handle shit too. Let me just pay for this, I'll even give you the money before we go in so that you can pay while we there. Ya money means nothing to me; it's all about the vibes. Plus, I know you'll spoil me one day anyway." I told him.

Kyrie nodded his head and got up off the bed. Once he was dressed, I handed him the money to cover our date. While he was hiding his box inside of his closet, I slipped the extra two hundred dollars he needed towards his car in the side of his dresser, where I watched him stash his money. He turned around, and I bent down to slide my feet in my shoes.

"You ready boo?" He asked.

Nodding my head, I got up and handed him my keys as we were walking out I heard voices. He looked back at me with a small smile.

"That's just my moms and aunties." He told me.

We walked into the kitchen, and the ladies sat around drinking beers and talking. Once they saw us, everyone was quiet, and

"Hello, I'm Zailah," I spoke to everyone.

"Hey, baby. Ky, you gone?" The lady I remembered from the hospital spoke.

"Shit, he got him a little cutie this time. That last little heffa, he had come out stinking up the whole damn house. Member Nikki, her little hot ass was smelling hot." I'm guessing it was his aunt that laughed.

"Yeah, I'm gone. I'll be back in a little bit, Aunt Pebbles you foul for that." He laughed.

"Bye." I waved.

On the way out the door I heard his mom saying how I was the same girl that held the door for her at the hospital. It almost made me want to turn around and hear what the rest of the conversation would be. If I knew them like I thought one small thing could turn into an hour long conversation.

"Look, don't pay Pebble's ass no mind, she be off that Steel Reserve and Mad Dog and don't know how to conduct herself. My mom's on another note she ain't that fucked up yet, so she wasn't gonna say too much. Had we left out about twenty minutes later and ain't no telling what you would have heard or saw." He admitted.

"It's all okay, it's nothing I haven't seen before. Almost reminds me of my mom when she gets to drinking. You better not crash my car, I'm trusting that you can drive." I said after a moment's reflection.

Kyrie looked at me and laughed before getting in the car. Nope, he wasn't no gentleman that came over and opened the door for me. I had to do that myself, but I was okay with it. I wasn't asking him to be who he wasn't or trying to change him. Once he was inside of the car, he pulled off. I grabbed Lil Wayne's drought three mixtapes and put it in the cd player.

"Turn that shit up boo, matter of fact cut on that *We taking over* track or *Upgrade you*." He looked over at me.

Switching the songs, I sat back in my seat and rapped the lyrics word for word. One thing about me was I was a rap fan and love to listen to the shit in my car like I was a street nigga when really I ain't know shit about the streets but what I heard.

"Okay, let me find out you gone be my little rider. I swore up and down you was gone have some Destiny's Child playing. Or some lil bow wow this jawn." He smirked.

"Boy bye, I love me some lil Wayne, TI, and of course, any State Property member. Especially the Young Gunz. Don't play with me. I be in the streets real talk." I put out.

We made it to the buffet had a blast. The entire time there, we laughed and ate. Most of the time was spent cracking jokes on each other or other people. If this was what love felt like, I wasn't sure; however, I knew that it was a feeling I wanted to feel over and over again. I was getting my very first feeling of puppy love and I was going to enjoy every bit of it.

yrie

SOMETHING WAS OFF, and I didn't know what. Today was supposed to be my last day working under Monty and me stepping out on my own. Of course Maine was gone bounce with me. I knew I had a big task, in front of me, and I was ready for it. Maine was already getting our baggies and things so that we could have a distinct look. Most people had yellow bags or clear ones with black skulls on them. We were going to do black bags for weed and green bags for the crack.

Zailah was gone have to understand that a lot of work was going to have to be put in for me to get where I needed to be. The only thing in my head was getting these niggas connect, and he was supposed to give it to me. I was digging her more than I should have, but our relationship was going to either have to take a pause, or she was just going to have to work with me in keeping us together.

"Man, I'ont think this nigga just about to give us his connect like that. He doesn't even really seem like he is ready to give up the game like he proposing." Maine sighed, cocking his gun.

"Word, but look, whatever happens, happens. I know you better walk out this door with me, if not Ima haunt yo ass till the day you die," I stressed.

"Same shit, we bout to come out this mufucka on top, and if you go or I go, the only promise we need to make is that if one of us walks out living, we killing off anybody that was in there, and to get this money." Maine laughed.

I nodded, cocked both my guns, placed them on my sides, and pulled my oversized black hoodie on my head. My dad had a bulletproof vest in his office, and I had to wear it. Opening the door, I looked at Maine and nodded. He stepped out, and we slowly walked to the door of the building.

"Just the two I have been waiting for, now let's get this shit started." Monty clapped.

Looking around, I only noticed eight people in total in the room. My palms were sweaty, and I was nervous as all hell. However, I couldn't let it show. If we had to kill him, this would be the second person I had ever murdered in my life. I wasn't like the niggas in those fairy tale books. I wasn't no straight killer, and I didn't need to be. I rarely got my hands dirty, but I would beat a nigga's ass if I had to.

"What's good with you Mont? What's up yall?" I spoke to everyone.

I got a couple head nods, and that was it. Monty took his seat before rubbing his hands together. I looked over at Maine to see if he was gone take a seat because I wasn't. When he didn't, I smirked.

"You guys aren't going to have a seat," Monty asked.

"Nah, we straight. What's up with ya people though? Why they surrounding us like some shit about to go down?" I asked. They're just hear for security purpose, you know the usual." he shrugged as if it was nothing.

"I guess, let's just get to what we came for. Let me start by saying that the work you gave us was bad for business. I don't know what type of time you on, but I ain't with that shit. I come to you because once upon a time, you had the purest shit in the city." I started.

Monty gave me a small smirk, and it pissed me off. I could hear Maine grinding his teeth and knew he wasn't feeling the shit either. I placed my hands behind my back, resting my hands on my gun. I knew at any moment somebody was gone bust they gun. Everyone knew I wasn't no natural born killer, and I wasn't trying to be. However, when I was placed in a kill or be killed situation, I would rather be the one that comes out just like anyone else.

"Yeah, I gave y'all that shit, and that's what was given to me. I had other shit, but I know y'all customers came to y'all faster than my other people, so I figured y'all would knock it off and get me a percentage back." He shrugged as if it didn't matter.

"Check this, our customers deal with us because we some regular ass niggas trying to make it out. We ain't scheming or none of that. We give out pure shit with deals and all. We came here for one thing, and that's cause you promised us your connect anything else you could leave that shit floating in the air. So what's up, can we get that information or no?" Maine barked.

Just like myself, Maine wasn't no killer. Yet, he would bust his gun with no questions asked. I looked around and noticed that a lot of Monty shooters were nodding they head when we spoke. I could point out the ones I was cool with and knew wouldn't shoot for him cause just like us, they were sick of his shit.

"You really thought I was going to give you two muthafuckas my connect? Y'all ain't worked hard enough yet. It ain't that easy y'all can either buy it from me or keep working for me. On top

MARRIED TO A PHILLY KING

of that, you both gone have to just take that other shit as a loss."
he smirked.

"Bet." Maine wiped his mouth.

I figured we were about to walk out of there and map some
shit out or even come up with a plan to take over even if we had
to step on his toes.

Pop pop pop

The shots made my ear ring since I was standing so close to
him. I watched as one bullet went through Monty head and the
other in his chest while the last one went into the wall. Quickly
ducking down to take cover as shots rang. I looked over and
shot at whoever I knew I was going to have to take out first.

My heart felt like it was about to beat out of my chest, and
all I wanted was this shit to be over so we could get the fuck out
of there.

"Yo, don't fucking shoot me after I just helped y'all niggas,"
Greg yelled.

I slowly stood up once the gunfire ceased. Pulling my Glock
22 from my sock and my nine from my back, I aimed it. I slowly
looked around to see if I could spot Maine.

"That's what the fuck I talking bout." He yelled, coming from
behind a wall with his gun aimed.

It was five of us standing in a circle everybody with their
guns pointed. We all stood quiet for a second.

"Look, we all were rocking for each other. We need to grab
what we can grab and get the fuck out of here," I said, putting
my gun down first.

Once everyone's guns was down, we went into the back
room and grabbed everything we could grab. I was kind of glad
that Monty had just gotten a shipment. We grabbed almost all of
the work and the entire safe since picking the lock was something we couldn't do right now.

"We gone meet up at Maine's house. If you don't want to

meet there, take the shit you grabbed and go off on your own." I shrugged.

Before we left, I doubled back thanking god for the gloves. I had then reached in Monty's pocket and grabbed his cellphone. Since he had two, I took his trap phone and ran out. Maine was outside knocking cans of gasoline over. Monty kept them in case he had to quickly burn the building down.

I lit a dollar bill and tossed it on the ground, catching the place on fire.

"Yo, What the fuck?" Greg yelled, hopping over the fire.

I laughed at him just as Maine peeled off. This was just the beginning for us, and hopefully, we made it to where we wanted to be.

"We up now." Maine smiled, fucking up my thoughts.

"Yeah, but check this. I was thinking we flip this shit as is without even cutting it up and then hitting his plug and grabbing more. If we can flip this shit faster than Monty, then it's guaranteed them Cubans gone want to fuck with us. Even if we get off half this shit, then use some of the money we got and grab some of them. We always gone be ahead and never run out." I suggested.

"You a fucking genius boy, we got to run this shit by them, and hopefully, just hopefully they with it. If not, we get rid of them and replace them if we got to. We gone have to stay war ready to cause, we just took money out a lot of niggas mouths, and once people see us getting some bread, they gone come for us." Maine stated.

"It's whatever from here." I let him know.

We climbed out of the car, and at this point, I was glad he lived on a small block with little to no traffic. As he went to unlock the .door, I began to grab the bags from the car. Hearing a car approaching, I stopped what I was doing and reached for my gun. Only to see Greg's car pulling up. Letting out the breath I was holding, I proceeded to grab the bags.

"We in this for the long haul bro, so stop reaching for your strap." Tray smirked.

I know he only told me that because he saw me reach for my gun, but I shrugged it off. I knew it would be a little while before I stopped going for my gun just because of what just went down.

"So y'all already know, we gone have to be ready for whatever. Keep y'all guns on you at all times if you fucking a bitch have that muthafucka in arms reach. This shit we just did don't get told to nobody we gone move this work, and if y'all want, we gone use some of that money to get more from them Cubans, so we don't run out. So it'll be like once we get low and waiting on a shipment if shit goes right with them, then we start using the extra shit. I don't think we should cook the shit down. However, we gone split this shit up, and everybody gone get they own packs, and you move it how you see fit. Each week we meet back here with a set amount whatever they say they prices are we split the bill down, or you get what you pay for that's all. Ain't no fucking boss 'round here. We are all our own boss and work for ourselves." I explained.

"That shit sound right, but I think you should holla at them Cubans since y'all were two of Monty's top workers and they know of y'all. You can say ain't no boss, but in every group, it's somebody that does most of the work and make all the calls. Since y'all two were the ones who got us in this position to be able to make moves like this on our own, then one of y'all should be the boss." Greg announced.

"Well then we gone have talk that one over maybe, I'll be the head of certain shit and Ky will take the lead on the other shit. Whichever we decide will be talked over, and y'all will have y'all opinion on it as well. We gone move like a family and respect each other's hand. If not, that means you gotta take ya cut and bounce now." Maine stated boldly.

No one moved or took their cut; instead, we all nodded our

heads agreeing with what was said. We all sat around talking, smoking, and breaking everything down. I was hoping like hell everything went our way. I was destined to be the King of Philly or at least one of them in this case, and I wasn't going to fuck it up at all.

CHAPTER 12

ailah

WALKING INTO THE HOUSE, I was on cloud nine. Kyrie had me smiling all night. It was now around two in the morning. I knew I should have been made it home, but I was technically grown, and normally I made it in before twelve. However, hanging out with him had me not caring about the time. I just loved being up under him. I still could feel the butterflies in my stomach that formed when he touched me. And my cheeks still hurt from the number of times he made me smile or laugh.

"Look what the wind finally blew in." My Father Zion's voice broke me out of my thoughts.

"What are you doing here?" Was the only thing that came from my mouth.

"I'm the one that's doing the questioning." He replied.

"You're right, I apologize. I was out with my friend, and we just let the time pass us. And before you start to say anything.

No, we wasn't out having sex, we were just hanging on his block. You can ask Bentley when he comes in." I let him know.

Had I just said I was with a friend, he would have sworn up and down I was out laying down and busting it wide open for Kyrie. When that wasn't the case. I mean, I would have loved to see if he could really move the way he be dancing, but I wasn't in no rush either. When the time came, I was pretty sure that I wouldn't be coming home at all.

"Do you hear me?"

"Huh? What did you say?" I asked.

"This muthafucka got you wide open. I said, who do you think you are that you can come in whenever you want to? And who is this boy that got you walking in my house the wee hours of the night? You ain't too old to get ya ass whipped." He voiced.

"His name is Kyrie, and he's a regular guy from the hood. That's just, for now, he got dreams to be somebody." I smiled just the mention of him made my heart beat faster.

"I really don't give a flying fuck who that nigga is, or who he think he gone be. And if you live up under my roof, you ain't gone be walking in this muthafucka later than me." My father yelled in my face.

"Says the man that barely walks in at all. You act like I told you I love him, I like him, and I want to build more with him so that I can say I love him. On top of that, I'm about to be nineteen. I'm technically grown and taking care of myself. You never bothered to ask before about what was going on in my life, " I replied.

I didn't understand my dad's problem, I had come in late from hanging with Kyrie, and for once he was home. In my eyes, it wasn't that deep. I was living my life and having fun. I guess it was because I wasn't there for the one family dinner he made it to this year, he had a problem. Just like always, my mother sat back with her glass of whatever alcohol was her choice tonight and said nothing. To her, that man could say no wrong unless it pertained to him telling his other bitches he loved them.

"I know one muthafucking thing. Any man that has you out this late only wants you for one thing, and if he has you mouthing back to me, I know he's getting it." My father fumed.

The more he yelled and kept me from answering Kyrie's call, the more irritated I grew. I didn't want to argue nor be disrespectful. Yet, for the life of me, I didn't understand why he wanted to bother me.

"You would know right, I guess that's how you keep leaving kids in every city you stop?" I stated boldly.

"Zailah, enough." My mother stopped me.

"Oh, now you have something to say. A moment ago, when he was down my throat, you had nothing to say. I'm the same person who fights with you when his random females pop up with their kids. You know the same ones who are almost the same age as me. And you don't have a problem with what I say and do then. When he not here, you let me roam freely. You could care less what Bent, and I do as long as we don't stop you from drinking." I shot back.

"If you know what's good for you, you'd better shut the hell up, and I mean now." He growled.

Closing my mouth, I stood there facing my father, my mom would never stand up to him, but I would. I was sick of all the hurt he caused just so he could come home and act like he was the perfect man. And maybe just maybe I could have continued to think highly of him had he not have tried to scold me on who I could and could not talk to. I didn't understand how he could possibly think he knew what was best for me if he didn't really know me at all.

"Zailah, go to your room." My mom sighed.

I was waiting on those very words to come from one of them. Quickly turning on my heels, I stormed off to my room. Slamming the door shut, I fell onto my bed a let out a breath.

This was some bullshit, here he was trying to treat me as if I didn't come and go as I pleased all the time. I didn't hear him searching for his son, who was still out partying, and he wasn't even legal yet.

Standing up, I decided to go take a shower, knowing that I could think and cool down at the same time. My dad had me heated, I could see if I was one of those kids who was out doing any and everything, but I wasn't. I had a job, I was in school and maintained good grades. Plus, I wasn't out here on no hoe shit, and I didn't come in late every night.

Bentley must have come in the house because I heard my dad ask him was he okay and how was his night before I heard a few doors close. He allowed Bent to come and go as he pleased. He even made sure while he was away, he left money for him to get condoms and whatever else he would need. I hated that it was like that. Because Bent was his son, he gave him this leeway he would never give me as his daughter.

He cherished the ground Bentley walked on, and Bentley cursed him out every chance he got. He would always say, "I give Bentley everything, so he doesn't have to go out in the streets and end up being a drug dealer or a stick-up kid."

My father didn't even know he was supplying Bentley with money for him to get high, and fly. He would never know that Bentley had dreams of being a dope boy, and judging by the people he hung with, Kyrie included, he was well on his way to becoming a drug dealer.

"Yo sis, you good. Ya pops low key tried to check me when I walked in, but you know I shut that shit down from the rip. So I can only imagine what he said to you." Bentley said, peeking his head in my room.

"You know he went in on me. I couldn't let it slide. Then ya mom ain't say shit until I started to pop my shit. Once she saw I was ready to give him hell, she wanted to step in." I told him.

I pulled my shirt over my head then let my towel fall so he

wouldn't see me naked. Once I had clothes on, Bentley came into my room. He sat on the edge of my bed while I climbed under the covers at the top.

"I should have come in with you. Then he wouldn't have said shit to you. I'm gone have to let him know he can't just be saying whatever to you cause you not out here on no hoe shit you doing what you are supposed to, and he should be proud of you. If anything, he should give you more than me and treat you better than he does me. You doing everything plus more so he shouldn't have shit to say about no moves you make." Bentley expressed.

"He gone say what he wants. You know he does that because I'm the good child your rebellious. Ain't too much he can tell you. Mommy just wants to be the perfect wife while she can and keep up that happily married image she portrays when that ain't it. Everybody knows how dad moves in her head; nobody knows though." I laughed.

"You need to hit this weed so you can loosen up," Bentley said while trying to hand me his chocolate Dutch filled with whatever weed.

I had just watched him pick seeds out of it and place it back into the bag. Whenever he got seeds out of his weed, his dumb ass would go and try and plant them. Pushing his hand back, I declined the offer. He grabbed my remote and cut the tv on. He turned on this Eddie Murphy comedy and lit up his weed.

Once he took a few pulls, he passed it to me. I puffed it and then began to cough. I tried it twice more and then handed it back.

"You can't be smoking my shit with them wet ass lips. Wipe them jawns before you pull anybody shit. You got my Dutch bleeding." He snapped.

He grabbed the scissors off my dresser and cut the back part off. I didn't care not one bit what he was talking about. I felt like I was floating and couldn't control my giggles.

"You mad, bro bro." I laughed.

"Shut the fuck up." He said.

It was funny until I felt my heart start racing. It was beating so fast it scared me. I also felt like I was floating. The shit scared me.

"Bro. My heart racing, you gotta feel it. I think I'm too high." I said.

"Yo, you high. Stop tripping and just relax." Bentley laughed.

"No, like look, feel my heart. It's beating so fast that it's not safe." I began to cry.

The way Bentley was looking at me made me laugh. So here I was floating with a racing heart while crying, and he was laughing at me. Which, in return, made me laugh.

"How the fuck you crying and laughing. Yo you tripping, you just high that's all." He reminded me.

"You right. I'm high and tripping. Brother, you got some food cause I'm hungry." I giggled.

"Man, you need to eat these chips and go to sleep. Shit watch the movie and laugh that shit off." Bentley threw a bag of chips from off my dresser at me.

Bentley got up and walked out of the room. He returned with a tub of ice cream and a bowl. I watched him place some of the ice cream in the bowl before he handed it to me.

"Eat this, it's gone help." He told me.

I grabbed the ice cream and began to eat it. I wasn't sure if it was from me being high, but the ice cream tasted amazing. It was like the flavors was enhanced or something.

"Oh my god, yo, this ice cream tastes so good." I hummed.

"Yeah you high." Bentley looked at me.

He finished his weed and then laid across the bottom of my bed. I ate the ice cream until I felt sleepy before I knew it I was fighting to keep my eyes open. Saying fuck it, I closed them and let sleep take over me.

CHAPTER 13

yrie

EACH DAY SEEMED like money was coming in faster. However, it was becoming too much for me, and I knew sooner than later, I was going to need a strong team behind me if I wanted to keep the money flowing. Even though we had a small group, we still carried our own weight and played the blocks like we used to. Now I found myself not even having time for school and looking more towards saying fuck college. I was getting mines, and by the time I finished college, I would already have the money I dreamed of. Every day I had been out until at least three in the morning only to take a quick nap, and shower then end up right back on the block.

"So you gone let me suck your dick tonight or what?" Tierra questioned me.

"Nah, I'm cool. I know how you are the moment you get a whiff of my dick you gone take that shit right back to Zailah. And I ain't losing my bitch over no broad like you." I snapped.

"You must be gay, what kind of nigga turn down head." She laughed to her friend.

"The kind that ain't fucking stupid, and watch ya mouth. Just cause I don't want no head from the neighborhood cum guzzler, I got to be gay. You a fool, stop swallowing so much dick, and maybe just maybe some nigga might fuck with you on that level." I shook my head.

Here I was trying to enjoy my night out with my right hand, and this bitch wanted to come fuck my night up. Grabbing my phone, I decided to shoot Zailah a text and see if I could see her for the night. I knew she had class in the morning, but her ass could go to school from my house. I knew by the time we got there, the whole house would be sleep. At first, I didn't want to invite her over because the place wasn't always in the best condition, and though my mother used to clean, she wasn't into all that now.

For the most part, when I got her to come over, I would be able to clean up and get help from my sister.

I was afraid at first that Zailah would judge me, yet she didn't. The last time she was over, I damn near ran her into my room so she wouldn't see the gang of roaches we had. The moment she texted me back saying that she would be over right after she was done her homework, I was over the whole club scene.

"Have you seen them niggas that went at you? I be looking to catch at least one of them." Maine asked.

"Not yet. It's gonna be a problem when I do." I replied.

I had been dying to catch one of them. I was praying to see all of them. However, God was hiding them from me. He must have known that I was going to end lives and make families suffer.

"Aye, I'm out. I'll see you tomorrow. See if we can get a few niggas that fucked with us from Monty's crew to be down, then we might start seeing a little more money." I stated.

I grabbed my drink downed it then got up. I gave Greg and Maine some snaps then headed home. My mom was on the couch, passed out. Picking her up, I carried her to her room. Once I had her in bed, I tried to clean up as best as I could. This was one of the reasons I didn't invite anyone over.

I looked around and grabbed the Raid off the counter, I sprayed it and then placed it under the cabinet. I lit a few incense in the kitchen to hide the smell. Usually, I would just fuck a bitch in my car and then drop her off home. However, Zailah was different.

"Who you got coming over? Cause you cleaning and in the house early? , but Zailah, cause if so, I already don't like the bitch, so don't bring her to meet me." My little sister Maliyah said.

"Since when you and Zailah become cool like that? Plus, she's my girl, not yours, so don't be trying to keep her in your room all night talking shit when I go run to the store." I told her.

Maliyah would wait until I left to go get Zailah chicken that she requested every time I saw her, and then have her in her room all night doing some kind of girl talk. Zailah's ass wouldn't even notice that most of her time was spent with Maliyah and not me. I was cool with it at first because I loved the bond they had formed, but at the same time, I was trying to get some, and my dick was hurting from not fucking in so long. Of course I didn't tell her that I just smiled and played it cool.

"Stop trying to be stingy. That's my friend, and we're just talking. She's like the big sister I never had nor wanted, but I got her. Relax, and don't do anything to mess that up," Maliyah smirked then walked off.

Since I knew she would come over and go straight to Maliyah's room, I had time to fix my room up and not let her see it. I stole a few of my mom's little candles she had around the bathroom and sat them on my dresser. I even stole her big candle off the kitchen table and lit it. Had my room smelling like apple cinnamon, that shit smelt bad to me, so I said fuck it and put that one back in the kitchen. I turned on my game and turned the music on from there.

Once I felt like I did a good job, I walked out of the house to go get her food. I was smiling hard as shit, and I hadn't even fucked yet. In my mind, a muthafucka was just happy I got enough courage in me to try. All we did was kiss, but she knew my ass wasn't about to keep that up for much longer, and I kept telling her I wouldn't either. My young ass was about to try and turn her out in the worst way.

"Yo, let me get ten wings, a small plain shrimp fried rice, and two shrimp and broccoli." Pulling my money from my pocket, I paid for it.

"Aye add on a homemade lemonade, two of them, and an iced tea," I called.

I knew if I didn't get Maliyah no food, her ass would be complaining, and Zailah would eat my food and hers. That girl ate chicken like she was a damn starving dog. It was cute and disgusting at the same time. I loved that she wasn't afraid to eat in front of me, but she ain't have to chew the bones.

"Yo, put me on. I'm trying to get some money, and you keep telling me to wait like I'm not ready, I will be out here all the time. I got your hundred dollars plus some."

"Young bull, I keep telling you, your sister doesn't want you out here doing that, and as my lady, I'm trying to respect her." I reminded Bentley.

"Fuck that, I was cool with you first, and you told me to do something and bring that shit back. I did that. I got the bread. Your word is bond, and you said if I get it, we can do something. I ain't the rest of these little niggas I promise you gone be proud you put me on. I mean, I can easily go get it from somebody else. You are supposed to look out for me though because I'm your young bull. If I fuck up, you can cut me off." He begged.

"Word?" I said.

"Word." He replied.

"Bet it, one fuck up you done. Come to the spot tomorrow, and I'm gonna give you your first pack." I promised.

"Cool, oh, your food is done." He laughed.

I gave him some snaps went and got my food then left. By the time I made it back to my house, Zailah, Maliyah, and her little friend were sitting on the steps laughing like they didn't have a care in the world. Meanwhile, I was low key hoping Bentley fucked up before his sister found out I put him on. Especially after we had multiple conversations about how she didn't want him being a part of that life.

"Hey, boo." She smiled when she noticed me.

"What's good, stink-a-butt," I smirked, pulling her up.

I wrapped my arms around her before placing a soft peck on her lips. She kissed me back but pushed me away before I could slip my tongue in her mouth.

"Eww, nasty. You better had got some for me." Maliyah's little friend smiled.

"Fuck no, you better eat some of Maliyah's shit." I frowned at her little ugly fat ass.

"Don't be mean." Zailah slapped my chest.

"What? Like it's cool to have a crush on your best friend's brother, but don't make that shit known. Plus, I heard about her little hot ass already, and she ain't even old enough to be doing the things she is doing. Maliyah, you better not try none that shit or Ima kill you, the nigga, and the muthafucka passing the message." I snapped.

"Shut up, Zailah, take him." Maliyah tried pushing us both in the house just as her phone started ringing.

"Who the fuck calling you this late?" I went to reach for her phone.

"Come on, boo, let's go chill." Zailah pulled my face to hers then kissed me.

Just like that, I didn't care about getting Maliyah's phone. However, I didn't miss the wink Zailah sent Maliyah way either.

"Leave my food, brother bear." Maliyah smiled.

Taking her food and drink out, I handed it to her, then pulled Zailah into the house. We headed to my room. I closed my door and locked it while Zailah, pulled her shoes off, and climbed on the bed.

"Come on, baby before my food gets cold." She pulled some hand, sanitizer out of her bag, and cleaned her hands.

She began to bounce on the bed as I pulled the food out of the bag. She rubbed her hands together and grabbed the brown bag with the chicken inside of it.

"Yes, with the hot sauce and ketchup, and it's still hot, oh god. It's about to be a murder scene cause I'm bout to kill these wings." She growled.

I watched her for a second as she broke the chicken wing in half, then stuffed the whole drumstick in her mouth. I wondered if she could fit my dick in her mouth like that.

"Stop staring at me, then you frowning. You better eat before your stuff get cold." She said with a mouth full of food.

"Your ass eat like a straight dude don't nothing about your eating says lady," I said.

"It doesn't taste right if you eat it all proper. This wings at your house we ain't out. Oh, and this set up cute." She pointed around the room.

I let her eat and then climbed onto the bed once she started to clean her hands off. Pulling her on top of my lap. I kissed her lips. She allowed me to slide my tongue into her mouth. My hands easily went inside of her sweat pants, and I began to rub her pearl in slow motions. Her head fell back, and she let out a loud moan.

"Shh, don't be all loud." I kissed her.

She began to grind into my fingers, so I rubbed a little faster. I placed my index finger and middle finger inside of her and made the come here motion while rubbing her clit with my thumb.

"Fuck." She mumbled as her body began to shake.

As soon as she stopped, I flipped us over, snatching her pants off of her. She looked at me with a small smirk on her face. I got us both undressed slid on a condom and went straight for the kill.

"Gosh, I think it's too big." She cried out.

"Nah, it's just enough for you," I told her, pushing into her tight center.

I slowly stroked her, and she clawed at my back. Her shit was super wet and tight. If it wasn't for the roach that ran across the top of my wall, I would have bust prematurely. I began to pick up the pace, and the bed began to knock against the wall. Grabbing a pillow, I placed it behind my headboard and continued my pounding on her pussy.

"Yess baby, fuck, oohhh shit." Zailah moaned.

Little did she know she was boosting my ego. Lifting her legs, I placed them on my shoulder, I pulled out of her, then slammed back into her. Repeating it over and over. She placed her hands on my waist, trying to push me back some causing me to have to hold onto them and began to roll my hips in a circular motion.

"Damn, that shit creamy," I growled, feeling my nut build up.

I quickly flipped her over then pushed her back down, giving her the perfect arch. I kept my hands on her back. Sliding into her wet tunnel, I gave her everything I got. While she screamed, I bit into my lip, making sure I didn't let out a moan that sounded like a bitch. The sound of her ass slapping against my stomach and her loud moans was all you could hear. If I'd known she would have been this loud, I would have turned my music up. Digging my fingers into her ass cheeks, I pounded into her.

"Shitt." She screamed as her walls locked on me, and her body shook.

"Argh fuck, damn Zailah, whoaaa." I let out as I filled the condom up with my seeds.

She fell down, and I fell with her needing to catch my breath.

"Get off me and give me my juice." She breathed.

Laughing, I rolled off of her and handed her, her juice of course after I took a big sip. Laying down on her lap, I closed my eyes, saying, fuck the food. For some reason her smell was intoxicating and I laid there enjoying the smell and thinking of how good her pussy was until sleep took over.

CHAPTER 14

 ailah

LIFE WITH KYRIE had been perfect, and I almost felt like something was going to go wrong. My father was still against me dating Ky, but I didn't give a flying fuck what he thought. I knew that he was pissed with me because today was his last day home before he got on the road, and he had yet to utter a word to me. I sat at the kitchen counter, staring at him while he hugged on my mother. Instead of interacting with them, I sat quietly, eating a plate of seafood salad like it would be my last.

This was the longest she could go without kissing the bottle. It was almost as if she needed him to function. I could tell by the way he kept looking over at me he had something to say. He pulled away from her and walked over to me. With each step that he took towards me caused my nerves began to act up.

"Zailah, we need to talk." He stated firmly.

"Okay." I barely got out.

The way he stared at me was as if he was contemplating his

next words. He stroked his beard a few times, and then my mom came over with tears in her eyes. At that moment, I knew whatever he had to say was about to be fucked up.

"Zailah, you know I love you, and I have stated rules that you clearly can't abide by." My dad started.

"It's not that I can't abide by them, I just don't think it's your choice as to whom I can date. Like how would you feel if someone told you not to date mom? You would still do it right because you can't help who you want to be with." I voiced.

"I didn't raise you to be with no drug dealing ass little boy. I'm a hardworking man, and that's what I see for my daughter. I see for you the man that you should have, not the boy that you have taken a liking to because of the name he has for himself in the streets. I want you with someone you can marry and build a future with not one that will possibly get you killed or have you visiting him in jail. I love you more than life, but if you can't follow my rules, you have to go get your own place so you can make your own rules." My father stated in a dry tone.

"What do you mean, go make my own rules? Are you putting me out? Like, what are you saying? I can't stay here anymore, where am I going to go? How can you say you love me yet put me out in the same sentence? Mom, you're okay with this?" I sobbed.

Looking over at my mom, she sighed. I knew deep down she wasn't in agreeance with this, but she loved her husband too much to go against him. I felt like the walls were closing in on me as they stood there staring at me. I had to grab my chest because it was becoming hard for me to breath. My heart was racing, and I began to cry hysterically.

"Zailah, calm down. Oh god, Zion, she's having a panic attack." my mom tried to grab me, but she pulled away.

"Zailah, your my daughter, so your always welcome to visit, but clearly, you feel as though you are grown, and since that's the case, grown people do grown things that include paying their own way." My father went on.

"Baby, I love you, and since I don't want to watch you leave, I'm going to go up in my room." my mother said in a low tone.

I knew he wanted me to beg him to allow me to stay or tell him I was willing to do whatever he wanted so that I could stay, but I wasn't. As long as I had my car, a job, and school, I would be fine. If my mother taught me one thing, she taught me to always save for a rainy day. If anything, I would get Kyrie to get someone to get me a hotel room for a few nights.

"I'm glad to know you feel that way. At least allow me to keep my things here until I find a place to store them, and can I keep my car? Or do you love me so much that you have to take that too?" I questioned.

My dad allowed me to have my two requests but I had an hour to evacuate the premises as he said. Grabbing the clothes that I knew I was going to wear along with a few coats and boots, I placed them in my car. My father or Zion shall I call him didn't even care that he was putting me out, and I had nowhere to go. I made sure I had my laptop since that was something I purchased myself.

Bentley probably was somewhere hanging with his friends, and I knew he would call me once he realized I wasn't there after a certain time. I was glad that my heat was working in my car because even though it had warmed up a little, the nights were still cold, and the spring weather hadn't fully kicked in yet. I started my car and pulled off. I drove all the way to the block I knew I would find Kyrie on and waited until he was done entertaining his customers. I got out of the car and walked over to him.

"Baby, what's up. Why my smile not on that face? Who you need me to go fuck up?" Kyrie stressed.

"I rather talk later, can I stay with you tonight?" I whispered.

"Yeah, you ready to go in now? I ain't been out here that long, but if you ready to go, we can." He said, pulling me into a hug.

"You good, I will just go sit in my car and do some of my homework. If I finish before you're done, I'll probably head over to the house. Then whenever you ready, just call me, and I'll come scoop you. Or you can drop me off there and then come get me when you done." I said with a note of relief.

"Do your homework first, and if I'm not done by the time you finished, just go ahead to her house, then come back and get me when I call you." He stated.

"Okay, by the way, thank you." I gave him a weak smile.

Kyrie nodded his head before bending down slightly to kiss my lips. He then sent me on my way. I walked back to my car and sat in the front seat, as I watched him do what he loves. While I silently cried for myself. I was hoping like hell that this thing with Kyrie went well. Wiping my tears, I looked up to the sky and told God I was going to place everything in his hands. I wasn't going to dwell on some shit that I couldn't change, nor was I going to drive myself crazy. I would explain to Kyrie the situation and see if he had an opinion, and after that, I was going to put that behind me. Opening my laptop, I began to do my homework.

"I told you I was gonna see you right?" I heard Kyrie say.

I quickly looked up to see who he was talking too. Kyrie swung before I could even see who it was. Tossing my laptop in the other seat, I hopped out of the car and ran over. Just as the guy went to swing back on Kyrie, I landed a punch to the back of his head.

"Chill, stay over there," Kyrie told me while watching the guy.

I then noticed it was the guy who stabbed him. Kyrie pulled his gun from his hip. He cocked it, causing the guy to turn to run, but Maine stopped him by sending his gun crashing down the side of his head.

"Arghhh, shit." He yelled out in pain.

That didn't stop them two from taking turns hitting the man with the gun. Kyrie must have zoned out because Maine had to pull him away.

"You trying to kill that man?" He questioned.

"He tried to kill me." Kyrie rebutted.

Turning to look at me, Kyrie frowned at me.

"Never do that shit again, you got me? I'm a man I can handle mines, had he hit yo ass back and knocked you out, I would have had to kill him. You handle the bitches that I can't touch, and I'll handle the niggas." He lectured.

Nodding my head, I made my way back to the car, too finish my work.

"You're ready?" Kyrie questioned a few minutes later.

Shaking my head yes, I kept my eyes locked on my computer screen. I had a few more words to go before I completed my essay, and I was trying to be done before we reached his house. I didn't want to worry about it anymore for the week. I was also going to call my supervisor in the morning so that I could pick up some more hours and also inquire about the manager's position that was open. I would make more money, and I would also be at work more and not cramped up in Kyrie's house or up under him too much.

I closed my computer just as he cut car off. Kyrie grabbed my bag from the backseat while I got out of the car and trailed behind him. Hopefully, his mom was asleep, and his nosey ass aunt wasn't there. We stepped inside, and god must have been tired of my hopes and prayers and finally answered one because the house was quiet and dark.

"You hungry?" he inquired as we walked into the kitchen.

I flicked the light on since it was next to me, and damn near jumped out of my skin at the number of roaches that scattered all over the place. I heard Kyrie suck his teeth before mumbling some incoherent things. He grabbed a can of raid and sprayed it before he began to clean up. I quickly grabbed my bag off the chair and took it to his room before returning.

"We can just order some pizza hut or some shit." He stated.

I could tell he was embarrassed by the expression on his face. Instead of saying anything, I began to help him clean up.

"Hey, there is no need for you to be embarrassed about roaches. I don't really care; we can just clean up and try to keep them down. Shit, I'm homeless, and now since my daddy just decided to kick me out because he doesn't see a drug-dealing boyfriend for my future, so shit, I should be the one looking like that." I let him know.

"Long as you have me, you won't have to ever be homeless. We just gone have to work hard as fuck so we can get out of here because we can't be living like this. Hell, it's bad enough I have to live like this, so I can't have you in this shit too long," he said.

I nodded in agreeance. We weren't in the kitchen for long before his sister came out. She gave him a hug and then came over to give me one.

"Hey Zailah, what you doing here so late?" she questioned.

"Staying the night with your big head ass brother." I joked.

"Yes, finally. Now when he leaves in the morning, we can go for breakfast and have girl talk like you promised we would." She smirked.

"We sure can." I laughed as Kyrie mean mugged both of us.

All of us stayed up for hours cleaning while his mother was passed out on the couch. After we were done, it smelled like straight bleach. Since it was only around midnight, Kyrie decided to order us some Chinese food and then go pick it up.

"Since he gone I can tell you. My boyfriend wants me to come over tomorrow, and you know how you always keep him company while I go over to the courts with him and his friends,

I'm gone need you to do that for me. They are having a dollar party, and I really want to go." she pouted.

"It got to be one or the other. I can't keep him in the house for that long because you know he needs to go make his money, and he ain't gone be mad at me." I smiled at her.

"I want to go to the party. It's over at midnight, but I'm only going until like ten. I love you, sis, you are the best. Now you gotta help me find something to wear or let me borrow something." She beamed

Maliyah and I had begun to form a relationship since I had been coming over more often. She was only fourteen, but Kyrie's ass had her on lock and wouldn't really allow her to do anything. I understood what it was like to be locked in the house wanting to experience the world as a teenager and do the things that the others were doing like parties and those sorts. So whenever she wanted to go, I would keep Kyrie in the house or with me. I made sure we stayed out late, and the moment he even spoke on wanting to go in, I would call her phone and hang up so that she would know to hurry her ass home.

"Fuck yall in here, all hype about," Kyrie asked, coming into the room.

"Girl things." We both replied.

Instead of him asking anything else about it, he left it alone. We sat in his room watching movies on his game while eating until we all fell asleep.

CHAPTER 15

ailah

"Maliyah, he really done got a bitch pregnant, and they having a damn shower while my stupid ass out her waddling around like a damn whale alone. He over there, smiling like he is having the time of his life. Girl either you gone drive this car faster or you gone let me fucking drive." I cried.

"You need to calm down, and before you go getting mad at me I kind of knew about what was going on. However, I didn't want to tell you. Nor did I know he was gone make me bring you so he could be there until this morning. I was looking out for the baby." She mumbled.

"You fucking what?" I yelled.

I heard her and everything she said, but I wanted my mind to be playing tricks on me. She couldn't have known and not told me. We were supposed to be sisters, and secrets were a big no-no.

"Whose sister are you?" I asked.

"Both of y'all." She responded.

"You could have gave me a fucking hint or something. I'm walking around looking stupid. That's not just some boyfriend I can leave or something like that. That man is my husband, and he can't step out on me, at a time like this." I bawled.

My heart was broken at the same time I felt like somebody knocked the wind out of me. I couldn't breathe, and it was hard trying to all I could do was cry. I thought he loved me and wanted to have a family with me and only me. I laughed at girls who were put in this position, and here I was in the same one. Yet, my man committed to me, he wasn't supposed to disregard our marriage like that.

"Just relax, you don't need to stress my baby out. I know shit is bad. However, you a queen, and you need to come out of this like one." Maliyah said.

To be honest I wasn't trying to hear shit she had to say. All I really wanted was for her to get me to the place they were holding this baby shower so that I could really see this. I needed to really see him in action. I was going to make sure everybody knew that couple wasn't as happy as they really looked.

IT FELT LIKE DAYS, but we finally made it back to Philly. Once we reached the baby shower, I wasn't sure if I really wanted to go in. Out of nowhere, I got a boost of anger and all but ran out of the car so that I could really make sure what I saw was real. I had to see it for myself to make sure I wasn't tripping. To make sure he wasn't really ripping my heart into pieces like it looked like he was trying to do.

"Sis, you can just approach him about it at home; you don't have to do this," Maliyah called chasing after me.

"That's my husband, Lee, and he got me messed up." I reminded her with tears falling down my face.

She nodded her head before placing her hand out. I knew what she wanted, and I wasn't sure if my gun was something I wanted to hand over to her.

"I just don't need you to go in there shooting nobody and having my little baby in a jail." She sighed.

Nodding my head, I decided it was best to just leave my bag in the car. Slowly I made my way back to the car and placed my bag back. I let out a breath before turning on my heels to head back to the building. I dreaded each step I took. I didn't think it could hurt anymore, but it did. As I got closer, my knees grew a little weaker. Opening the doors to the building, we walked inside, and I looked around. I knew by now that the eyeliner I wore was running down my face along with the mascara. Stepping inside, it looked as if they were opening gifts. I excused myself until I made it to the front.

"This what we doing Kyrie," I uttered.

Kyrie looked up at me as if he saw a damn ghost. He looked around for Maliyah and then frowned at her. The girl that sat beside him looked from me to him as if she was confused. Just like I was, she waited for him to respond to me. I regretted ever thinking this wouldn't hurt anymore because at the moment, I felt sick to my stomach. My body was feeling a pain that was completely foreign to me. All the times I thought he broke my heart could never prepare me for this or this feeling I was having.

"Zailah, what the hell are you doing here." He questioned as if he should have been there himself.

"The same thing you doing here, welcoming my stepchild. Kyrie does this girl, no, you have a fucking wife? Does she know that your wife is pregnant as well with your child because, from the looks of it, she doesn't." I yelled at him.

I was ready to hop up on that stage and bust him in the face with the box that held a little baby rocking chair. Yet, I knew that I would have to walk around to the steps to get to him, and by that time, his ass would have gotten up and hopped up there was something I couldn't do at the moment.

"What? Kyrie, you ain't tell me you had a damn baby on the way, nor did you mention anything about a wife. Why would you not tell me, you got me thinking we ready to start a family, and you already have one?" The girl looked like she was about to cry.

"Yo, man fuck. Look, my bad, if shit was not supposed to happen like this." He apologized to her.

For a minute, he actually looked like he cared for her. On top of that, he was apologizing to the bitch and not to me. He had me messed up, grabbing the centerpiece off the table that was closest to me. I launched it at his head. He ducked just in enough time for it to miss him. Stupid bitch, it was like God wasn't on my side because I wanted that little glass vase to knock him the fuck out, then shatter into a million pieces like he had just done my heart. Instead of doing both, it did the latter. It was in that exact moment I realized I couldn't be mad at her if I wanted to. This was all on Kyrie and his infidelities. She had nothing to do with this, so I would not direct anything towards her.

"Are you fucking crazy, I know you did that shit because I told the girl my bad, damn I owe her an apology just as well as I owe you." He barked.

"So you really just gone step out on our marriage like that? Huh, did I not give you enough? Did I not mean enough to you? I just had to come see this with my own eyes, to make sure the shit plastered all over social media was true. You had the nerve to send Maliyah and me on a trip out of town so you could do this. God, Kyrie, I want to fucking murder you. Like with my bare hands, I want to bash your fucking skull in. You ready to lose everything we got because that's where we at right now." I hiccupped.

"Man, Zailah, don't do that to me. You know I wouldn't want

to lose you over nothing. I really love you. I apologize, this wasn't supposed to happen. However, I knew that you wouldn't allow this, so I had to do what I had to do. That doesn't mean I don't want you or our family." He said in a small panicky voice.

"That's exactly what it means, don't expect me at home, and congratulations on the baby boy." I turned and made my way out.

I could hear the low talking and gasps as I headed out, I even heard the girl beginning to yell and scream at Kyrie. I almost smiled in satisfaction that their day was ruined just like mine.

"Maliyah, please just drop me off home. I don't need you to stay until your brother gets there," I told her.

She nodded her head, and we drove to my place in silence. As soon as she pulled up to the house, I grabbed my bag and wobbled as quickly as I could into the house. I sat on the bed for a while, contemplating if I should leave and never look back or if I should stay. Moments like this, I wished I could call my mom. The day I choose to be with Kyrie was the day my family cut me off, and I damn sure wasn't about to call Tierra. I rubbed my stomach in small circles while letting out a frustrated breath.

I wanted to leave, run away, and never look back. I wanted to give up and just get a divorce, that bitch could have him. However, I wanted to ask him why? I wanted to make what we have work. I wanted to fight for everything we have built.

Grabbing my suitcase, I decided that a break and some time to think was what would be best. I just couldn't think of a place to go. Had I not been pregnant as hell, I could have easily took a flight.

Once the place I could go clicked, I began to pack up my suitcase. I was grabbing all of the stuff I could fit now and leaving the rest. Hopefully, my heart led me back to my beautifully built home, but if not, I was ready to face the world.

"I know your ass ain't about to pull a disappearing act, not while my baby is in there," Maliyah said, scaring me.

"I thought your nosey ass left, and what do you want me to do Lee? I can't face him, I can't look in the face of the man that I loved with every ounce of me and see that he stepped out on me. I'm not that woman, I told him already all the bitches and hoes before the marriage were left in the past. Once we said those vows, I gave him a clean slate. I erased the thought of him stepping out on me. I forgave him for all the random bitches that popped up or ass I had to beat. And he turns around and does this?" I cried to her.

"I wish I had the answer or even knew what to say to you, but I don't. I just hope and pray that y'all can fix this." Maliyah stated.

"He broke my heart, he did more than break it ain't no words to express what he has done to me." I sobbed.

My stomach began to churn, and I felt like I was going to pass out. Wiping the sweat from my forehead, I slowly stood to grab my water bottle. Taking a sip, I sat down.

"Sis, this not good for the baby. I know you're upset, and I know you're angry. However, it ain't just about you right now. You gotta stay strong because the baby doesn't need to come early or anything. My brother is a dickhead, and he just so happens to be the man you married. Things will work themselves out, I'll love you no matter what." Maliyah told me as she rubbed my belly.

I laid back on the bed, closing my eyes, I knew I had to take a nap before I dealt with Kyrie because I just know his ass was going to pop up. I was surprised he wasn't here yet, and in a way, I was glad he wasn't. I just needed one last peaceful moment because I knew life for us was going to be anything but, after this shit.

CHAPTER 16

 yrie

"What the fuck was that Kyrie? A wife and a baby, how the hell did you forget to tell me something to that extent." Sky yelled.

"Skylar, look as much as I want to stay, I love my wife, and I don't want to lose what we have. I know I led you on, but I'm sorry. You was a night at the club gone wrong. Well, not really wrong because I actually grew to like your bald head ass. How you got pregnant off that one time, I don't know. However, I'm not gone just leave you high and dry. I'm gone handle my responsibilities. Hopefully, we can remain cool." I told her right before she slapped the shit out of me.

"I deserve that one." I laughed, licking my lips.

"Go after your wife, just know this conversation is far from over." She sighed.

"You right, We will talk later," I promised.

I would tell her what was up later; right now, I was worried about my wife and the things I would need to do to fix our relationship. Grabbing my keys and my coat, I hurried out the door not giving a fuck what anybody had to say. I was doing well over the speed limit to make it home. If I knew my wife like I thought I did she was going to be sitting on the bed with a shit load of clothes ready to leave me.

"Baby, baby," I yelled as soon as I got the door open.

When I didn't get a response, I skipped up the steps running straight towards our bedroom. I didn't know what I would do if she was gone. I quickly wiped the tears that threatened to fall at the thought of her being gone. Zailah was seated in the middle of the bed with her suitcase. I snatched it from her before speaking.

"Fuck is you doing? You not leaving me. Not now or ever, but mainly now. You got my baby in your stomach. I can't let you away from me. I know I fucked up, but it was a one-time thing. I never meant for it to go this far. I was drunk one night we were arguing I ain't even gone hold you, I was folded. My ass was hurt for real, it was that night your ass decided you wanted to go shake ya ass on that nigga in the club. I saw you and went to a strip club, I met ole girl, and from there I drank until I couldn't really focus, and I'm not completely blaming the liquor cause I knew what I was doing a little bit. I remember waking up at her house she was cooking breakfast, I got up and left. She hit me a few months later telling me she was pregnant. We did that little shit where they draw fluid from your stomach to get the DNA, and he was mine. I had to step up. I was scared to tell you afraid that I would lose my marriage, so I kept it hidden. I also didn't tell her about you because I needed to know what kind of girl she was and if she would be causing problems for me. She's not that type though, so I feel fucked up. I ain't just let yall both know what it was from the very start." I confessed.

Zailah just stared at me, she didn't say anything at all, and that is what got to me the most. It's like she was a mute or some shit and the more I talked the more she stayed quiet. I wanted her to respond, curse me out, shit I would be happy if she kicked me out. anything besides just looking at me like I broke her heart beyond words.

"Baby, talked to me. your my wife I love you more than anything please I'm sorry I didn't mean to cause you this kind of hurt especially now that you pregnant with my seed." I begged her to talk to me.

"That's it kyrie, I'm your wife and your busy doing things worse than you did when I was just your girlfriend. How I'm supposed to deal with this? knowing you share something so special, the same thing we created out of pure love with someone else?" She struggled to get out.

The way her voice cracked did something to my mind, body and soul and not in a good way. She continued to look at me and I wanted nothing more than to fix it. I tried to climb in the bed with her and just hold her but she jumped away from my touch like I had burned her.

"Fuck you Kyrie, don't touch me. You should have been thinking about the fact that I was your wife the moment you thought about sticking your dick in someone. Yeah I danced with someone but you entertained that bitch enough to give her a fucking baby. Imagine how it would feel if I went out and fucked another nigga, sucked his dick? Huh, am I not good enough for you? Do I not make you happy anymore?" She sniffed.

"Woah, Woah, suck whole dick? See now you trying to cause real bad problems. Like why would you say that?" I snapped.

"That's all you heard. I swear to god you so slow. After all this and the one thing that gets you mad is hearing about me sucking another person dick." She snapped back.

"No, fuck, yes you make me happy, and yes you are enough. Shit you are more than enough and if you want the honest to god truth. I don't deserve you, but I need you, I can't live without you. And think about fucking or sucking another nigga and Aint no need in making threats because you know how that will turn out." I tried to reassure her.

I watched her reach over and before she could sit back up I had my gun aimed at her. Zailah, thought I was stupid but I knew her very well.

"You thought you were about to catch me lackin? I know you all too well and I know you keep that gun there. I see you place it there every time you come in the house." I let her know.

"Tell me one reason why I shouldn't shoot your ass right now." She questioned.

"Cause I'm gone shoot your ass back, I would hate to cause harm to my baby but if I gotta go you gotta go too. Shit ain't no muthafucka bout to be saying that got my bitch. Won't be no widows left round here." I replied.

She sat the gun down, and I placed mines on the dresser. Once I sat it down I laid down on the bed. She didn't say anything however she moved over slightly.

"Look ain't no need to pack your bags. I really love you, you know this. Zailah and Kyrie ain't nobody else gonna make you feel like me, love you like me or even give you the kind of history we got. It ain't always been all bad nor has it been all good. I'm willing to change." I admitted.

"No the fuck you not, you say this same bullshit every time I'm ready to leave your ass. I swear I'm the dumb one for keep taking your shit. I allow you to walk all over me and for what?" She stressed.

"Don't say it like you really gone, arghhhh!" I screamed.

The shock that went through my body caught me off guard and I couldn't even move as my body twitched. I finally got enough strength to jump up. My legs were shaky and I had to catch my breath.

"You gone fucking tase me, for real I should smack the shit out of you. You better thank god you pregnant." I barked.

"No, bitch, you better thank god I'm pregnant. Cause had I

not been, you and that yellow ass female you was with what have been in the hospital with holes in y'all. Fuck you mean, you really thought you was about to lay up with me spilling your sad ass apologies. Fuck you, fuck your softy's, fuck this marriage, and fuck both the families you thought you was about to build." She stated.

"You know what, I'm just gonna leave because you asking for me to beat yo ass in here." I threatened.

I grabbed a few things, and then slid my feet into my Nike slides. I didn't even trust her enough at the moment to not do some shit when I bent to pull my shoes on. I looked up and she was struggling to get off the bed instead of helping her I got my keys and walked out of the room.

"I fucking hate you so bad, I'm gone hurt you one day too. I want to make you feel everything you ever made me feel and mark my words one day you gone feel it." Zailah yelled after me.

"Bet." I shrugged.

"You done even ducking care." She cried

"I do but what the hell you want me to do. Huh Zailah, you want me to sit here and let you beat my ass and tase me until I knock the fuck outta you? Or be a man except my wrongs and walk away? I made shit bad I ain't trying to make it worse." I admitted.

"If you walked out and died right now that shit would make my day." She shouted.

"Now just wish death on me. You know if that happened your dumb ass would be the one fucked up the most. You would be hurt because deep down inside you really don't mean that. You got it though don't worry about me trying to make shit right for a while because I'm not. I'm gonna give you the space you dying to get."

She was screaming her head off about what I didn't know because I damn near ran out the front door slamming it behind me. I knew i fucked up I admitted it and I was feeling it every bit of it. I felt like Bow wow on that outta my system song she used to always listen to back in the day. I knew I hurt her and she didn't know it but I hurt me too.

Getting in my car I pulled off and headed to Maine house. I drove at a reckless speed limit not even caring about the consequences. Whatever happened, happened. I made it to his house in all of fifteen minutes. Climbing out of the car and taking my time to go inside because I was more focused on rolling my weed. Once I stepped inside I could hear the moans from a female and him grunting. Ignoring the shit I quickly jogged down the stairs to the basement and turned on the tv. I played pandora and turned it up as loud as I could stand. Lighting my weed up and grabbing the bottle of Hennessy I sat down and drank from the bottle.

"You know why we here Kyrie, we don't have to do all that, do we? Just know you have the right to remain silent anything you say or do." The cop spoke.

"Yeah I know cut the shit and take me in. Baby I'll be back home to you in no time." I shouted over to Zailah.

Instead of responding she just looked at me and nodded, she knew her silence killed me however she had just found out I tried to fuck the girl that lived down the street and she was pissed. I had been telling her all day how I didn't even fuck just was going to if she let me. However, the niggas had to go run their mouth to her and I knew it was because they had been trying to get at Zailah for the longest but she was mine.

They took me to the precinct on 55th and pine and I had to sit for a while. I knew since I was still on probation I was gone have to do sometime however I wasn't worried about a small sit down. Especially since I was up in the game.

The moment they let me out that cold ass cell to make my phone call I dialed my baby number hoping she would pick up. When I heard her voice a smile broke onto my face.

"Baby I got you no matter what, just do your time and let me worry about the rest of the shit." Zailah spoke into the phone. Sliding down the wall I sat on the floor and sighed.

I promised myself at that moment that I would always keep her by my side and do as little to hurt her as possible because a nigga wasn't perfect. That was the same day I told her I would make her my wife.

"Aye cut this shit off, I told your ass don't fuck that girl, I can bet my last dollar that Tierra sat that shit up. Your drunk ass ain't want to listen. Either fix the shit or leave sis and let her be happy. I mean either way she deserves it. But what you ain't bout to do is drink up all my shit while wasting that good ass weed. I been said Zailah was something different and a keeper. You want to go fuck that up so deal with whatever she hand your ass. I surprised she ain't shoot you after she tried to the last time." Maine yelled cutting the music off.

""Fuck you. I'm gonna get my wife back, and how you gone preach some shit when I never even saw you take a bitch serious." I laughed.

"One day I will until them I'm blessing hoes with big dick and a good time nothing else." Maine told me.

"I'm gone give her her space. Not for long though. I love her too much." I replied.

"Don't seem like it sometimes and if it ain't that it's cause you do some shit that will contradict what you say." He admitted.

I had to look at him like he was stupid he knew how much she meant to me but maybe just maybe what he was saying was true and I would have to make a drastic change and I was willing to.

CHAPTER 17

 **ailah**

"I TOLD your sprung over dick self when we were kids his ass wasn't no good." Tierra sipped her wine.

"How do you know? You been with him, like don't disrespect my brother in front of me." Maliyah snapped.

Maliyah could talk shit about her brother all day long and even I could in front of her but nobody else did it, and she would go off. Prime example why I didn't want to have this conversation in front of Tierra. I knew Tierra wasn't a fan of him, however, she was still my friend and they didn't have to like each other. Long as they didn't disrespect each other I was fine.

"You know it's always that one family member that won't tell the nigga he ain't shit. I know ya momma and daddy know he ain't shit." Tierra laughed.

"Zailah, get your friend before I reach across this table and smack her with this bottle of wine. This broke ass always need to borrow something ass, bitch, don't got no room to talk about ain't shit. Your momma wasn't shit and you don't even know your daddy to know if he wasn't shit but I bet you he wasn't. Now speak on my brother again I fucking dare you." Maliyah sat her bag on a chair next to her.

"Listen little girl, you ain't come across a bitch like me before. I'm telling you now touch me or even jump stupid and ya brother gone have to come pick you up." Tierra smirked.

I was going to stop them because things were escalating quickly. However my belly was growling and my food was too good. I just hoped no fists were thrown, Tierra knew how I felt about Maliyah so she knew that laying as much as a finger on her was not going to sit well with me.

"I'll beat your ass and have my brother come tear this bitch the fuck up now, what's up? What you want to do?" Maliyah stood up.

Maliyah was so hot headed it wasn't funny. I was surprised she hadn't thrown any gun threats because she never left home without one. Tierra looked at her and laughed out loud. I took a sip of my lemon water then sat it down.

"Alright, listen I was just venting because for some reason I want to go home to my man in my house, yet, I want the nigga to suffer like he has never suffered before because what he not gone do is keep playing me like I'm a damn fool." I sighed.

"Girl, this the same shit you kick every time. You say you gonna leave then two days later your ass right back with him. That's why I'm glad I got me a young Bent because his ass know not to play with me." She spoke.

" A young who?" I replied because I knew my hearing had to be off. Either that or this baby had me hearing shit.

"Bentley, oh you ain't know. She would tell you all about my brother fucking and whatever else around the city or even bash him but forgot to let you know she been fucking your little brother for years. Old pervert ass." Maliyah laughed.

"Bitch please Bentley is grown as hell and always have been. I ain't start fucking him till he moved out of your momma house." Tierra spoke.

"He was seventeen when he moved out of my mother's home. Tierra how you fucking my brother and forgot to pass that info on. you know what go ahead because clearly that's what his ass wants to do. But let me tell you this if something happens to my little brother because of you. I'm going to fuck you up." I snarled.

Tierra was a good person underneath the bitch she portrayed to be. Which was why I remained friends with her for so long. I also knew that she was always on her own and had to grow up faster than most people.

"Ain't nobody gone do shit, everybody knows who Bentley run with and they don't want that kind of action. You know for Kyrie to be known for not killing people he put a lot of fear in people." She said.

"You ain't got to be a killer to get respect." I repeated the words Kyrie spoke all the time.

"Fuck that, any person I knew at the top was fucking ruthless and would shoot a nigga quick. Kyrie real difference." She smiled.

"Don't smile when you talking bout my husband. Bitch, look regular." I frowned.

Even though she said her little crush on him was gone I still ain't want nobody smiling when the talked about him but me. I felt like I should be the only bitch that spoke his name and it bring a huge smile to my face. However, at the moment it caused my heart to ache at the mention of him. I didn't know how long it would be like that. Yet he was my husband and giving him away to these thirst traps wasn't about to be that simple. If I felt like we needed to separate then we would but divorce was just something that wasn't going to happen. There was no way I was giving anybody the legacy that I helped create.

"Sis, your food." Maliyah said breaking me from my thoughts.

I looked over at the waitress and she stood there holding my steak tacos. I was greedy and always had to have an extra meal. I thanked her and the man dug in.

"Zai, I can't tell you what to do with him. I mean y'all are married but what I can say is you keep letting him walk all over you so he gone keep walking without a care. You too pretty and it's to many niggas out here willing to treat you how you supposed to be treated. Or you can just join the hoe club." Tierra shrugged.

"Hoe, my ass. You know I can't do that. Kyrie would be out here going bat shit crazy. Instead I can keep him guessing for a while and then see if he's really going to change. Because this is it for me, I honestly don't think I'll be able to accept this child." I spoke.

"Can we just enjoy the food, I don't need you to keep talking about it and bringing yourself down. If you want the real, then here it is. What you and Kyrie do or decide to do is between y'all. Nothing we say can or will change that because we are not married. We can have our opinions but that's all. It's about what Zailah wants not us. If you want to be with him shit go ahead I won't judge and if I do have something to say I'll tell you. And if you don't fuck it you took all you could we will always remain sisters. I can say that girl said she ain't no shit about you and since she has found out about you she hasn't even been a problem." Maliyah responded.

"You're right, I'm ready to go now. My hair appointment is in an hour." I sighed.

Getting up I slid a hundred dollars on the table to cover the bill and grabbed my bag. I wasn't in the mood anymore to sit there and continue that conversation. Maliyah stood up and threw a twenty on the table for a tip.

"Ain't no need in me still sitting there if you leaving. Call me later I'm gone come by or whenever you need me just hit my line." Maliyah smiled kissing my cheek.

"See you later niece." She said to my overgrown belly.

"I guess that calls for me to go as well. Zailah, you know I don't mean any harm in what I say or do. But you and Bent, are the only people who ever looked out for me or even taking me serious. I mean honestly, I kind of have some type of love for him I don't really know how to explain it because I never felt any sort of love from a man before. I didn't want to tell you because I know you would have been mad. Bent, doesn't care and it's not like we hide it from the world just from you. If I hurt you in any kind of way I apologize." She stated sounding sincere.

"I understand, and it's okay to tell me things. Yes it may hurt my feelings but let's be honest we have been friends for well over fifteen years you know how forgiving I am. Just don't do shit else for a while because I don't know how much more I can take." I replied.

I gave her a hug and then pulled away. Tierra phone began to ring and we both looked down. I saw the name "Skylar Bug" flash across the screen and she quickly snatched her phone off the table. I waved goodbye and walked off just as she answered. Sometimes I thought that girl was gay because each time that number had called for the last few months either she took the call outside or she wouldn't answer it.

"I have to go, call me so we can link again. Don't be putting too much stress on our baby." She stated.

"I got you, aye you ain't gotta rush off when your little girl-friend get to calling. I won't judge you." I joked.

"Girl, stop ain't shit bout me gay. I love dick." She replied scurrying off.

I wobbled my way to my car and then climbed inside of it. By the time I got my seat belt on I was out of breath. I didn't see how people could have kids back to back because in this moment I knew that I would never have another child. I would be those people who were one and done.

Starting my car I pulled off and headed to the hair salon, I was hoping it wasn't crowded because I didn't feel like hearing about the latest gossip. Sometimes I loved it because you would hear about any and everybody who was cheating. The only time I didn't want to hear it was when my husband's name came up. Getting out of my car I wanted to curse God for not answering my prayers. The salon was packed and I just knew some shit was going to either go down or be discussed.

"Hey La La, you ready to let that hair free or we giving you another wig today?" Jewel greeted me.

Anybody who was anybody knew that Cherish Daniels ran the best salon in Philly. Many travel to come get slayed and I was one of them. Jewel was her best stylist so it was only right that I only allowed him to play in my hair that I loved so much.

"I'm thinking I want to get some color in my weave, I need like a blunt cut bob. You can take this wig and redo it then sell it for a discounted price. I need some fresh bundles and a brand new fucking look. Make sure it's says you done fucked up and loss yo wife." I spat.

"Highly noted bitch. I have been hearing about that shit you know it's been the talk of the shop but I ain't speak on it because it ain't came from the horse's mouth. All I'm gone say is watch the company you keep and keep your ears open. Other than that I hope you been putting that degree to work while you can because that baby bump is just growing and besides all the extra shit baby you still glowing." he smiled.

"You know I'm gonna look good regardless, ain't no way in hell I'm gone allow my husband to have me out here looking any more fucked up then he already has me." I admitted.

"I admire your strength, and what God has planned for you is what he has whether it's you leaving him or yall working it out. however, follow your heart and don't go off your emotions. Now come on so I can have you looking like something delicious." He laughed pulling me to the wash bowl so he could get me right.

CHAPTER 18

yrie

"SHE REALLY LEFT your ass this time? I remember my dad made her choose, home or with you. Her ass decided to pick you ain't have a place to stay or nothing. All she kept saying was how she had you , her job and car and she would be cool." Bentley spoke.

I remembered that shit and it made me feel even worse then what I was already feeling. Grabbing the bottle I turned it up to my lips. Here I was missing my wife in a club full of bad bitches. I figured since I was single and my dick was hard I could fuck one of them. Of course my wife kept popping up in my head making shit hard for me.

"Shut that shit up. Cause your chick here popping pussy for your man's right over there in the corner." I laughed.

Bentley head snapped around so fast that his ass probably had whiplash. He jumped up when he spotted his homie and Tierra in the corner. She was in his lap giving him the dance of his life. In fact from where I was it looked like they were fucking. Bentley was pushing through the crowd of people. I picked my bottle up off the table and headed over so I could get a better view. Bentley snatched Tierra off of Dutch and threw her on the floor.

"Fuck is you out here doing ?" He snapped.

"Bent, Bentley baby it's not even that serious." Tierra tried to explain.

Bentley turned around and slapped the shit out of her before turning back to Dutch who was placing his dick back in his pants. Bentley reached for his gun but I grabbed his hand.

"We in a club full of people." I told him.

"I don't give a fuck, I'll blow this bitch up." He growled.

Bentley was in rare form, he turned back to Dutch and smacked him with his gun wherever his hits could land. Tierra started to cry and Bentley turned towards her.

"I should shot your dumb ass. Get the fuck up you gone bust it open for a nigga in the club? You really still on some hoe shit." He snapped.

"I ain't even fuck him, he was showing me his." Before she could finish Bentley punched her in the mouth.

I wasn't a fan of domestic violence so I pushed him away from her. Granted I probably would have killed both of them while they were still in action however he didn't. And there was no way I was about to let him turn into Ike Turner over no basic ass broad. What he saw in her was beyond me.

"Fuck I miss?" Maine asked.

"Where the fuck did you come from?" I replied.

Bentley pulled Tierra up off the floor and pushed her towards the door. We all watched on for a moment until they made it out.

"You foul as fuck, it don't matter what you bout to say either. Nothing should have been able to have you fucking your man's girl in the middle of the club. I would have killed you instead of just beating your ass." I told Dutch.

Dutch sucked his teeth before pulling his shirt to wipe at his mouth. He quickly stood to his feet and got the fuck out of the club. I took his seat and waited for the waitress to bring me a bottle. Maine was staring at me and I knew he was waiting for me to tell him what had happened.

"Bent caught Dutch fucking his hoe." I stated while rolling my weed.

"I told his ass to leave that hoe alone. But check this, guess who I ran into on my way here causing me to add another name to my count." Maine looked up from his own backwood he had began to roll up.

What he said had caught my attention and I was all ears. He paused for a moment as we watched one of the bottle girls walking over to us with a big ass bottle of Henny. I was wishing she stopped with her sexy ass walk and hurry up so he could tell me what was going on.

"Member that shit with Monty, his men he used to work with finally grew enough balls to come holla at me. Instead of talking to me like a grown man he figured I was still that same young bull that needed work from him. Whole time I'm relaxed and shit, this nigga was talking big shit bout how he was gone send some lil niggas at us on some takeover shit. He was spitting and all that, so I smoked the nigga with his own strap after I beat his ass." He shrugged.

"Seriously? Where the fuck Rob old ass even come from?" I questioned.

"Dead fucking serious. He pulled up on me like he was my age. I was cracking the fuck up at first until he started getting carried away." Maine replied.

I lit my weed and inhaled as he continued on with his story. My mind flashes back to the day we last seen Rob.

"WHAT THE FUCK *just happened in here?' Rob barked looking around.*

The entire stash house was cleaned out. It had been three days since Monty funeral and this was the third stash house to get hit. The last two was us but this one was handled completely different. Bodies were sprawled out everywhere. To the naked eye on the outside you would have thought this was just a regular house that was being fixed up to sale. However it wasn't, we all looked around as Rob stared each one of us down. Of course I would rather be laid up with my girl counting money but I was here to not make myself look suspicious.

"I know it was you two, it ain't like I haven't seen how since my man just up and got killed the same day he was supposed to meet yall, how yall been flossing around this bitch. You two bastards got the whole hood copping from yall and how the fuck is that possible when I know like hell he ain't give up the connect. the moment I get solid proof it was you two I'm gone have a few niggas at ya heads" he threatened.

Instead of responding to him I just laughed and lifted my shirt to show him I was always carrying. Have whoever you want come for me whenever you find out whatever it is that you are looking for. I ain't ever feared a nigga in my life and I damn sure ain't bout to pick today too. Fuck is you talking bout." I reassured him.

"Real talk boy, don't no bitch run in our blood in fact we can have at it right now you got your team and we got who we need so what's really good?" Maine snapped.

I could laugh a threat off but Maine took them very personal, however I was rocking however my boy was.

"You really want to see me bout something young bull? Fuck you mean, ill beat your ass real good like your dumb ass daddy should have instead of playing Casper your whole life." He spat at Maine.

"Look is we here for this or here about what the fuck was taking?" One of the workers yelled.

Maine not being one to let shit go calmly took a few steps forward before sending a punch Rob's way. He connected to his face before anyone could react. I watched as Rob's tooth went flying across the room. Rob stumbled but gained his footing quickly and threw his hands up.

"Fuck that now you got to rumble me." Rob swung a left followed by a right.

Only one of the hits caught Maine but it didn't faze him. He stepped back and circled around him a few times. Rob was fighting off of anger and ran up on Maine swinging wildly. Maine took a step back and sent a powerful uppercut knocking Rob on his ass.

"God damn, aight, that's enough. you asked for that shit Rib you know we too old to be out here fighting these young muthafuckas you should have shot his ass." Rob's friend laughed as he helped him up off the floor.

"Don't put know thoughts in his head. The moment he would have reached both yall would have been dead." I let him know.

"I'm gone see yall around." Rob let us know that this was far from over before heading out.

"That weed got you spacing out on me bro." Maine laughed.

"Fuck you I was thinking bout that time you knocked that nigga tooth out." I reminded him.

Looking over at Maine I noticed his eyes were looking in the direction of the entrance , I noticed exactly what had his attention. Three girls that looked the exact same was heading our way.

"Hey, I noticed yall from our VIP section and instead of having a bottle sent over to yall we decided to bring it. "I'm Lena, that's Mena, Tina. Were triplets and sometimes we like to share." Lena flirted.

I licked my lips as I looked them over . Tonight was my lucky night because I never fucked triplets before and if I had it my way I was gone bust all three of them down.

"Okay, well I hope yall came to share this bottle with us. now that yall got us that it's only right we show yall a good time." Maine smirked.

"If the price is right we will show yall and even better one." Lena let us know.

"Money never been a problem. Just drop yall price." Maine flashed her a wad of money.

"Hell yeah, yall smoke?" I questioned. In that moment I was happy as hell to be single.

"Yeah, before the night over that bottle ain't the only thing I want to wrap my lips around." Tina I think she was whispered in my ear.

"If you that bold, wrap your lips around that muthafucka then." I nodded to my semi hard dick.

I was glad as hell security was in front of our section because Tina squatted down in front of me and pulled my dick out with ease. She wrapped her hands around me before licking my dick from the base to the tip. I watched her for a second as my dick grew to its full length. She placed me in her mouth and began to bob while twisting her hands and my eyes closed.

"That's right baby sis, suck that big muthafucka." One of her sisters coached her on. In that instinct it was like she began to suck spit and kiss my dick like she would never suck one again.

"god damn bro, she looks like she at a hotdog eating contest." Maine jokes.

" Yall want to see a contest, I'll be the judge." Mena asked.

I was enjoying the feeling too much to even want to know what she was talking bout until I heard Maine groan out loud. I looked over to see Lena head bobbing and twirling. Mena was sitting on the couch opening the bottle. With my head tilted back she poured a shot into my mouth before turning to do the same to Maine. She then gave her sisters a shot before telling them to switch. Lena latched onto my dick and I almost came. Her sister head was good but she was a fucking pro.

"Bro, her shit the devil." Maine stated pointing to Lena.

I could only nod my head in agreeance I grabbed the back of my head and began to pump into her mouth. I couldn't even let out a moan because Mena was back to pouring a shot in my mouth as I came.

"Fuck that shit it's a hotel like ten minutes away. what's up with it?" I questioned them placing my dick back in my pants.

It was known way in hell she was gone suck my dick like that and I do not see what the pussy was about.

"Let's go then." Mena shrugged pouring liquor in her own mouth. She tapped Tina to let off of Maine. He went to stand but she pushed him back down.

"argh fuck." Maine screamed out and jumped up.

I reached for my gun until Mena stood up with a smirk. I paused for a second not sure if I wanted to shoot the bitch or let her suck my dick to see what the fuck she just did to my home oy.

"She got a different kind of throat." Maine let out trying to catch his breath.

Taking my hand off my gun, I nodded my head for them to lead the way. We damn near raced to the hotel once we were inside we gave them half of the money with a promise to give them the rest after we fucked. We ended up staying all night fucking and drinking until we all passed out.

CHAPTER 19

 yrie

"BENTLEY, I'm telling you. Watch ya self with that bitch. You be out in hoods that don't fuck with you busting dope moves on my streets. You can't be doing that. I'm telling you, ya bitch gone get you hurt." I tried to reason with Bentley.

Bentley was and will always be my young bull, and I was glad he came to me about these streets. Not because he made me extra money but because I would protect him with my life. He was more than just somebody on my team he was my little brother and I'd be damned if anything happened to him out here. I would feel like it was my fault and I knew damn well Zailah would blame me. Tierra was Bent's downfall. She was the one who took his virginity and sucked his soul from him. Bentley was head over heels in love with a bitch everybody smutted out at some point in their life which is why I would never touch her. On top of that she was Zailah best friend and even though I did my fair share of shit touching her would never be one of them.

"Man, you saying that cause you don't like her. Tierra love me just like I love her and we wouldn't put each other in harm's way." Bentley expressed.

I wanted to knock the damn love sick look he had off his face. Talking to Bentley was like talking to a brick wall hoping to get a response.

"Bruh." I palmed my face thinking of the right words to use.

"She loves what you possess, she loves that you out here on the streets, she loves the money you give her, she loves the house that you brought and put her in. She loves the fact that you keep her on a higher level than what she could be on her own. That's all ways you show ya love. Name some shit she has done for you or can do for you. If you got knocked today, you think she gone visit, send you bread, or even write you a letter. Let alone keep that pussy fresh and waiting on you? She gone jump to the next nigga, and that's straight facts." I told him.

"That was the last mufucka, and he wasn't no Bent, she does shit for me. I ain't gotta tell you though. Look bro, I love you and I value your advice. Yet, I don't speak on you when you in the clubs making love to strippers, fucking triplets, or how you got two ladies pregnant at once and one happens to be my sister, YOUR WIFE. So while you preaching to me remember that shit and take your own advice." He snapped.

"Bet, I won't speak on that shit no more. So when that shit blow over don't come with them broken heart stories, cause I'm gonna be the first to say I told you." I shrugged.

Handing him the package he came for, I grabbed a back wood off my desk and rolled it up. Little bro was gone have me stressing and warring over a bitch that wasn't worth it. He was to head over heels to think straight and she was to money hungry to even think of what will happen when he finds out about her and her multiple side hustles. On top of that I was praying to God to send him a little female his age that was doing right or at least wanting to his way so that he could see the difference in the bitches.

On top of that I had to deal with my own shit, Zailah being out of the house had me staying out later and being in the office more. I couldn't sleep in our bed because her scent was still fresh in the room. I was glad I had clothes for days because I hadn't done laundry since she left, since I was so used to her doing it. It wasn't no food or snacks because she went food shopping. It was about three rolls of toilet paper left that I knew would last because I was rarely there. My house isn't a home anymore because the star player was missing. I couldn't wait for her doctor's appointment to come so that I could see her.

I wanted to do good by her and be the perfect husband I just didn't know how to be. The more I felt like I was losing her the angrier I got. I didn't understand how she could just up and leave me after all that we had been through. Once I finished getting high I thought about taking my ass home and laying in my bed. I grabbed my phone and watched videos that Zailah and I had made in our phones. I had to beat my dick to the sound of her and her gushy pussy.

It was no doubt in my mind that when I saw her I was going to at least taste her if not fuck the shit out of her. I knew Zailah and it had been quite some time since I done her body right so just like me she was in need of some good love making. I had been getting pussy elsewhere yet it wasn't hers. Nor did I eat any pussy and I was dying too, since I loved to eat it so much.

Each time I fucked up I felt bad but I knew eventually she would forgive me. It didn't matter what I did Zailah always came back to me. Which was why at times it was so easy for me to step out on her.

Standing up from my desk I made my way out of my office to my car. I had one problem in this world and it just so happened to be my wife. I had come up with so many ways to be a better man to her. However, the feeling I got from cheating did something to me and the feeling alone kept me doing what I was doing.

Instead of going back to our house, I headed to my sisters. I knew she would have some information about how my two babies were doing. On the way there I stopped by Sky house just to check on her and see if she or my son needed anything. Knocking on her door she slung it open with a tired look on her face.

"What the hell do you want Kyrie?" Sky asked in a frustrated tone.

"I was just trying to come through and check on you and my young bull, that's all." I sighed

"We good." She stated before attempting to close the door.

I placed my foot in the way so she couldn't close the door. She pushed for a moment and that shit began to hurt my foot.

"Yo chill the fuck out. damn man, let me at least talk to your ass and apologize." I snapped.

She let go of the door and I pushed it open. She took a few steps back and I walked inside. Looking around I saw a bunch of boxes.

"You moving?" I asked.

"No, that's my son stuff." She replied.

She stood there staring at me with a foul look. Her hand was placed on her hip and she leaned all her weight on one foot. I wanted to go to rub her belly and talk to my son but that didn't look safe at the moment.

"I know you not here to stare at me or question me about boxes so what do you want Kyrie? I don't have time for your wife to pop up on me either. I'm not a fighter, I have never been one and I'm not about to become one. So please let her know she doesn't have to worry about me." She begged.

I nodded my head and then let my eyes roam over her. she looked good as hell and I could admit that even though she wasn't dressed. She almost, gave my wife a run for her money in the looks department.

"I came to apologize, I know I should have told you I was married but all honesty Zailah had me in my feelings. Plus you approached me I didn't approach you. That's on me though because I should have been up front with you, and even afterwards I could have told you. I just ain't know what type of chick you were and at the same time I was trying to figure you out I was trying to protect my wife and you. I don't want any drama knowing yall both was carrying my babies. I ain't gone lie either I was making sure you wasn't the messy type to do all the extra shit. Skylar, you having my son so we gone be around each other and he's also gone be a part of my family that includes my wife. I would like for that to happen and whoever you end up with just make sure he treat my lil dude as if he was his. I don't love you but I got love for you and I wish you nothing but happiness. We can be bomb ass co-parents." I admitted causing her to smile.

"You're right, I don't want no problems either Ky, so let's just do what we have to for the sake of our son and tell your wife that if and whenever she wants to sit down and talk I'm open to it. I know she will eventually and I'm all for it of course as long as she doesn't try to beat my ass." She shrugged.

"I got you, now take my son and take me off the block list so I can continue to make those appointments. Oh and stop eating all them fucking snickers." I pointed to the box she had on the table.

"Yeah whatever, now go fix shit with your wife so my son can have a healthy little brother or sister and step mom." She smiled showing me the door.

I nodded and walked to the door before pulling her into a hug and placing my hand on her stomach feeling my son kick.

" love you lil man." I spoke to her stomach.

Walking off I headed to my car and then drove to Maliyah

house. using my key to get inside I heard her on the phone laughing. It was late as hell so I figured she was asleep and that's why she hadn't responded to my calls .

"Yo, my dirty little nigga. this why you couldn't respond to me. What nigga got you all happy like that?" I questioned.

"Fuck you, don't be just walking in my shit like that scaring the fuck out of me. I should have shot your dumb ass." She glared at me placing her gun back in the kitchen drawer.

"You weren't shooting shit with your scared ass. I just came to spend a little time with my favorite sister." I told her.

"I'm your only fucking sister. and wash your hands before you go in my fridge." She warned me.

Turning to wash my hands I looked into the pots on the stove and licked my lips. Her ass had made some ribs, bake mac and greens and I was about to get me a healthy serving. I looked over and saw her ashtray which held a freshly rolled blunt and knew she was gone curse me out. Pulling weeds and wraps from my pocket I set it on the counter in front of her as she finished her phone call. I made my plate and placed it in the microwave before grabbing her shit and sparking it up.

"I knew you loved a nigga." I said while letting smoke out my mouth and nose.

"You didn't." she turned to face me.

"Just roll up while you're talking, then I need to rap with you anyway. I need to make sure work and school good for you or I'm shutting down that business account I sat up for that damn book store you want to open." I told her grabbing her full attention.

 ailah

TODAY WAS bittersweet I got to find out what I was having which also meant I had to see Kyrie. Plus my hormones been all over the place and I was dying. Not literally but if I didn't get any dick soon I was liable to. Since we had called it quits I hadn't had an ounce of dick and this baby had my hormones jumping. I couldn't even read a sex scene in a book without stopping to grab my vibrator. For some reason my toy wasn't doing it for me and now that I knew I would be in the presence of Mr. good dick himself I wanted the real thing. Shit even if it was just to get a quick one off.

Since it was hot, I put on a white and yellow off the shoulder sundress with a pair of white sandals. My 360 lace unit was curled to perfection and I even applied a little makeup. My goal was to allow Kyrie to see what he was giving up on. I was looking good as hell and that pregnancy glow helped a whole lot. Grabbing my wallet I headed out the door early so I could grab a bite to eat. The walk to my car was a long one and I could tell I was getting big because I was out of breath by the time I started my car.

After getting some food from a little breakfast store I headed to the hospital for my checkup. When I pulled up I saw Kyrie car which meant he was either sitting inside waiting or still inside of his car smoking. With the mirror tent it was no way I could tell. Grabbing my food I got out and made my way to the side entrance.

"Damn girl, you looking good as a muthafucka." Kyrie said as I walked by his car.

Just like I thought his ass was in there smoking. I knew because the moment he rolled his window down a cloud of smoke came out. Ignoring him, I continued to walk putting a little pep in my step. Shit I was scared to look at him in fear I would be in his car with my dress hiked up letting him do whatever he saw fit. The sound of his voice had me dripping like a melting ice cream in a hundred degree weather. I heard Kyrie door slam followed by his footsteps. He grabbed my arm and pulled me into a hug I didn't return.

"I miss you baby, and I just wanted, nah fuck that needed to hug you." He whispered in my ear.

My body shivered from the chills that ran through me. His arms felt so good around me that if I didn't step away I would forgive his ass. So I stepped back and looked up at him with a frown.

"You looking real fucking beautiful, I might need to put another one in you soon as you drop." He threatened before he licked his lips.

Lawd how I wished he licked me like he just licked his lips. Hell he didn't even have to do that good of a job. If he just licked me period I would be happy. And the way I was feeling he could put another baby in me or down my throat long as I got a fill of that devil dick.

"You know, I know that look. My wife need some of daddy in her life. It's cool, after this appointment, I'm gone glaze that hole for you." He smirked.

"Shut the fuck up, you ain't glazing Shit." I replied.

In all honesty I was wishing this doctor's appointment was over so he could make good on his word. Sex with Kyrie was amazing however making love to him was so much better. Kyrie was not only rough in bed but he was a complete gentlemen at the same time.

The nurse called my name and we stood up heading to the back. She took my weight and gave me a gown to put on before leaving. Once I had my gown on I came and sat on the bed. Waiting for the doctor was the longest part of the appointment. Kyrie looked over at me and then stood up. He walked over to me like an animal about to attack its prey. Kyrie grabbed me by my legs and snatched me to the end of the table like I was about to get a hysterectomy . He squatted down and raised my legs over his shoulder.

At this point my breath was caught in my throat and my eyes were glued on the door. His lips latched onto my pearl and he swirled his tongue around my clit. I swore he was drawing figure eights or whatever he wanted on my pussy. I had to bite down on my bottom lip to keep myself from moaning out loud.

"Ky, somebody might walk in here." I let out between moans.

His tongue lashing was feeling so good that my legs began to shake, and I swore I was light headed. He kept on licking and sucking on me until I came then he proceeded to lick me dry. Kyrie helped me down on the table, so that I could use wet wipes I kept in my bag to clean myself up.

"You feel what you caused." He whispered in my ear.

I was pinned against the trash can with his third leg stabbing me in the back. He had his hands on my stomach rubbing small circles while keeping me still.

"Knock Knock." Someone said as the door came open.

Kyrie took a step back from me and the lady smiled.

"Hi, I'm Veronica and I'll be performing your ultrasound and telling you what your little one is. If you haven't already could you turn off your cell phones or silence them. Thank you." She beamed.

I climbed onto the table and she placed a white paper towel cloth like thing over top of me. Kyrie sat next to me. Kyrie was looking at the screen with a big smile on his face he wanted a girl and I really didn't care what we had as long as my baby was healthy.

"Okay, this is going to be cold." The lady smiled placing the gel on my stomach.

I sucked in a breath then looked up at the screen. at first I couldn't see nothing but as she moved the thing around my baby popped up. I was a ball of nerves, I had been waiting on this day for months and it was finally here.

"I already know that's my girl in there. Watch, that's my Demi momma." Kyrie voiced.

The baby must have heard him because he or she began to move around and kick me.

"Woah, she must know her daddies voce." Veronica said as she got a picture in between Demi legs.

"I fucking told you, that's my girl." Kyrie shouted.

"alright, relax you got your girl. Now we have to come up with a middle name." I told him.

Kyrie glared at me. "come on you already know her name is Demi Maliyah."

I nodded my head in agreeance I always promised Maliyah that if I had a girl she would be named after her so I had to fulfill my promise and I was glad Kyrie was okay with that name. I was so caught up in staring at Kyrie and how he was so into the screen I hadn't even realized the lady had began to wrap everything up until she was wiping my stomach off.

"alright you can go out to the front and make your next

appointment for about three months unless the doctors order you to come back before them. But from what I seen baby girl is healthy and right on track."

we walked out after thanking her and went to make another appointment. Once we had everything schedule we headed to our cars.

"I'm gonna follow you to your spot or you can follow me to the house." Kyrie said.

"It don't matter and I'm gone follow you either way. I need some cause them toys just ain't cutting it anymore." I stated boldly.

I was so ready to show him why he should have never fucked up and what he had been missing. Wobbling to my car I climbed inside and waited for him to pull off. I followed him back to my place and was happy. I wasn't exactly ready to go back to our home. If he had gone there I would have stayed. I had invasion of privacy blasting and I rapped along to it the entire drive. This album was explaining my life and feelings at the moment which was why I was so in love with it.

"Come on." Kyrie told me.

I allowed him to help me out of my car and up the steps to my little condo I had been staying at. The moment we made it inside of the house he was all over me. Pushing me ack against the door while locking it he kissed me. Slipping his tongue into my mouth, I wrapped my leg around his waist. Kyrie took that gesture and slid his hand up my dress and palmed my ass.

"Stop playing." I mumbled into his lips.

"Shut the fuck up and let e enjoy my time, you already know how shit about to go." He reminded me.

Being the good girl that I was, I shut up and let him have his way. Kyrie picked me up and carried me to my room. He placed me on my feet and then pulled my dress over my head leaving me in my panties and bra. He stood to his full height, licking his lips as his eyes traveled over my body. Kyrie looked at me with so much lust in his eyes I was almost scared yet excited as to what he was about to do to my body. Kyrie pushed me back slightly so that I could lay on the bed. Crawling on top of me he was careful not to place all of his weight down on me.

WE KISSED PASSIONATELY until he broke it and traveled his kisses down to my neck. I sucked in a breath he knew that was my spot. He licked and sucked on the spot right below my ear causing a waterfall between my legs.

"Ky." I breathed.

Kyrie ignored me and continued to kiss on me. He kissed down my body pulling my left nipple into his mouth. He twirled his tongue around it while lightly biting down. He did the same to my right nipple and then made a slow trail down to my neatly waxed kitty.

"Oh you got her waxed for me?" He asked.

Kyrie slid down the bed until he was kneeling on the floor. He took one of my legs and told me to wrap my hands around it just below my knee, making me hold it up into place. Once he had me how he wanted me he placed light kisses on my thighs. I was soaking wet at the point and ready for all of his four play to be over with.

He licked my folds before using his fingers to separate my lips. Sucking my pearl into his mouth he used his tongue to make figure eight movements. He used his knuckle to follow behind his tongue causing a crazy sensation to shoot through my body.

"argh fuck." I moaned out.

He didn't even have to eat me for long before my body was shaking. I let out a scream and tried to push his head away. He held me in place and continued his tongue lashing as I tried to get away from him. I began to feel like I couldn't breath and tears left my eyes. I began to feel like I was about to pass out just as he let me go.

Kyrie climbed up the bed and turned me on the side. He laid me on my left side and straddled my leg. Bending my right leg he wrapped it around his waist rubbing his mushroom shaped head against my clit before entering me. We both gasped at the feeling of his entrance. His strokes were deep and slow I reach down to push him back a little but he slapped my hand out of the way. He kept up his slow pace for a minute.

"Shit, Ky.Ohh you too fucking deep." I let out.

"You better take your dick." He growled.

He rubbed circles on my clit as he picked up his pace. The feeling of pleasure and pain he was sending my body through had me screaming out as loud as I could.

"You better not take my shit from me again you hear me." Kyrie mumbled while slapping my ass.

"yes fuck." I cried out.

My body began to shake as well as his, I could feel his strokes pick up and his dick pulse. He shot his seeds in me just as my cream coated his dick.

"I love your ass I swear to god." He hissed as his body jerked.

"I love you more." I said as my eyes closed and I meant every word.

CHAPTER 21

 yrie

ZAILAH HAD BEEN out the house for a while and not talking to me. I hadn't seen her since we found out that she would be blessing me with a little girl, and she let me get some of that golden stuff god blessed her with. Since I followed her to her little apartment I decided to stop watching her from my car and knock on the door. Getting out the car I slowly walked to her door and knocked on it.

"Who the fuck is it." She barked swinging the door open.

"Why you ask who is it, if you were gone open the door before I could respond." I laughed earning a mean mug from her.

She smacked her teeth then looked at me with her hands on her hips. We stood there just having a stare down. I grabbed her and pulled her into my arms. She didn't hug me back but I didn't care I held on to her, until she attempted to push me away.

"Let me go." She mumbled.

"For what? I miss you Zailah, you my wife. I'm tired of these games you keep playing with me. for some reason you think that this is a joke and that I won't flip the fuck out if you keep this shit going. I'm trying to respect you and give you space because I know I caused you a great amount of pain but how long you gone keep this shit up." I asked.

"This not no joke nor do I think this a game. You think what I feel every day is a game? Ky, we were supposed to be a family this is supposed to be a moment that we remember and not in a bad way. this was supposed to be the part where we forget about everything and became the family we always talked about the one you always wanted. However, you fucked that up when you created a family with someone else. The crazy thing is because unlike most females my anger is completely towards you. I don't have an ounce of hate or dislike for that girl for the simple reason she ain't no you had a wife." Zailah frowned.

Seeing the hurt pour from her eyes made me feel like shit. the fact that every day I felt defeated because I couldn't fix the one thing that meant the most to me broke me more and more each day. I finally let her go and she took a big step back away from me. Giving me enough room to step in and close the door. Looking her over I noticed that she was only in one of my shirts. I was praying to god that she ain't have no panties on because if I knew my wife she was missing me like I was missing her.

She turned and walked to the kitchen I watched as her ass jiggled with each step that she took. She leaned over the island and continued to eat her fruit she stared at me as she stuck the banana in her mouth and my throat feels dry. She was trying to tease me and it was working. I licked my lips and she smirked at me.

"stop looking at me like that. On the real though I miss you too, I'm not gonna lie to you either I'm not too sure if I'll be able to accept your child. I mean I know if I take you back then I have no choice but to accept your baby. You know I'm not that mean, the little baby don't have shit to do with what you did. however, it's gonna be hard for me to look him or her in the face knowing you stepped out on me and created that." She admitted

"He is going to grow on you and you are going to love him like your own. I know you will one day, that's all I'm asking, and as much as I want to be with you, you know that if you don't accept him, I won't accept you. I understand what I did and I hope like hell we can fix it, but I love my kids more." I sighed.

I needed her to know that if she took me back then she wouldn't have a choice but to accept my son. If she felt like she couldn't we would need to part ways. There would be no way in hell I could be with her if she would act funny towards my child. I know I was wrong but if she could forgive me she could accept him.

"we will just have to see since I still have a few months. I guess we can work on us and if I don't accept him when the ties come we will call it quits. I also would like to have a sit down with your baby mother just so she knows that I'm not looking for any drama as long as she isn't, I just want to know where her head is. and if she would be okay with the whole co-parenting thing because if I do decide to accept him we will all be in this together and have to deal with each other." she replied

I looked at her with a small smile, my bitch was growing up and I was pretty sure that she was already accepting the situation she just didn't want to come right out and say it. I hadn't planned on today going like this so while she sat there eating up all the fruit in the kitchen. I looked for things to do to show her that I cared and was willing to make things right.

"You better not have my house all fucked up either." she warned.

"nah, I barely be there. I know the clothes and shit need to be washed and I painted the baby room and put some shit up there." I told her.

"You what? I need to see this you taking this whole I got my daughter thing to far. You better had did a good job too. Or I'm going to hire somebody to come and put my demi stuff together like it should be. here room needs to be fit for a princess." Zailah let me know.

Grabbing her hand I pulled her to the door. It was only one way for her to find out if I did a good job or not . I had her room decorated in gray and white and it had an enchanted mural on one side of the room. On that wall was a bookshelf full of baby books, because Zailah just knew he wanted to read to her every night. There was also a gray rocking chair on the side of the books. I had her name painted over top of where her crib would be. She had a dresser and shelves for her clothes and soap and all that stuff she would need.

"Dang, you must miss me being home. You can slow down, my big ass not about to jump out of the car and run back." She giggled.

I hadn't even noticed I was driving that fast I was so used to driving by myself that I started not to care about the speed limit altogether. Slowing down I pulled into our driveway.

"You got here in record time. Now come help me out of this damn car so I can go see what you done did to my baby room." Zailah said.

Getting out of the car I made my way around to her. Pulling the door open I helped her out of the car and lead her into the house. once we were inside I locked the doors behind us. Zailah looked around as if she was inspecting the house to see what was different.

"Everything is still the same I told you I ain't have nobody in here. It's just been me when I come by to change my clothes or just to go to sleep." I told her.

"Okay. Now after I see Demi room, we need to sit down and have a talk. I need everything out in the open and hopefully you waited for me to forgive you like I have you. I'm just hoping you took the necessary steps to win me back like you have been claiming you were. Especially since you have been blowing my shit up nonstop every day for me to come back home."

I followed Zailah up the steps thinking if I needed to tell her how I been real cozy with them triplets. I couldn't get enough of the freaky shit they were into. Now that my baby was back home I would cut them off, yet I was going to take that secret with me to the grave. I just couldn't risk losing her again. Plus what was the chances of her finding out, and if she did Maine would have to take the fall for that shit. She opened the door to the room and gasped.

"Oh my Godddddddd." she screamed out of breath.

"You can thank me now, fat ass." I smirked.

She walked around the room and took everything in. The smile on her face made me proud of my own work as if I wasn't already. I knew I did a good job but she had just confirmed it.

"Your ass can't paint so I know you ain't do this." She said.

"Hell nah, I had her god dad Maine come do that shit. It was my idea and I even tried to sketch the shit out on paper it doesn't look like this but he got the idea of what I was trying to do." I grinned.

"I ain't gone fraud, you did an amazing job. Thank you so much for doing this because I have been stressing about what I was gone do to her room." She sighed as she turned to look out of the window.

Walking up behind her I wrapped my arms around her. Placing my hands on her belly and rubbing small circles. We stood there for a moment in complete silence, I was content just how we were. Zailah laid her head back on my chest, tilting her head she kissed my chin.

"Let me go start the damn laundry." She stated breaking our silence.

"You just trying to get away from me."

Zailah nodded her head then stepped out of my embrace. Walking around me she headed towards our room which was right across the hall. She looked around in disgust.

"I swear you smoke more weed then a little bit." Zailah said while grabbing the Ziplock bag off the bed.

"*I'm in love with Mary Jane she's my main thing.*" I sang playfully.

Grabbing my dirty clothes hamper I took it down stairs for her. I jogged back up the steps just so I could watch her clean. I knew she was about to get into it when I heard the music starts to blast. Plopping down on the bed I grabbed my weed and backwoods and began to roll up. I smoked while watching her. A small smile appeared on my face as I thought about how I even missed the little things like this. I had been doing this same shit since we got our first apartment. I would travel from room to room with her and watch her clean. I used to try and help but she would get mad and tell me I was in her way.

"I hope like hell you over there thinking about what you're gonna feed me for dinner, while you smiling." she frowned.

"Actually I wasn't but, what do you have a taste for?" I questioned her.

"Some cereal." She smiled.

I knew like hell at that moment my Demi wanted cereal because Zailah wasn't too much of a cereal fan. She would only eat that if it was nothing else sweet in the house and she didn't feel like going out. Or if she decides to smoke some of my weed with me on the late night she would end up eating a big ass bowl of Cap'n crunch like she would never be able to get some again.

"Whatever you and my daughter want y'all gon get. I

promise I'm gone do my best to keep you happy from here on out. You already know I'm gonna be the best dad in the world. I just have to work on becoming the best man for you." I made it known.

CHAPTER 22

 ailah

KYRIE and I were doing good and as much as I didn't want to admit it, I was glad he was because I missed him. I hadn't had any contact or any drama for the matter with his baby mother. That was a plus for me and was also making it easier for me to accept what he had done.

"Excuse me." Kyrie randomly started to Tierra.

"Why you say that." Tierra asked him looking up with a frown attached to her face.

"Because bitch, you always in the way." He barked.

"Ain't that the fuck right." Maliyah laughed.

I tried to hold it in but I couldn't, I doubled over laughing. Causing Tierra to shot me a look that could kill even then I was still laughing.

"Brother Bear, that was one for the books." Maliyah stated and I agreed.

"You know what fuck this I'm just going to go. You think

because he gives you dick and yall on good terms, that now he can just come back and play me? like when was that shit cool I been here for you when he was out with his other family." Tierra shot.

"What? Just because I fuck him from time to time don't mean shit all good between us it just means that it isn't all bad either. Bentley, you better get her because she was not about to try and upset me because what yall got going on. I'm not a part of those problems, regardless of how Kyrie made me feel I never took that shit out on you. So go ahead boo, leave if you want too. Oh and Tierra, while you at it make sure you keep them uptown niggas far away from my brother I'd hate to have to add any more names on my baby father list of bodies." I threatened.

"You on some bull shit now Zai, them niggas ain't moving nor scaring shit. If they know like I know they will keep quiet like they been doing and leave my bitch alone because I don't want to start an unnecessary war." Bentley growled.

"You always defending her Bent. You know she was just dead wrong for getting mad at me over some shit he said." I let him know.

Tierra had to put the pussy on Bentley because he would take her side over any ones. Even the times he knew she was completely wrong like now. she had known reason to be mad at me for laughing at a joke.

"Check your man then. He shouldn't be able to call me a bitch or disrespect me. I swear if Bentley and him wasn't so close." She stomped.

"You swear what? You got me messed up. I ain't pregnant nor am I your friend. On top of that I don't give a fuck how Bentley gone feel about me running in your shit. Whatever kind of open threat that was I promise you, you better leave that shit right where it's at. Bent, on everything you better get her I swear to god I will beat this bitch ass." Maliyah snapped.

"Beat it then." Tierra yelled trying to get from behind Bentley.

Maliyah went around Bentley and he pushed her back. I knew like hell that was the wrong thing for him to do because Kyrie gripped him up so fast, that nobody had a chance to react. Giving Maliyah the chance to run around him and land a punch to Tierra face.

"You gone disrespect me like that bro, you know how I play over her and you gone test the fucking waters huh. You must believe it's fuck family cause that's how you acting." Kyrie barked.

Bentley tried to pull away but Kyrie hold remained on him. I could see Bentley jaws clenching and knew that if I didn't step in right away things would go left.

"Bitch. I told you, you wasn't fucking with me." Maliyah yelled.

I looked over to them to see Maliyah hand wrapped in Tierra hair and both of them swinging wildly. Tierra bent her knees and I knew that she was going to use her weight to slam Maliyah or at least try too.

Maliyah delivered a few punches to the back of her head before she started to uppercut. Just like I thought Tierra would, she swung Maliyah in a circle causing them both to go tumbling to the ground.

"Whoop her ass Maliyah, you better fuck her up. I swear to god or Ima beat both y'all ass." Kyrie coached.

"You better let my brother the fuck go now." I warned.

I didn't care who was fighting or what was going on. I did know that he wasn't about to have him gripped up against the wall, while he coached his little sister on. I also didn't care about who was more dominant or who disrespected who. I did care about my little brother and right or wrong I was going to protect him if need be.

"Not until he calm the fuck down. I know his lil dumb ass

and if he swing on me Zai, you gone have to be mad at me."
Kyrie spoke boldly.

"Let him go now so that y'all can stop them. They fucking up
my damn living room Ky." I whined

"Okay damn, Bent if you swing on me Ima fuck you up so
think straight and fast mufucka." Kyrie let him go and slowly
backed away.

They kept eye contact for a second before Kyrie grabbed Tierra
hands trying to pry them from Maliyah hair. I knew he would grab
her and not Maliyah so I went to step in. However Bentley rushed
over and scooped Tierra up. Sitting down on the couch I almost
wanted to grab the weed off the table and smoke the shit myself.

"When yall done we all gone sit the fuck down and get some
understanding around here. All this shit is not healthy for me
and my baby." Rubbing my temples I waited for everyone to sit.

The moment everyone sat down I handed Kyrie his weed. I
took a second to look over Tierra and Maliyah. Maliyah had
blood dripping from her lip and a bruise forming on her forehead. Tierra on the other hand would be sporting a black eye
soon and a hickey on her head.

"So now y'all just gone be walking around all fucked up.
What was supposed to be a sit down for my baby shower turned
into a fight because you all have yall own personal issues. It's
not about any of you at the moment it is about my child
though." I sighed.

Kyrie stood there looking over his sisters face the more he
looked angry he got. I shot him a look that said not right now
and he took a seat next to me. I was going to have to do as much
as possible to keep them from going at it. If I knew Kyrie like I
thought I did then he was over there contemplating on
Knocking Tierra the fuck out.

"Man, Ky, I ain't trying to be beefing with you but if you grip
me up like that again we throwing hands bro. That's real shit

like on my momma." Bentley looked directly at Kyrie who smiled at him.

"Touch my sister again I'm gone do more than grip your little ass up. And that's on your sister my boy." Kyrie smirked.

"Fuck that what's good then." Bentley stood up and pulled his pants up.

"Woah, woah." I screamed.

Looking between them I almost begged Kyrie with my eyes to not get up. He ignored me and stood up throwing his hands up.

"Wait one fucking minute. You both are not about to do this. Your brothers come on y'all gone really do this right now. Out of all the stuff you both could have fucked each other up over y'all choose this?" I questioned.

Kyrie was the first to drop his hands and sit back down. I hope that they could have a conversation about it and do what was right. I didn't want it to be awkward every time they came around each other.

"As for y'all two girls, please try and keep your hands to yourself, as well as your smart remarks. You may not care who y'all fighting effects but I do. I want my husband and brother to continue to have the good relationship they have been having for years." Looking between Maliyah and Tierra I could tell they were listening.

"I'll be the first to speak up, I apologize to my brothers and my sister for putting y'all in this situation. I ain't mean for that to go down. Tierra I don't like you and I'm not going to pretend too, what I can do is be cordial and that's all I have to offer." Maliyah shrugged.

I had to look to the sky and silently thank god. Maliyah wasn't one to apologize or be cordial with someone she didn't like but she was willing to do so. Looking over at Tierra she just sat there as if she was debating.

"I mean what do I have to apologize for she put her hands on me." Tierra spat.

"Man, you drawing. Just agree to disagree, at the end of the day this my family and I fucked up by touching little sis trying to protect you. When you can't even be an adult about the situation when everyone else is admitting their wrongs." Bentley spoke up.

Tierra stood up and wiped her hands on her pants . Turning to look at Bentley she giggled.

"It's supposed to be you and I against anybody. So for you to sit here and make it seem like I'm wrong or I have to apologize to that damn girl for touching me." Tierra said with a sigh of irritation.

"See god this why I don't be being the bigger person. Lord only you can save this bitch now." Maliyah whispered.

"It's not even about whose right or who is wrong Tee, it's about my baby shower and is being a family. If you can't understand that and put your differences aside for that then are you really family?" I asked her.

I didn't want her feeling like she was wrong or that she wasn't family. I wanted her to be a part of things just like everyone else. However she was making it very hard.

"Look babe, shit will get easier don't worry. My baby gone have the best baby shower in the world because we gone make sure of that. So stop frowning Tierra just having one of her moments. It'll be cool she'll come around." Kyrie pulled me to him kissing me on the forehead.

I nodded my head while watching Tierra walk out. I looked over at Bentley and he stayed in his seat. He grabbed the zip of weed and began to roll one up. Maliyah smiled at that because just like her brother she was a damn pothead.

"I guess we can get started now. I want it to be inside of a big building, and I need it to be sometime next month. I want a candy land theme but I also want it to be a little girl with a colorful tutu on. I want big lollipops and all kinds of candy, don't leave out no chocolate either. I need a big bucket of Ice cream so it can last me throughout the time I'm there. I don't want no chairs placing us in-front if anyone. I want to be mingling with the guess. I want games and amazing prizes. I also want to do a fifty, fifty raffle." I smiled while mainly telling Maliyah who was taking notes.

Kyrie and Bentley just sat back smoking not saying a word. If Kyrie didn't like something he didn't bother to say it. He just let me have my way and that was how I liked it for the moment.

 yrie

"Come on Maliyah, you need to tell your little girl friend to hurry up. I need to make it to the damn market, you know how Zailah, gets if I don't make it home on time for her damn shows. She needs her Ice cream and her hot fries." I sighed.

Here I was waiting for Maliyah friend to get out of work so I could take her to the shelter. I wasn't up for it but Maliyah had talked Zailah into letting me help her out. I was only here because Maliyah was in class and the poor girl had just gotten fired. Her baby dad had popped up and was in the damn place showing his ass. In result of all that she got fired. She was currently living in the shelter with her one year old baby. I thought it was none of my damn business but of course my little sister had to drag me into this shit.

"I'm about to try and call her again hold on." Maliyah voiced through the phone before hanging up.

Since it was a supermarket across the street I figured I could run inside of there since we were I had already been waiting twenty minutes. Stepping out of the car I almost wanted to get back in. It was hot as shit and I would rather be in the air. I began to walk across the street with thoughts of leaving the girl and just going home to lay up under my girl. however I didn't want to disappoint Maliyah ugly ass. stepping inside of the market I quickly made my way to the isle with the ice cream and grabbed a tub of cookies and cream ice cream. I also grabbed a box of sneakers and Twix ice cream bars. I then made my way to the chips and got the biggest bag of hot6 fries I could find. Once I had all my stuff I headed to the cash register to pay for my items.

"ma'am you gotta pay for that milk." The cashier told the girl two people ahead of me.

"Listen I need this milk. I can't just give it back." She snapped.

the girl snatched the milk and went to run out but was caught by security. The guard snatched the milk out of her hands and slammed her to the ground. I watched on contemplating what I should do. On one had I wanted to just give her the money for the gallon of milk and on the other I just wanted to pay for my shit and get back outside to wait for this slow ass girl who was going to end up getting cursed the fuck out.

"Please I need this for my baby I'll pay it back just let me get my check first." The girl cried on the floor.

"Aye look I'll pay for the shit. Just let the damn girl get up off the floor and go. Shit its only like what six dollars or some shit." I stepped up.

I couldn't take people pulling out their phones and beginning to record I know later on this lady would have saw it somehow and been embarrassed. I walked up to the cash register and added my stuff then paid it. The guard let her go and I handed her the bag with the gallon of milk inside of it.

"Thank you so much. I'm waiting for my friend's brother and

I decided to come get some milk so my baby wouldn't be up all night crying and we end up being put out of our place." She thanked me.

"No problem, it's crazy I'm waiting for my little sister's friend and just so happened to run over here to get some shit for my wife." I laughed trying to lighting the mood.

"is your name Kyrie?" she questioned.

I nodded my head.

"I'm Nina, I'm who you were waiting for. Sorry to make you have to wait and then witness that. My life isn't so great right now and I have to do what I have to do. Again thank you for all of this because you honestly didn't have to do anything." she smiled.

I had to admit, Nina was easy on the eye. She should have been out here fucking for money instead of being about to go to jail for stealing. I mean if I were her I would be. I looked her over once more and took in her body she was definitely stacked in all the right places. The only thing that was fucked up was her shoes and her weave. Had she let that shit go she would definitely be a badass jawn.

"I know you have a wife so can you please stop staring at me like that. Your married one not me." She flirted.

"my bad and you right. I know a few people who wouldn't mind throwing some cash ya way if you let the bust you down." I admitted.

We walked to my car and she got in. I asked her for the address she need to go to and then dropped her off in complete silence. Soon as she got out of the car I headed home.

"You finally came in. I hope you got my stuff." Zailah smiled.

"I do," I said, handing her the bag.

My phone began to ring and I looked down to see it was Maine calling. I frowned my face up because him calling from his burner phone could only mean one thing, and it wasn't good.

"You already know what time it is, I love you." I let Zailah know showing her my phone.

I sat my regular phone on the table and walked out the door without saying goodbye. The reason was that I didn't want to jinx myself. As if I was never coming back when I knew I was going to do everything in my power to come back.

Making my way to the garage I got in my all black impala and cruises through the streets. I grabbed my phone and dialed Maine to see where he was at.

"Uptown." He spoke before hanging up.

I knew exactly where he had to be, it was only one place he could be. Pressing my foot on the gas, I decided to take the highway instead of the regular streets. As soon as I got on the highway I lit my weed up. Tonight was about to be a long night.

Pulling up to one of our loyal customers Sap's spot I parked and grabbed my gun from up under the seat. I cocked it back placing one in the head. I was about to have to cock my gun if anything I was just gone let shit fly. I grabbed my nine from the secret compartment in between my car seat and did the same.

Stepping out of the car, I looked around, checking my surroundings then headed inside of the house. Maine was seated with his gun on his lap, smoking. I took a seat next to him then lit my own weed up.

"What's good? Why are we here? This shit just better be important." I let them know.

"Look, you need to get your man under control. His bitch gives us the drop every time I slide a few dollars and some dick her way. I keep telling you he getting real beside himself. I do business with you and I don't come short, nor do I ever have any fuck-ups. Our line of work with each other is great. I know he ya people though so I'm coming to you now. I don't want no beef with you. Shit, I don't have any with you. Yet I know his ass family to you, so if I move on him how I want, it's gone bring bad blood between us." Sap stated.

"Bro. I told him holla at you. I stay out of all this shit, but you know whatever move you willing to make, so am I." Maine told.

"All I can do is talk to him and see what he gone do. I can't make known moves for him, and I know how the game goes. I won't say that if you make a move on him, it won't be personal for me cause it will. With that being said, I respect you for coming to me like a man. Ima rap with him, and if he keeps it up, I only can respect you if shit gets out of hand." I spoke honestly.

I would be dead wrong if I told him not to fuck with Bentley. I knew the game and what came with it. Bentley had crossed lines that could have gotten him kilt. He didn't care nor fear the consequences. Standing up, I gave everyone a handshake and made my way out the door with Maine close behind me.

"Man, that nigga called me to re-up then hit me with that shit. We gotta get Bent, to stop this shit or we gone have to murk some of our best workers. Meaning he gone have to step his shit up and work on this side and his. Lil bro doing some shit that would have gotten him killed if you asked me. Ain't no way I would have let no shit like that slide. Tierra got Bent head gone, ain't no way no thot pussy got you out here ready to risk ya life. Especially one that's giving niggas the run down on you." Maine sighed.

"Real shit, it's fucked up cause he know I ain't gone let shit happen to him. Hurting him will hurt my wife, and you already know how I feel about that. What's messed up is because he doesn't even care who he dragging into this shit." I was really fucked up about the situation at hand.

"Give his little ass an ultimatum, either he cut the bitch off, or he gets cut off. I know that's family shit he family to me too. However, we ain't about to get into all of this over no bitch, nor over no shit that can be avoided. You know Id bust my gun over y'all with no hesitation, but we can avoid this, and we ain't been in jail or had no beef since we made it to this position I ain't about to get into it now unless we really need too." Maine stressed.

Nodding my head, I relaxed against the car and thought about it. Hopefully us giving him this choice would make him realize this shit wasn't as big of a deal as it could be. I was no bitch by any means however, I knew how to pick my battles wisely, which is how we made it this far without too much trouble. Maine was right, and I just hope like hell that Bentley listened this go-round.

"Aye, somebody blowing ya phone the fuck up." Maine pointed out.

Looking at my trap phone, I noticed Skylar's name. Something had to be wrong for her to be calling my business phone.

"Yo," I answered.

"I need you, baby dad." She whined.

"Fuck, is you talking bout?" I questioned.

"I think my water just broke." She cried.

"Fuck, I'm on my way. Send ya location." I said before hanging up.

Without telling Maine anything I hopped in my car and pulled off. My son was about to be born and I wasn't going to miss it for nothing. God must have been on my side because when I pulled up to Skylar house she was being placed in the back of the ambulance. I quickly parked and ran over.

"I ain't miss nothing did I?" My breathing was fast and I was sweating at this point.

"No, Ky, you didn't. Arghh." She screamed in pain.

"Try to relax, don't be scared either I'm here and I got yall no matter what." I promised.

My stomach began to hurt and I began to feel nauseous. My nerves were kicking in and I wasn't sure what I was going to do. However, I knew I was looking at Sky a little different for some reason I felt more attached to her. It had to be because she was having my son. I didn't know much about being a parent and as she screamed louder the more worried I got. My son was coming and all I wanted to be in the moment was the best father in the world. Or at least that I could be.

CHAPTER 24

 ailah

"Where is your brother? How's he been?" Maliyah's little friend asked her.

I had to do a double-take at her. I knew she felt me stating like she had just lost her fucking mind. I placed a mouthful of ice cream in my mouth to keep quiet. Here I was offering the little girl a job, and she was inquiring about my damn husband.

"Didn't I tell you he had a wife?" Maliyah snapped.

"Okay, and what that got to do with me? He fine as fuck, and I would love to see how." She started.

"He mines as fuck, and you won't love to see shit, especially not me knocking ya fucking head off your shoulders. Now you can look, however, let that be all you do." I cut her off.

Yeah, I had enough, and if she kept going I was gone chuck this damn spoon across the table and clunk the bitch in her head.

"Oh that's you, my bad. He helped me, so I was just willing to help him if need be." She smirked.

"Yeah, and he'd have to help me hide a dead body," I smirked back.

"Relax, aye. You know Sky having the baby?" Maliyah questioned.

Her eyes never left her phone, but my heart broke with those words. It was like the pain that I thought was gone came rushing back all over again. My husband was really sharing a moment that we planned to share together with someone else.

Getting up from the table, I replied. "Nah, I ain't know."

Grabbing my bag, I quickly rushed out of the food court. I dialed Kyrie's number a few times, but he didn't answer. Yet, he did respond with a text saying he would call me soon. I headed back over to the table and sat down.

Sighing, I looked over at Maliyah. "So that's why his ass ain't come in last night. Lee, I ain't gonna lie. I might have taken him back to fast."

"No, you didn't, y'all gone be together forever. It's just tough right now. I'm pretty sure you'll accept my nephew in due time." She smiled.

"I don't know if I can, and right now I'm not feeling like I can it's literally making me sick to my stomach." I admitted.

Maliyah's little friend was looking in between us, taking it all in. I wanted to get up and have this conversation else-where. My head was spinning a little bit, which caused me to grab the water and take a sip. Since he wouldn't answer me, I faced timed him from Maliyah phone and watched from the side.

"I don't know why you got me in the middle of this shit." She sighed.

Kyrie's handsome face popped up on the screen, and he had the widest smile. In all my years of knowing him, I had never seen him smile the way he was in the moment.

"Sis, look at my little nigga. He handsome as shit right. He came out weighing seven pounds even." He beamed.

"He is handsome, what's his name?" She asked.

"Truth Kyrie."

"Aww baby Truth." Maliyah cooed.

I watched as Skylar grabbed Truth from Kyrie. She held him close to her. She kissed his cheek then gave him a small baby bottle. That made me smile, but what made my heartache was the way Kyrie was looking at them. He had so much love filled in his eyes. There was a look on his face that he hadn't even given me yet. And I felt something I hadn't felt in a long time. Jealous.

"Sis, I'm so fucking happy. I haven't felt this feeling before it's like for him I want to be perfect. I never want him to look at me like I ain't shit. He just makes me want to be better already. I can't even thank Sky enough for having him." He stated with pride.

Maliyah looked over at me and gave me a sad smile. She must have known how I was feeling at that moment. What made it worse was when he walked over and kissed them both. Making Skylar smile at him and tell him thank you as well. The same kiss that made them smile was the one that broke my heart into a million pieces.

"Congrats Kyrie." I finally spoke up with a shakeup voice.

It killed me that the entire time I stood there looking in the camera with his sister, he hadn't even noticed me until I said something. I was torn. On the one hand, I was happy for him. I was happy that he loved his son and the way he looked at him. I knew he would never let him down.

On the other hand, I was hurt. Hurt to know that somebody had given him a feeling that I waited my entire adulthood to give him. I was upset that he created life outside of our family and that he was enjoying it so much.

Walking away, I headed for the bathroom. With each step I

took, the more my heart broke. I was trying so hard to contain my cries until I reached the bathroom, but it didn't work. It was hard not to cry, and maybe if I wasn't pregnant, I would have been able to not cry about the situation.

Here I was blowing his phone up all night and morning only for him to be there and not answer me. He could have at least picked up and let me know what was going on. I would have had no choice but to be okay with it. Instead he told me he was going to handle business and from the looks of it that was not business.

Inside the bathroom I looked into the mirror and cleaned my face. I stared at myself for a second just taking in my puffy red eyes.

"My mom used to always tell me be the best version of that girl that's looking back at you in the mirror. In fact, if she's looking back at you with a sad face, then you be better than the one that's looking back at you. She would say, it's not enough love in the world that should ever have you looking at yourself like the way you are now. It'll either get easier or harder. Just remember you are the person who will decide that. So no matter what, always look at yourself with as much love as you want to receive. Because you and only you will be able to give yourself the amount of love that will ever count." Maliyah's friend said from behind me.

"Thank you, and I apologize for my behavior towards you earlier." I cried.

I was thankful her mother told her those words because I needed to hear them myself. I was going to store what she had just said into my memory so I could tell my daughter that. I also apologized because I could have handled it better.

"If you want my opinion, then it's fuck him. I don't know y'all history though. But if it's deep enough for you to be wearing that wedding ring then you have to decide if what you're going through is deep enough for you to let go." She with a small smile.

"That's the thing one minute I feel like I need to let go, and the next, I remember how much I love him and what we been through. The promises, the vows. I don't want nobody to reap the benefits of what I helped him build. I don't want anyone to get him to be the man that he was supposed to be for me." I admitted.

"If you wasn't the one to fuck up them vows, promises, and whatever else, why beat yourself up about it? I know you don't know much about me, but I was married too, and I'm only twenty-two. My soon to be ex-husband took me through the worse. And I would say I didn't want anybody to have him because I knew he had the potential to be the man of someone dreams. You know how fucked up I was when I found out my four-year-old sister is my child's aunt and sister? Once I found out that my mother was the same person who had him put me and our child out. He was the man I prayed daily he would be to me for my own mother. I didn't let that faze me though I'm homeless with a child and a wealthy ass husband. I say that to say this, I'm worth more right now than I ever was."

I listened to her, and we both were in tears at this point. I didn't know this girl really, but I knew she would be someone I held close to me. She had me feeling like my problems weren't even as big as hers.

"It'll be alright. I help you as long as you promise to keep giving me these inspirational ass talks. I'm gone help you get on your feet; that's my word." I promised.

"Bet." She wiped her tears.

I heard sniffles from behind us, and I looked in the mirror to see a lady I didn't know and Maliyah both crying with us.

"I'm sorry, but both of y'all stories were so touching that I tried to walk out but just couldn't. God has something great planned for the both of you. Just remain positive and keep pray-ing." The lady told us before walking out.

"Man, y'all come fucked up my makeup. Zai, you know I love you right, and even though I love you for my brother. I'll still love you no matter what you decide. We will always be sisters, and nobody can change that. I'm not sure if you upset at me for loving my nephew already, but you know I love kids and can't help it. He's a baby, and he's innocent. I don't want you to be mad at me though, or feel like I don't care about your feelings because I do, and my niece will always be my favorite. That's why I need you not to stress that much. I know that's asking a lot, but everything you feeling so is she and we need to welcome a healthy baby." Maliyah came over and hugged me.

"I love you too, and what the hell is your name because you never told me," I asked the friend.

"Nina, my name is Nina." Nina extended her hand.

I grabbed it and shook it while replying.

"Nice to meet you, Nina, I'm Zailah." I smiled.

"Nice to meet you as well. Now Maliyah, can we get the clothes you promised. Cion really needs some new stuff. And once I get paid more, I'll pay you back." Nina said barely above a whisper.

I looked back and forth between the both of them. I knew Maliyah was nice, but sometimes she wasn't that nice. That girl loved to save money and then go on a big shopping spree on herself. That let me know she really cared for Nina because she didn't help anybody she barely liked people.

"Don't insult me. Pay me back by giving me a closet in your place when you get it. I know that right now, your savings to get a house or apartment, so if I can help, I will. I wish you would let me give you the last thousand dollars you need." Maliyah huffed.

"I just want to work for it, that's all," Nina replied.

"How about this, since we shopping and you look cute,

letting me know you can dress. I'll pay you a thousand dollars you need to baby shop for me. Like bottles whatever you think I'm gone need. I'll cash app you the money as soon as we leave out of the mall." I smirked.

"Seriously, oh my God. Thank you pooh. "I love you." Nina cried.

"Girl, hush. Just don't cross me, and we will remain cool. Now come on and make this money." I smiled.

For now, I was happy, and all my sad feelings were placed in the back of my mind. I knew once I face Kyrie, I would be back to feeling hurt. So, for the time being, I was going to enjoy the moment.

yrie

"Kyrie, you know you gone have to talk to your wife. I don't have a problem with her, and I know that Truth, will be a part of y'all family. Meaning that she will have to be around him. I just don't want her hating my son over something that had nothing to do with him." Sky voiced.

"Chill, I already told her that if she doesn't accept him, then we wouldn't work. Wife or not, my son will be my main priority, and when my baby girl comes, then so will she. My wife follows behind that. She wouldn't do anything to him or anything like that. Zai is just hurt, and I'm pretty sure you understand that." I sighed.

I could hear how broken Zailah was from her voice. So even though we had just taken what felt like fifty steps forward, I knew now we had just taken hundreds of steps backward.

"I really wish shit was different. I don't regret my son, but I do regret the position you put us in." Sky teared up.

"Look, baby mom. Right now we are about to enjoy this time as a family. We are not about to give my son any negative vibes. I know I fucked up, that's something I have to deal with. My son here now and you nor Zailah can change that." I stated.

I really wanted everyone to shut up and feel however they were going to. As far as myself, I would deal with whatever consequences that came from my actions. However, I was going to enjoy every minute of the time spent with my son.

"You just being so nonchalant right now, it's crazy. Kyrie, we gone have to deal with it, and I rather deal with it now then for the next eighteen years. You were supposed to have us sit down, and you have still yet to do so. And don't say it's because y'all wasn't talking because both of y'all rings are back on." Sky said.

"You right, but that's cause that shit wasn't on my mind at the time. Don't think it was ever brought up when it was. She agreed to do it as well. However, I, myself, ain't ready we just got back on good terms, so I was busy trying to fix shit as well as handle some other things. Now, if you want to sit down with her that bad, I'll give you her number, and y'all can do that. I would rather wait it out though until my daughter is born, so she doesn't get too stressed out." I admitted.

Yeah, I was stalling on them having a sit down, but my intentions for stalling were good. I knew that Zailah, said she would behave and act like an adult. However, she had said that in situations millions of times and acted the complete opposite. I knew it was going to have to happen one day because it wasn't no way in hell my kids wouldn't know each other or not be able to spend time with each other because of their moms.

"Hand me my damn son." I reached for Truth.

Sky swatted my hand away before frowning at me. I had to pinch the bridge of my nose because she had me pissed off with that move.

"Don't play with me. Give me my damn son." I growled.

She handed him over with a small smile attached to her face.

She was beautiful as hell, especially with her natural look. Her hair was all over the place instead of in the neat bun she originally came in. Her lips were full, and the beauty mark on the side of her mouth was so sexy to me.

Sky was the complete opposite of Zailah. Zailah was small but thick in all the right places. She had one deep dimple and hazel green eyes. She kept her hair in the latest weaves, but when it wasn't, it reached just a little past her shoulder.

While Sky was straight thick. She had thunder thighs, ass for days, and her stomach wasn't flat. Sky's eyes were a dark brown color so dark you would think they were black. She had really thick and long hair that she wore out all the time. She was very natural and pretty as hell.

Just like Zailah she was short; however she was much taller than Zailah. While Zailah was a firecracker, Sky wasn't. She was always calm in situations, and she never really went against my word, usually what I said went. She was easy to talk to, and I could just sit around her for hours without much arguing or talking for the matter.

My wife still had insecurities that I knew was my fault. Yet, I felt like if she forgave me, then she shouldn't keep bringing it up.

"So when you gone allow her to meet your son. I just feel like you pushing all this shit back. I'm not trying to nag you or anything, but I want to get to a point where there isn't any confusion, and the sooner, the better." Sky went on again.

"Now you starting to irritate me. I said shit would happen soon. I know it's better for it to happen now. But she's still carrying my daughter, and I don't want to add anything further to stress her out than I already did. Why you can't just leave the shit alone for now." I barked.

"Okay, no need to get loud. I'll leave it alone." She put her hands up in the air as if she was surrendering.

I took my son and played with him. I gazed down into his

eyes and wanted to give him everything his little heart would want. I wanted to protect him from any evil. It was like I wanted to shield him from the life I loved the one I lived every day. God willing, I would be able to make sure his savings account doubled the money I had put up already, also making sure college was paid for anyone he wanted to go to. I wanted him to have the chance at life niggas in the hood never thought they could get.

Shit, I was proud of him already, and he didn't even do nothing but hold on to my finger and give me a small smile. My heart was almost full. I just needed his sister to make it complete. With them, nothing else in the world would matter.

CHAPTER 26

*K*yrie

"Man, Bent, I told your ass about coming up here and doing all this shit. Now how many times you think I'm going to be able to just talk to these niggas about you moving on their turf. You not thinking straight, and it's only so much I can tell you about your bitch. She gone fuck around and either get your hurt or killed." I snapped at Bentley.

Here we were five in the afternoon in another person hood and he was having beef. Now granted, I was the plug and could cut all this shit, but why lose out on some money over some shit that should have been stopped. On top of that, even if I wasn't the plug to these niggas, it was only so much disrespect a person could take. And these weren't Bentley's corners, nor was this his hood. Sap already made multiple attempts on solving shit. Bentley just couldn't get it together and was slowly but surely about to start some shit up.

"Bro, they tripping over a few measly ass dollars. They act like I'm coming down here busting all they trap." He shrugged.

"You one hard-headed muthafucka," I told him, and he smirked.

Walking away from him, all I could do was shake my head. To prevent any further problems, I was just going to have to call on my wife to get her friend in check. Because if I had to, I was going to send a group of bitches to beat her into submission. Had she not been throwing pussy to the highest bidder, we wouldn't be going through this. On top of that, I would much rather be chilling with my son.

"Look, what can we do to fix this shit and keep the money flowing," I asked Sap.

"I'm tired of talking to young bull. Every day it's the same shit and the nigga acting untouchable. I'm telling you now control him for some shit happen to him. Especially over a bitch the whole hood then smutted out." Sap stated boldly.

"First of all, calm the fuck down. Now I'm here cause you called me. No need for the threats because it ain't gonna happen." I replied as calmly as I could.

"Ain't shit, and I mean shit gone happen to me. Fuck you talking bout. You calling big bro on nut shit, if you was really bout it why you ain't holla at me. I'll beat you the fuck up out here." Bent roared.

"Chill the fuck out. You on some bull shit, and I keep telling you that." I told him, pushing him back.

I was real close to fucking Bentley up myself. I was even more ready to curse him the fuck out, but I wasn't gone do it. Not now anyway, he knew the moment we wasn't around people I was gone give him hell.

"See, you can't control your little niggas. I'm about to have to take my business elsewhere." He replied.

This was something I continuously told Bent, him acting like this when I was in his face telling him to chill was complete disrespect. Each day I was leaning closer to cutting ties with him. Outside of the bullshit, he was in, he made good money and fast. I valued him as a worker and little brother. He just didn't know when to relax.

"Elsewhere? Who shit you gone find pure like mine? In fact, go ahead. I ain't missing out on shit if you do. Now, if you want to be on that shit with me, this can go however you want it to. Now either we can squash this shit and Bent you stay off their streets, or it can be whatever." I said, not really in the mood to deal with it no more.

For a while, I had been trying to keep shit cordial and even keep Bent away; however, he was hard-headed and didn't understand the problems he would cause. Bentley was a prime example of a person who had to lose someone close because of his shit or damn near lose himself before he thought of his actions before taking them.

"All I'm saying is keep the little nigga on his blocks we ain't coming down there fucking with his money, stepping on his toes or nothing. I expect the same shit back from him. You right ain't nobody shit pure like yours, but I rather cut ties then to have to kill a nigga. Or have a young dick head trying to kill me over some dirty ass bitch. Ain't gone be too much more of this going back and forth shit before a whole lot of blood is shed. Ayo Bentley next to you run up pussy nigga you better swing cause I'm gone clean yo ass ain't no more words from here on out. This the last of them. I put that on my mama grave. I catch you busting a trap on my shit we gone have some problems." Sap snapped.

"Oh yeah? Ayo, what you said you needed?" Bentley asked a smoker.

He served the fiend the turned in looked at Sap with a wide smile on his face. This boy was bold and disrespectful as hell.

"So what you said was gone happen?" He questioned placing his phone and money inside his car.

Instead of interfering, I watched to see what would happen. Sap nodded his head at his squad, causing them to start moving in on Bentley. I was thinking about shooting all they asses, but I quickly thought against it.

"Check this, you got a problem with him, you handle that shit. He a grown ass man, you don't see me making no moves. What you not bout to do is have ya people go at him while I'm standing here. Like as if I won't be willing to sit a few of ya folks down." I jumped from off the top of my car and wiped my hands over my head.

Sap called his people off Bent, before stepping into the street with him. Bentley was smirking and already in his fighting stance. Sap pulled his pants up, then swung. Bentley wasn't quick enough, and the punch landed making him take a step back.

Sap had to be mad and ready to get some shit off cause he didn't come to play. Bentley squared up again, and this time, he swung twice, catching Sap with the first one and missing the second. Circled around each other before swinging wildly. Bentley was getting the best at Sap until he picked him up and dumped him on his shit.

"Damn," I muttered at the sound of Bent hitting the ground.

"Get the fuck off him." One of Sap's men yelled.

I had to be seeing wrong because what I thought was Bentley hitting the ground was actually Sap's head. Bentley somehow got him in a head lock, and as he was going down, he held on to his head. Reaching for my gun, I quickly headed over.

"Nah, don't touch him. Grab ya man, and I'll grab him." I eyed the guy.

I didn't know him nor worked with him. I knew that he worked under Sap, and if he knew what was best for him, he would follow my instructions.

"Best believe you gone see me." Sap threatened once he was back on his feet.

"It's whatever bull, go get some ice for that lump on ya shit. Plus, that muthafucka bleeding. Go get ya shit together, then we can do whatever you want." Bent spat blood on the ground.

"Let's go," I told Bentley.

Turning on my heels I got inside my car watching Sap and his crew like a hawk. Bentley hopped in his car and sped off. I followed him until he pulled up to his apartment. I jumped out of the car and snatched him up by his shirt.

"You see what the fuck yo bitch caused. Matter of fact, I can't even blame the hoe to much anymore; it's you. You don't know when to walk the fuck away. How you plan on reaching the level of a boss when you still picking fucking fights that have now turned into a war. I know because he has been speaking on it. I couldn't dead the nigga in broad daylight with a bunch of kids and shit outside. Or start a fucking shoot out. I rarely get my hands dirty, so adding a kid to my list of bodies wasn't happening. I don't wanna see you on NO blocks until your hotheaded ass cools down." I snapped.

I was shaking him like a child that pissed you off and you didn't want to hit them. I gave him one finally shake and let him go. I was sure what I said got to him because he had a look of defeat on his face.

"How I'm pose to make money if I can't hit the blocks? Look I'll go fix the shit man." He pleaded.

"It's too fucking late to fix the shit. You done disrespected that man on multiple occasions, then you beat his ass in front of his crew. He gone have to redeem himself or his respect and name in these streets won't mean shit. So what you think he gone do? You seem to forget niggas be willing to die over respect man. You weren't worried about your blocks while you were out on another man's block. So don't worry bout it now. I'll have Rock take over until you ready to come back." I told him.

"Come on bro, you supposed to be my brother you really gone do this." Bentley said on the verge of tears.

"That's exactly why I have to do this. I rather lose money then you lose your life. Your life is worth more than money to me. It's not a permanent thing unless you make it." I shrugged.

Bentley snatched the perfectly rolled weed out my hand and stormed off into his spot. Had he not been upset, I would have snapped on him, but I let him have it.

After everything was said and done, I found myself sitting in my car, blowing back to back. I was outside of my house thinking of all that shit that was going on. I was trying to convince myself that Sap would let this shit go, however, knowing the streets and how they worked led me to believe someone was going to have to die. If I had it my way, Sap would have to go.

Neyo's voice came through the speakers causing my thoughts to shift. Now all I wanted to do was get out and go be with my daughter and my wife. I needed them more than anything, and it was killing me that I couldn't give my daughter the family she deserved. I knew I fucked up, but I was honestly ready to change. Zailah had to know that this time, I felt how serious she was. That I didn't want to fuck up anymore and I would honor my wife.

She's always considering my feelings
Thinking' of me before herself
Most of the time I'm so damn selfish
I don't even realize she treats me so well
She's so much better than me
I'm so unworthy of her
Oh, Why does she stay

Neyo was proving points when he made this Cd, and I wish like hell that I would have been listened to this damn song and changed my ways before it was too late. I wiped the tears with the back of my hand and got my shit together. She would understand soon that I wanted her and only her. I was willing to do whatever needed to be done to make her feel like she was supposed to. I just pray that it's not too late. I could see in her face that she thought I was feeling some type of way about Sky, and honestly, I was. But I was comfortable with Zailah. I knew her in and out and didn't have to learn things about her. I also knew that I loved her deeply and not just because she gave me a child. However, with Sky, she just was a breath of fresh air, and I think my feelings grew for her because she gave me my first-born, my son.

No matter how it things went I would always love and protect the both of them. I needed to get my shit together and fast.

CHAPTER 27

 ailah

STANDING at my mother's door, I kept telling myself I shouldn't be here. This was something I did once a year and got the same thing. Knocking on the door repeatedly, I waited for someone to open the door. I wanted to check on my family and tell my parents that they were going to be grands.

"Get the fuck off my porch Zailah." My father yelled through the Ring bell that held a camera and speaker.

Turning around, I walked off the porch and headed for my destination. Trying to suck it up like it didn't matter was no use. The tears fell once I sat in my car. I was parked outside of their home, bawling my eyes out. I couldn't believe he was still acting like this after all these years. I failed at every attempt to talk to them; however, no matter how much it hurts, I couldn't give up. Wiping my eyes, I pulled off and headed to the nail salon.

I drove slowly through traffic just to get myself together since where I was going wasn't far from my mother's place. I got myself together, and before I stepped out, I used a baby wipe to clean my face. Once I looked presentable, I made my way inside. I wasn't at all surprised to see Tierra because we always came here on the same day since our teenage years.

"What you been up too? You just call yourself being mad at me for nothing." I smiled at Tierra.

I hadn't seen her since the fight, and I kind of missed her. Though she couldn't stand Kyrie, I had someone to talk to who wasn't on his side. As much as Maliyah loved me she loved me even more for her brother.

"Girl, I just been hanging with Bent. He been mad though. Kyrie took him off the blocks because of some shit he got into, and he's been laying low." She stated.

We were currently sitting side by side at the nail salon. My eyes popped open at what she said.

"He what? Since when? I ain't know nothing about that. Bent, had to do some shit though if Kyrie and Maine agreed to take him off his blocks. That ain't something they would just do." I replied.

I was glad today wasn't as packed as usual in fact, we were the only two people here at the moment, and I was glad for that.

"That's what I said. It has something to do with some nigga name Sap from round my way." She downplayed the situation.

"You talking bout Sap with the dreads? The one you used to fuck with while you and Bent was going through y'all little shit? That ain't got nothing to do with you, right? I know how Bentley gets over you. Please tell me you ain't get my little brother into no dumb shit." I was now turned in the seat facing her.

"It shouldn't have nothing to do with me. From what I heard, Bent been moving on Sap's space, and Sap wasn't feeling it. I also heard your stepson was born, how's that going?" She tried switching the subject.

Usually, I would have went with it. However, I heard about

Sap. I knew that he was one of Kyrie's best workers. I also heard how he and his crew got down. Now I wasn't doubting my brother, not one bit, especially if it came down to him having to fight. As far as a shoot out though, he had never been in one, and I prayed to God daily that he wouldn't have to.

"Girl, we will get to that, but right now, I'm worried about my brother. So is this fixable like I can get Kyrie to step in?" I questioned.

"Kyrie knows about it. He was there when they threw hands. Bentley fucked Sap shit up too, and he didn't like that. You know how that goes. I have been keeping my eye on Sap. Regardless of anything, Bentley is my baby, and I honestly love him. He's always had my back, I regret doing some shit, and ever since they beef escalated, he takes it out on me as if it's my fault." She cried.

I almost just almost felt bad for her. I knew that she loved my brother or had to have love for him. They were together for years, but it didn't mean she would protect him or that she loved him more than she loved money.

Tierra was a person that would be willing to do anything if the price was right. Or if it was to make her feel like she had one up on somebody. Which was why the constant thought of Kyrie and I always played in my mind. After finding out she wanted him first, I knew she was going to do something to hurt me. She tried many times back in the day to sleep with him, but when he didn't budge, I guess she gave up. I used to be mad yet, I moved passed it once she offered an apology and got her ass whipped.

"I just can't wait for you to pop, then we can go out every here and there and have fun like we used to. Being stuck at home with your brother is driving me wild."

I nodded my head at her and took a sip from my homemade Iced Tea. She was doing all this talking, yet my mind was on my brother and seeing what Kyrie could do to handle this before someone got hurt.

"Eyebrow done?" The lady asked me.

I shook my head no, getting up I went and paid for my stuff and headed out the door. I was trying to hurry up and get to Kyrie and figure out what was going on. Dialing his number, he didn't answer just like it had been for the last few days. It was like once his son was born, he completely forgot about his home. And as much as he begged me to stay and promised to do right. I felt like he wasn't even holding up to his end of the bargain.

Instead of heading home, I drove by Bentley's place. Somebody was going to give me answers as to what the fuck was going on, and since Kyrie wanted to not respond, I was going to go straight to the source. I was driving through the whole hood just to see if I see Kyrie. For a minute, I was mad at myself because this was some shit I did when we were younger. I would circle the block for hours at a time any place I knew he hung I would ride there checking for him. It was plenty of times I went by Maines house and banged on the door at wee hours in the morning. I always told him nothing should ever stop you from coming home. Unless he was dead in the hospital or in jail.

Parking on the street, I got out and walked the few minutes to his house. Since his block was always full of cars, I wasn't able to park in front of his house. Wobbling up the steps, I knocked on the door while catching my breath. I waited a second before the door was swung open, and the smell of weed-filled my nostrils.

"What's up fat ass?" Bentley greeted me.

"Fuck you," I stated while stepping inside.

"How's the little one? I can't wait for you to pop. I'm gone finally have me a little baby." He rubbed my stomach.

I swatted his hand away. He knew I really didn't like anyone touching me. This little baby would go crazy the moment someone rubbed my stomach, and the kicks were powerful.

"I'm pretty sure you know why I'm here. Why I had to find

out shit from Tierra? When were you gone fill me in on what the fuck was going on? Why didn't Kyrie handle this shit, did you even tell him before this shit escalated? Bentley, I'm not about to lose you to these fucking streets." I yelled in his face.

I was fuming mad, how could he put himself in a position like this. He was the only family I really had left. I thought about going over to my mom's house, but the one time I did had me questioning myself every time I had a thought about visiting.

"Man, them niggas was telling me what I wasn't and was gone do. You know I ain't ever been one to follow directions. Then I felt like that dickhead thought he had one up on me because he fucked my bitch. Like out of all the niggas in the world, she could have fucked she gone fuck a nigga in Philly." He barked.

Taking a seat on the couch next to him, I watched him place his head in his hands. Instead of rubbing his back and consoling him, I sat there watching him.

"So you are saying all this because he fucked Tierra? Bro, you knew when you first met her how she was, you thought she was gone change because of you? Let me be the first to tell you just because you love someone and are willing to change to make your relationship with them perfect, doesn't mean they will be willing to do the same. If they are willing to do it, it will be on their time, not yours. Bent, that's shit you watched me go through for years even after marriage and doing bid after bid. I did everything in my power to make him be what I wanted, and he's still is who he wants to be." I confessed.

"I hear all that, I'm saying though. When it's just us, shit seems so perfect, she understands me. We vibe on a whole nother level. It's just that baby girl got a pussy that's mighty friendly. I mean, I know I can't erase her past but got damn if that shit don't gotta come back to bite me in the ass. Then Sap's nut ass talked all this beat my ass bullshit until he caught these hands, and the outcome wasn't what he thought. Now Kyrie got me laying low until we figure out just what moves he gone make." Bentley sighed.

"I get how this shit goes, and I know I need to be strapped at all cost. I also know that he took me off the blocks because if something happens to me, that will fuck you up. He gone want revenge. But at the same time, its money out here to be made, and I'm missing out on it." He went on.

"Look, I know he took you off the blocks, and you know like I do, he has a valid reason. What I want to know is, what are you going to do after everything blows over? Are you going to take this as a lesson learned or not?' I questioned him.

"Hell yeah, next time I'm gonna kill that bitch. I don't even know how it got to this point I swear I heard what Ky was telling me. However, that man was testing my hand like don't wave ya white flag and at the same time throw threats shit just call it quits and walk away. I was trying man, the fucked up part is because I care about losing money more than I care about any of this shit." Bentley was now standing up and pacing.

"Just calm down and think shit all the way through. I know right now shit ain't going your way, but it will if you think before you react. Even if he threw silent threats after he waved his flag, he still waved that muthafucka and copped out. You should have left it alone. He was not supposed to not fuck your bitch it was free pussy thrown his way, and if you were in the position, you would have glazed that hole as well. You gotta take that out on her, not lose out on no money. You smarter than that now you out here spending savings and smoking up all this got damn weed. Gone have me high as a kite before I walk out this damn door." I expressed.

Since we had been here and was talking, he had smoked at least three times. Yet he still hadn't told me what he was gone from here. I hoped like hell he left my friend alone, but if not, I would be happy for him.

"So again, after this what you gonna do?" I questioned

"I'm gone do shit the right way this time I'm not gonna be out here beefing with nobody unless I have to. Ain't gone be no more doing no petty dumb shit. Man, this shit really fucking me up. I have goals and money that I want to save. I'm trying to be hood rich by the time I'm twenty-five." He smiled.

"You still got time baby bro, you just gotta get your shit together and fast. Don't let this stop you just take it as a learning process and move forward. You got potential everyone sees it. I love you, Bentley; don't forget that. You're smart, now, you got to make smarter moves. I'm bout to get up out of here, this baby got me tired." I stood up, hugged him, and made my way home to an empty house.

CHAPTER 28

yrie

"BITCH, GET THE FUCK OUT," Zailah yelled out soon as the door closed.

"Zailah, chill the fuck out. This my house just like it's yours. I apologize for not being here for all those days. My son was born, and I can't help it, but I want to be with him all the time." I smiled, just thinking of Truth.

"Well, that's an even better reason for you to leave. I'll call you when your daughter decides to make her presence known. You know her baby shower would have been even better had her dad shown up yesterday. That was strike three for you. Kyrie, please go. I ain't trying to fuck with you like that no more, and quite frankly, I don't want to. You have done enough. Like come on, you really forgot about that. Knowing I was planning that day for a really long time. You so caught up on not answering my calls because you think I'm gone trip on you.

Then you completely forgot to tell me about my brother. Who the fuck is this person you're becoming." She screamed.

Rubbing my hand across my mouth, I looked at her. I was so caught up in my son coming home yesterday and getting his room together. I forgot about the baby shower. By the time I remembered it was over.

"It wasn't like that, Truth came home, and none of his shit was put together. I went over to help and got caught up. We can have another baby shower. Damn man, why you ain't text me or some shit." I replied, trying to find ways to have been reminded.

"You trying to make me go upside your fucking head right? You ain't even answer your sister's calls. On god, you need to fucking go. Go back to wherever you came from. Then you got the nerve to be staying the night out. Oh, you really playing family. You got me messed up." She shouted.

Each time she came around the island in the kitchen, I made my way to the other side to stay out of her reach.

"Yeah, bitch, he got you fucked up," Zailah said out loud.

This muthafucka was talking to herself. I knew she had to be tripping now. My best bet was to get the fuck out of dodge; however, I wasn't near the door. And if I went into the back yard, she would just follow me.

"You need to sit the hell down and relax," I told her.

She frowned her face at me then took a sip of her cup.

"What you not bout to do is waltz your ugly ass in here and tell me what I need to do. Since you want to talk about what people need to do, let's talk about you. You need to get your shit together. Kyrie needs to remember he has a child on the way. Oh, and you also need to attend to your wife. Let me see what else, you need to have your baby mother meet me real fucking soon. In fact, nah scratch that at this point, I may beat her ass just because you getting on my nerves, and I can't beat you. You also need to remind yourself where home is and if you want me to be here when you make it. Cause right now, I don't want to see your face. I real life hate you if I could kill your stupid ass right now and not miss you, I would. You also need to figure shit out with Bentley and Sap so that money can get back to flowing the right way." She spat.

"For one, you let me handle that street shit. You know I don't even want you in that or out there granted the concerns are your brother, but he gone have to learn. I have been telling him for a while what was up. He decides to handle shit how he wanted. And now we got to handle shit. Honestly, you should be thanking me cause I really don't have to place myself in the line of fire I could play the background and still collect my money." I shouted.

Sometimes I tried to play it cool with her and remind her that I always wanted her happy even if I failed to do it at times. Zailah knew how to piss me off, and that's exactly what she was doing. Instead of arguing any further with her, I let her go on and on yelling about how I wasn't shit and how I created a new family and was gone leave ours.

"You hungry, or you need some dick?" I cut her off.

"Oh, you care about what I need. Well, let me tell you since you can hear me or you even care to know for the moment. I need my so-called husband to be that my husband. I need him to come home at night, I need him to rub my feet after being out and making sure all his shit is running smoothly. I need him to remember that I have needs too, Oh, and I need him to remember that while I'm out of work because he asked me to, that I can go back to my job instead of having someone else run my shit and I just collect money. I haven't been to my own shit to actually sit in it or do any work from it because you keep me here. How do you think I feel having a whole daycare that I haven't seen in months. All I know is what I'm told. I need my husband to remember I put him first before anything, and he supposed to cherish me for that." She cried out.

"I get all that, you gotta understand that I want to be around my son. I don't want to miss a moment. When Honesty is born, you gone see how I feel. I would bring him here, but I don't want you uncomfortable or to cause you any more stress than I already do. I'm afraid you gone look at my son different and not accept him. Then I won't have no choice but to walk away from the only girl to have my heart. Zee, don't think I won't put you first but if I had to choose you or my son, I'm picking him. I love you to death, but I love my kids more." I expressed.

"Kyrie, it's just fucked up. Why you do this to me? Huh, to us? I know you don't regret him, and I don't want you to, but I regret you ever put us in this situation. Kyrie, do you love that girl? I saw how you looked at her, with pure amazement. You looked at her how you used to look at me. I can't take that. I feel selfish, and I don't want to. I'm scared to I'm scared that I'm losing my husband. The man I gave up everything for." At this point, Zailah was crying so hard that I ended up shedding a tear with her.

"No, I don't love her. I have love for her, even though she had my kid. I'll always make sure she good for that reason, and that reason alone. I don't fuck that girl we don't kiss nothing. I will be there with my son, and that's it. I can call her right now on FaceTime, and she will put the phone directly on Truth." I said honestly.

Zailah looked at me and then walked out of the kitchen. I decided against following her and allowing her some space to cool off. Reaching in the cabinet, I grabbed my weed and rolled up one. I also grabbed my bottle of Henny and took a swig straight from the bottle. I needed to get fucked up so that I could deal with shit. I wanted to take my mind off of everything and just have no worries if only for a minute.

Truthfully I was stuck I wanted everything to be okay and for me to have the perfect relationship with both of my baby mothers. I wanted them to get together and allow my kids to have an ideal relationship with each other. It seemed like the more I did, the more I fucked up and I didn't want to do too much damage.

Losing Zailah would put me in another space, and that was not where I wanted to be. I had been in that place one time, and I didn't want to go back. I remember the shit like it was yesterday.

"Oouuu fuck Kyrie, give me that dick." A girl whose name I didn't know moaned.

I was high as hell of some blues, and I was feeling myself. I had just made my first ten thousand, and the money was still rolling in.

Her pussy was so wet, but her head was even better. I had her bent over the couch while Maine fucked her friend on the other couch.

"Gawd, it's too much." She screamed I was hitting her with the death stroke.

"Shut up and take this dick. You been begging for it all night." I groaned.

Rotating my hips, I hit places that had her screaming. Her moans were driving me wild and boosting my ego all at once. Lifting her leg over the couch, I dig into her deeper. Her juices were dripping down my dick, and I was tempted to make her suck it off and swallow my nut.

"Ky Fucking Rie, are you fucking stupid. You really a dickhead." Zailah screamed out.

My dick went soft immediately, and I pulled out of the girl. Before she had a chance to react, Zailah snatched her over the couch and began to whoop her ass.

"Blame him for this ass whipping," Zailah yelled.

The girl grabbed Zailah's hair and swung wildly. None of her hits seemed to faze Zailah. I grabbed the girl, hands off of my baby's hair, and pushed her towards the door.

"Grab ya friend's shit and leave," Maine told the other girl.

"Ima kill you," Zailah said to me.

. . .

I WAS TOO high to even try to run from her. She jumped over the couch and punched me in the face. Had I not been fucked up, I could have blocked it.

"Chill the fuck out." I pushed her.

She stumbled back, and when she gained her footing, she ran up on me. Grabbing me by the shirt, she pulled me to her and began to swing on me. A few hits connected to my face, and I didn't like it. Reaching back, I slapped her hard enough to let her know I wasn't about to be a punching bag, but not hard enough to hurt her.

"You gone hit me cause you fucking other bitches. Watch me go hop on the next dick and see how you like it. You know niggas been trying to holla at me." She smirked.

"You want to die?" I had her by her neck and was shaking her like a rag doll.

"Get off her, bro." Maine pulled me off of Zailah.

"Fuck you and you too," Zailah yelled at us both.

Maine and I were standing there looking dumb, so we never noticed the two-piece that connected to both of our jaws from Zailah.

When she walked out the door, that was it. I didn't talk to nor see her for a few weeks. I popped more pills and drank more lean. I didn't even bother to go home, or I wouldn't make it. I would sleep in my car. I searched for her high and low and came up empty each time. I felt like I couldn't do anything without her, and I didn't want to.

"Man, her ass will be back, next time don't get caught. You were supposed to give that broad the best three minutes of her life." Maine jokes.

"I know, and when she comes back, I ain't cheating again." I lied.

"Your backwood stale." Zailah pointed out, bringing me from my thoughts.

"Look, I'm gonna make sure you get your happy life. With or without me." I promised.

That was a promise I couldn't break. Her happiness meant a lot to me, and I wanted that for her she deserved it. And the easiest way for her to get it along with my approval was to stick by me.

CHAPTER 29

 ailah

Laying on the couch, I did not understand why I was in so much pain. I knew that I was preparing for labor and learning more at my appointments. Two more weeks was a lot of time, so I wasn't understanding why I was feeling all kinds of pains. I thought about calling Ky, but any other time, the pain would pass after a few hours.

"Fuck," I shouted to no one in particular.

My mind kept on running back to thoughts on how I needed Kyrie not to miss this like he had missed my baby shower. Everything was perfect until he didn't show.

Walking into the building, I heard the music before I saw anything. I had paid my DJ Telly D, seven hundred dollars to come and show out. Beyoncé's new song was playing, and I just knew everyone would be up and dancing. I invited my mom and dad, but they kindly declined my offer to come.

Maliyah had been here all morning, setting things up and making things perfect for me. I offered to pay her because I knew she decorated parties for people for money on the side; however, she didn't take my money. I couldn't wait to see the inside, all the plans I made were taken into consideration until a few weeks ago. Maliyah had a theme she had been dying to do and just couldn't allow her niece not to be the one to have it.

"Oh my God, this is beautiful." I uttered, looking around the room.

The theme was a little mermaid baby Afro puff princess. The colors were teal, gold, and lavender. There was a slideshow playing on the wall of Kyrie and me. The candy table was amazing, there was also a fruit table. The cake was big with four tiers and a little baby mermaid in a clam on top. The bottom Tier said Honesty. They just had it all planned out that my baby's name was going to be Honesty since her brother's name was Truth. I wanted her to be named Demi, or Ava. My maternity photoshoot pictures were on full display, and I knew I would be taking them home to place on the walls.

"How you like it sis?" Maliyah asked.

"Like it, bitch, I love it, and check you out." Smiling, I looked over Maliyah.

My sister was dressed down in her Auntie gear. She had on a shirt with her and me while she kissed my belly and some teal colored jeans with lavender sandals. Even though it was a simple outfit, she rocked it.

"Me, bitch your glowing. Weave on fleek, and this white dress girll-lllll." She hipped me up.

I did a little twerk then went to go greet guests. Maliyah guided me through the place. Each table was set up nicely for people to eat. Instead of centerpieces, she had pitchers of juice.

"My Honesty has so many gifts; it doesn't make no sense. You do not have to buy anything. They came out and showed out you hear me?" She smiled.

We walked up to the stage, and I took a seat. My feet were hurting, and I hadn't even walked for that long. Maliyah grabbed the mic from the DJ and began to speak.

"Hello, I'm pretty sure y'all all know me by now, and if ya don't, I'm Maliyah. The proud and only auntie, I'm also the host of tonight's event. For starters, I would like to thank you all for coming out as well as for the gifts. We are highly appreciative. Zailah, say hello to everyone. Her dogs were barking so she couldn't make it to each table y'all." She said, earning laughs from the people.

"Hi, and thank you all for coming. I'll be around to rap with all of you. Just give me a minute. There's also a photo booth I would love to have pictures with everyone for the baby's photo album." I spoke then handed the microphone back.

"Okay, now that that's out of the way. We have a lot of games to play. If everyone would go to their seat, there is a cup at each table. There are also more at the bar, but those cups won't win you a prize, and I have several. Those cups have an ice cube inside with a baby in it. Pour you some juice right now, or whatever you drinking. Once your ice melts, and you see the baby floating yell out, my water broke as loud as you can. The person who does this first wins the first prize, which is a Kindle. With each game, the prizes gets bigger. I also have raffle tickets for two dollars, all the money will go to the start of Honesty college funds. However, half of the money will be given to whoever ticket is called." Maliyah grabbed a bag and a roll of tickets and handed it to Nina, who I hadn't seen when I came inside.

"That is Nina, and she will be collecting money and handing out tickets. Bentley, the wonderful Uncle, will be pulling the tickets and he and I decided to give you Zailah a surprise. I mean, it's really for Honesty, but ya know." Maliyah handed the mic to Bentley, and he stepped up.

"What's good y'all, I'm Bentley, the uncle and the co-host. I'ont really do this shi... I mean stuff but I ain't really have no choice. I hope y'all have a good time and make it an even better time for my sister." He stated.

"While we wait for that Ice to melt. Bentley, Nina, and I will be coming around with a piece of paper and a pencil. When they are done, I will be playing a slideshow. A lot of you here gave us some pictures to show. Each of you will guess who the baby's picture is, being as though it's a lot of people we only selected ten people who are known by everyone in here. I did place a list of names to help you with a thought of who it could be. Write down your guest, and once it's over, we will collect the slips, and whoever has the most correct answers will receive the gift."

Maliyah handed the mic back and jumped off the stage while everyone went around and played games I looked around for Kyrie. I texted and called him back to back only to get no response at all. The more I waited the more frustrated I grew.

"Where the fuck is your brother?" I asked Maliyah once she came back.

She started the slide show and then turned to me. I looked her in the face, ready to burst into tears. For some reason, I knew he wasn't going to show, and that hurt. Especially when I had to pop up on him at a baby shower, and he was having the time of his life. Here I was his wife, carrying his child and alone.

"You know he's probably with Truth, I called him multiple times already, but he ignored my calls. He probably thinks it's you, or I'm calling for you." She sighed.

"It's fucked up though Lee like he really not here," I whined.

Nina walked over with a big smile, but when she noticed we weren't smiling, she frowned.

"I was coming to give you some love, I can come back if you want me to." She said in her small voice.

"No it's okay, I like you. I'm pretty sure you know why I'm upset. And where is Maine ugly ass at? He gone be a horrible god dad. His ole fucked up tattoo having ass a come speak." I tried switching the subject.

"Let me go get him, he here somewhere. You know he probably

snuck off to go get high." Nina walked off, and I looked back at Maliyah.

"Look, don't you cry, no matter what you enjoy your day it's all about you and my niece deal with him later," Maliyah told me.

I agreed to let it go for the moment, yet, it didn't mean the hurt went away. It actually got worse as time passed.

"Fuckkkkkkk." The contraction that hit me brings me out of my thoughts.

I laid there until my panties felt very moist and the feeling of me needing to pee became unbearable. Pulling myself up off of the couch, I held on to it and guided myself to the hall. Once I was at the hall I held onto the wall and slowly made my way to the bathroom. I was clenching my phone in my hand just so I could call Kyrie once I sat on the toilet. Finally, making it to the bathroom, I pulled my panties down and relieved my bladder. Dialing Kyrie's number, I prayed like hell he answered.

"What's up Zai, you good?" He spoke into the phone.

"No, I think I'm in labor. Oh God, it hurts so bad." I cried.

"Where you at? You okay baby, don't do anything until I get there. Remember to breathe," He said calmly.

I COULD HEAR the wind blowing through the phone, so I knew he was driving.

"Ughhhh," I screamed.

The pain shooting through my body was one I never felt or wanted to feel again. I stood up and then slowly slid down the wall on the floor. I was sweating, and I felt like I needed to shit.

"It feels like I need to push Ky." I got out between breaths.

"Relax, take slow deep breaths, and don't push. Fuck hold on okay, don't hang up. I'm gonna get you an ambulance." He said.

I tried hard not to push, and it only caused me more pain. I had to place my hand on my treasure box to feel like I was pushing her up. I knew that there was no way I would make it to the hospital. Baby girl wanted to come, and she wanted to come now.

"God, help me please this hurts so bad." I let out.

Saying fuck it, I pushed a little too hard and I swore it felt like I was about to take a big shit. I felt like when a person is constipated, and the shit wouldn't come out, so you found your-self holding on to whatever was next to you to help you push that shit out. Each time I felt like I needed to push, I did, and each time, I pushed a little harder. I heard tires screeching, and Knew Kyrie had made it.

"Zailah, where you at ma?" He called.

"Bathroom," I growled.

Kyrie came running into the bathroom and looked down at me.

"Shit, I see her head, the fuck y'all want me to do now? Yo, how long you say cause my baby don't wanna stay in there no more. Oh, shit, my guy she coming out." Kyrie spoke on the phone.

He got down on his knees after grabbing the white hand towel from the closet and placed one on the floor he grabbed another and kept it in his hands. He rubbed the side of my face and then smiled at me. It was fucked up because that same smile that used to make my heart melt didn't make me feel anything anymore.

"Look, she's gone come out, and it's cool cause the ambu-lance will be here in about four more minutes. I need you to stay calm and push when you feel like it. No matter what, you have to stay calm." He said.

I didn't give not one fuck about staying calm. I wanted her out just as much as she wanted to come out. So each time I felt the need, I pushed. It was just Kyrie and me when my baby decided to pop out. Seconds later, the paramedics came rushing in. They helped Kyrie cut the cord and clean her mouth out. My baby had a set of lungs on her. Kyrie covered me with the towel, and I was picked up and placed on a stretcher and then handed my beautiful baby girl.

The moment she opened her eyes and stared at me; I felt a different kind of love. I knew that nothing else would matter and if it did, it wouldn't be more important than her happiness.

CHAPTER 30

ailah

"Aww, Honesty, mommy loves you." I smiled down at my baby.

I couldn't get enough of her. Even though she hadn't been in this world for more than three weeks, today was her first day home. Of course her father could only bring us home and then had to rush out because his son Truth had an asthma attack.

At first, I was against naming my baby Honesty. However, he wanted her to be named after her big brother, and while I was sleeping, he filled out the rest of her birth certificate and gave it to the nurse. We did all of the work together and left her name blank because we weren't sure what we would name her. She was so tiny, and I was scared to hold her to tight or even pick her up sometimes.

The smile on Kyrie's face when she was born was priceless. Yet, it was the same one plastered on his face when his son was born. I was happy for him at times because he had his son and daughter. I knew that he wanted kids more than anything, and though I wasn't the one to give them all to him, I was grateful that he had them.

Honesty was latched on to my breast. I tried to give her a bottle, but she would not drink it for me. Her nurses said she would take the bottle for them, but the moment I came up there, she wouldn't take the bottle at all.

My phone ringing brought me out of my thoughts. However, To see my mother calling was a shock to me. I was upset with her because she hadn't seen her only grandchild yet, and I knew it was because of her husband. Grabbing my phone, I sent her to voicemail before shooting Kyrie a text asking was the baby okay. Hearing my phone ding, I opened the text reading it, I dropped my phone and covered my mouth. I had to sit my baby down and catch my breath.

My head began to spin, and the tears began to fall. I had to do something I couldn't sit still. Grabbing my phone off the floor I dialed the number I hadn't dialed in a while. My hands shook as I waited for someone to pick up.

"Come to the hospital now. Please." My mother's voice was frantic.

Hanging up the phone, I quickly dressed Honesty and placed her in her car seat. I rushed to my car and strapped her in. I drove as fast but as safe as possible all the way to the hospital. I left my car at the front and grabbed my baby out. Running inside, I went to the front desk.

I didn't have to stop because Tierra came rushing from the elevators.

"Your mom told me to come get you." She said through tears.

We went up to the fourth floor, and my mother screams could be heard through the hall. It felt like it took us forever to get to the waiting room when really it was only a minute or so.

"God, please let him make it through this." She cried.

"Mom, what happened?" I asked, sitting on the floor with her.

Honesty was sound asleep in her car seat, so I sat her on the floor next to us.

"He was driving Bentley's old car. They meet around 52nd street and switch cars so Bentley could be safe. Your father made it a few blocks, and the car was shot up. They shot my husband up, he didn't deserve that he wasn't perfect lord knows he wasn't but to shoot him seven times." She wailed.

Hearing this only made me cry with her. I held onto her as she cried into my shoulder. At the moment, I didn't care about any bad words that were said or any ill feelings. All that was on my mind was God allowing my father to be okay.

"What the fuck happened? Where my dad at?" Bentley snatched my mom off the floor.

"You're what happened. That wasn't meant for him it was for you. What the hell are you out here doing boy? I gave you everything you didn't have to go out there in them streets. You see what them streets have done to our family? If he doesn't come out of this, I'll never forgive you. I'll live this earth in pain every day because of your reckless actions." She pulled away from Bentley and went to slap him.

Being the sister that I am, I caught her hand and gave her a death stare. Judging by the look on Bentley's face, her words had stung enough. As long as I was standing there, nobody, mom, or not would put hands on him. Unless it was me, and I wasn't in a slapping mood.

Pulling Bentley into a hug, I whispered it wasn't his fault into his ear. I mean yes, it was his beef, but he didn't pull the trigger.

"Oh god, you sent the devil here instead of a miracle." My mom screamed.

I didn't even have to look up to know Kyrie had blessed us with his presence. I could smell the cologne I loved so much, and my mother always called him the devil. She liked to believe he was the reason her family split, and Bentley was in the streets the way he was.

"Ma'am, we did all we could. We even tried to resuscitate him. However, nothing worked. The bullet that struck him in the stomach traveled to his heart, hitting a main artery on the way." The doctor told my mom.

My knees grow weak as her screams grew louder. The pain that shot through my body was unexplainable. It felt like someone came and punched me in the chest while at the same time, sucking the air from my body.

"Damn, man. Fuckkk. I told him I would just leave the fucking car and get somebody to come tow it. I should have made him listen to me." Bentley said to no one in particular.

"I hate you, Bentley. I swear I do, I don't ever want to look into your face again. You look just like the man that was taken away from me. It shoulda been you." My mom cried.

Just like that, all the tears and sympathy I felt for her went out the window. I was no longer hurting for my mother and father but for my brother.

"Are you serious? That's your damn son, it's one thing to blame him, but all the other shit was uncalled for. Maybe it was for him, maybe it wasn't. Your precious husband was out sleeping with any bitch willing to bust it wide open for his ass. Maybe one of them bitches was scorned or one of their husbands. Or maybe it was some shit that had to do with my brother. However, he was our father, just like he was your husband. So standing here yelling you hate my brother ain't bout to go on too much longer. Now you gone be a miserable old bitch instead of one with a husband. Them words gone come back to bite you in the ass. So when my brother decides to forgive you, so the hell will I." I stood in her face.

I couldn't believe her, and yes, I knew nine times out of ten, this was all because of Bentley's mess. Now wasn't the time to bring that up, especially with the cops lurking. I knew instead of them coming to ask what had happened or if we had any information them sitting back and watching my mom shout out all this shit was better for them.

Kyrie walked over to me and pulled me into him. He hugged me tightly, and I melted into his hold. I let all of the tears I had in me go. I cried for the relationship we had, I cried for my brother, I cried for my dad losing his life. But most importantly, I cried for my daughter. She would never meet her grandpa. Though he was a fucked-up person, his heart was pure. Now I was seeing just how important family is, and even if we didn't get along, staying in each other's lives while we were on this earth was a must.

CHAPTER 31

yrie

"Bro, I fucked up. I fucked up bad. Man, how the fuck I let this happen. Nigga shot my fucking pops cause Tierra's ass. I mean damn how the fuck I'm supposed to face my mom or my sister. I told the bitch not to pull up on me, and she does the shit anyway. It's like the niggas were following her. Then on top of that, I begged him not to take the car. I swore he could just have somebody come pick it up like he was supposed to and tow that shit." Bentley roared as he paced the floor.

Fredrick was driving Bentley's car for the day because he was supposed to be getting it junked. Being as though he didn't know Bent was into street activity, he thought nothing of being in the car. Of course Bentley had the car tinted, and Mr. Frederick had been the one to catch the bullets instead of his son. How he didn't know what Bentley did was something I probably would never know. Everyone but him knew that Bentley loved the streets and fast money more than anything.

"You know Freddie's ass did everything himself. It's only one thing to do now. We gotta shed some blood through these streets. We not just taking that. Somebody gotta die behind that. If war is what Sap wants, then war is what he gone get." Maine shrugged.

"Bet it, and where the fuck you been, Mr. MIA," Bentley questioned Maine.

"In the house getting pussy and counting money. Ayee, Nina ass a cold freak. She be trying to suck the skin off my dick. I ain't gonna lie I'll play step daddy if I have to just to keep her swallowing my dick. Plus, she pretty as shit. I had to thank God for allowing me to see her that day leaving from y'all house." Maine smiled.

"This muthafucka finally got some in house pussy. On some real shit though. We need to go at these niggas head on. Since they want to take one of ours, it's only right we take anybody on they team that's not willing to get down." I stated.

"So when we gone move out?" Bentley asked.

I knew he wasn't gone be ready for my answer, but my mind was made up. It had already been a few days since Freddie took his last breath. Usually, I would wait things out and catch niggas when they least expected. However, I wasn't on that type of time right now. Somebody made my wife cry now. It was only right I handle things the way she wanted them handled.

"Now, I know where they are at. I already got the drop. Listen, if you let that bitch get you in one more situation like this one here, I refuse to help you. You gone have to take ya chick and do whatever." I said while placing the duffle bag on the table.

I had called up my old headache and got him to supply me with some of his best work. I also told him not to do any more dealings with Sap and his people. I met up with him and paid a nice check for the new toys we had.

"Don't even think about it," I told Maine.

I knew he would go for the gun I had specifically picked for me. And the fact that he only had two of them meant I needed them both. I was dying to test it out, so I would use one for tonight, and the other would be put up in my gun shelf.

"That shit nice bro, come on you got two let me get one, I'll give you ten stacks for it right now." He smirked, knowing how I loved money.

Shrugging my shoulders and saying, fuck it. I handed him the PGS MFG 5.56 Nato AR-15 7.5" Barrel SBA3 Pistol and took the money from him. That was money I would split in half for my baby mothers to go shopping for my kids.

"You ready ?" I asked Bentley.

This was his first shoot out I ever let him be in. I was only allowing this because this was his beef, and his father was the one who took that L for him. So even if he wasn't ready, he had better get ready. It was no time for backing out or his nerves. He was just gone have to deal with it all later.

"Born fucking ready." He grabbed the gun and cocked it, surprising the hell out of me.

"That's what I like to hear, y'all got me out of the house, and I'm glad it's for a good reason." Maine smiled, showing all thirty-two.

This was just like him, while I hated the feeling I got before it was time to go handle some nigga, he loved it. I wasn't scared, but just like before a person got into a fight, that nervous feeling that shoots through their body, I got every time.

We each grabbed two guns and extra clips. Me being me and needing to make sure I was extra prepared, tucked my Nine inside of my boxers, and pulled my shirt over it.

"Look at this gotta be extra ready ass. Bent, relax, and don't overthink this shit. We gone have to smoke on the ride cause you look like you bout to shit on yourself." Maine jokes.

"I ain't gonna lie, I feel like I got bubble guts so can we get this shit over with." Bentley frowned.

I smirked remembering that very same feeling I got the night we decided we were really gone takeover and Monty had to go.

I grabbed the entire Ziplock bag of weed and backwoods and headed to my all black Monte Carlo, I had got a smoker to get it in her name back in the day and just kept up with it. Maine and I, had two cars we drove when it was time to catch a body. Afterwards we drove them back to a garage we had that couldn't be traced back to us.

"Sit in the front pup, it's time to see you back all that shit talking and smoking niggas up. You might fuck around and go get you a tear drop after this. Aye, bro, you know I gotta take advantage of this shit because that nigga finally quiet. Bent, you known for talking shit and you quiet as a church mouse right now." Maine was cracking himself up.

As much as I wanted to laugh I held it in, I sympathized with Bentley I knew he had a lot on his mind. However, this was all a response to some shit that he created.

"Man, look just go in there and smoke anything moving. Relax and let the gun do the talking for you, you been to the range you know how to shoot." I reminded him.

Bentley wasn't new to shooting guns, yet, he had never caught a body. Once he did it he would be fucked up for a few days and then it would do one or two things. Turn him into a straight killer or make him never want to kill again unless he had too. I was hoping for the latter, but with Bentley that might just not be the case.

Pulling up to the small block right behind Wayne Ave we cut the lights of and got our guns ready. I said a quick prayer as the nervous feeling filled my stomach. I knew just as it came it would leave. I looked over at Bentley and he looked like he was about to back out on us at any moment.

"Smoke some of this and relax." Maine said now serious.

Everyone was quiet in their own thoughts as we faced our own blunts. I said a quick prayer asking God to protect and forgive me. I asked him to allow me guidance through this situation and for my brothers safety. I asked him to watch over my kids and their mother's.

After an hour or so with no one coming in or out of the house I was ready to move. I figured we could wait it out a little more and then go in with guns blazing.

"Fuck it, let's go." Bentley got the courage to say.

I looked at him like he was crazy, and the look on his face let me know that he really was. He jumped out of the car and stormed down the street with his guns at his side. Hopping out, I quickly but quietly ran up behind him. Once we were close to the porch, Bentley wasted no time. He aimed his gun directly at Sap's head and let his piece do the talking for him.

Aiming my gun, I hit anybody moving. I knew we had to be quick and hopefully take out more than we injured. I was hoping we made it back to the car, and none of us got hurt. Maine went in the side alley, and I knew that was for security purposes. He was making sure nobody ran from the back of the house and shot at us. Bentley was letting his bullets rip through everything I wasn't even sure if he was looking at his targets. I took a step back and looked around when I saw nobody moving. I tapped Bentley's shoulder and nodded for him to come on. We backed up down the steps, and I let off the whistle that Maine knew. It was a call we had done since kids. The moment he emerged from the side alley, we took off running. Hopping in the car, I pulled off before anyone could even close their doors.

The ride back to the garage was completely silenced. I parked the car in the back and climbed into my Audi. Pulling out, I saw Maine looking over in disgust. Bentley was bent over, throwing up everything he had in him. That was one of the after-effects of killing someone.

"Bro, this little fucker, ain't no virgin no more. He got his first one. I think we birth a killer, we gone have to keep him out of shit now. You saw how he was busting his shit? I don't even think you hit as many niggas as him. He was in another world with that. The look in his eyes was like he found a new love. Bent loved power, and I know he was just feeling real powerful." Maine said.

"Yeah, I saw, we gone have to get him high and tell him about closing his eyes and picturing that shit, and how to get it off his mind," I replied.

Bentley finished up and walked to the car. He slowly got in and sat with his head in his hands. He let out a deep breath.

"I need to smoke something crazy. That shit keeps replaying in my head, the look in his eyes was like he wanted to beg me for his life and the fucked up part was that I wanted him to beg, I wanted him to apologize for doing my pops in, then I was gone put a bullet in his head. I wish I could kill the nigga over and over again." Bentley stated barely above a whisper.

"Whenever that shit pops up in your head, just think of something else, now that you killed somebody each time gets easier and easier. You can't dwell on it, or you gonna make yourself crazy. You did what you had to do. It was either you or him, and you chose to save yourself like anyone would." I reminded him.

"Yeah, man, I know I keep fucking with you and joking around, but shit gone get easier. That doesn't mean you go out there and just shoot anybody you arguing with or anything like that. Remain humble, and always keep in mind if you pull it, you better use it. Don't just pull it though, if a nigga reaching, then you bust his ass first. You ain't even really gone need to pull it you got hands, always make them your first option that gun won't gain you no respect." Maine spoke.

Nodding my head in agreeance, I thought back to all the times people swore I was pussy and thought I only carried a gun because I didn't fight. However, that wasn't the case. Before the shit, with Monty, I never carried a gun, and I didn't have to fight because people respected me. Which is why I was gone teach my son you earn your respect or you take it. I would buy him his first gun and let him know that having a gun won't make you a man, and just because you have one doesn't mean you're untouchable. I would teach him to clean the gun, store it properly, and also to understand that a gun is to protect you and your family. To see it for what it was and to use it only when needed, not to toy around with it.

CHAPTER 32

ailah

KYRIE HAD BEEN BLOWING my phone up, and I chose not to care. Usually, I would entertain him, but my feelings for him were disappearing by the days. The only thing I wanted him to do was to continue to be a good father to his daughter. It was so hard watching him father and love another child. Though I loved kids, I still had yet to accept the fact that I really had a stepchild out in the world. Most women would be able to do it, especially if their marriage was on the line, but at this point, I could care less about the vows we took. In my head, he didn't care nor respect them, and if he had, we wouldn't be where we are today.

"Girl turn that phone off or silence it. Hell, pick it the fuck up my brother calling you like it's a damn emergency. He bet not be letting my niece cry or no shit like that." Maliyah stated.

Looking down at my phone, I silenced the call again. It wasn't nobody I wanted to be bothered with. Plus, I had been texting my baby father since I had walked out the door to check on my little baby every chance I got. It was crazy how I hadn't been gone a whole hour, and I was missing her. I didn't even drink anything because I didn't want to do the whole pump and dump thing. My breasts were leaking, and I just knew that it was time for her to eat.

"That's not your brother. That's some guy I met in the damn store and gave him my number. I'm not gonna lie I gave him my number to see if I had it in me to talk to someone outside of your brother. However, I'm not even ready to step out there again." I sighed.

"Your ass finally giving up on Kyrie, I ain't gone lie I thought his ass had gold swinging between his legs the way you always was hooked on him." Tierra jokes.

"I'm pretty sure you always wanted to know what that gold tasted like too." I snapped at her.

Before she could respond, I heard a familiar voice. One I wasn't familiar with but a voice that I would never forget. I looked around until I spotted the person it belonged to. We locked eyes for a brief moment, and then she looked over at Tierra. A small frown appeared on her face. Standing up with her baby, she made her way over to us. I was confused, but my heart raced the closer she got. Whatever her reason for coming over was didn't matter to me because all I was thinking was that I was about to be face to face with the baby that my husband created.

"Hey, cousin." She spoke directly to Tierra.

"Cousin, oh fuck no," Maliyah said.

I was too shocked to say anything. Tierra knew this whole time and had probably set shit up for them to end up together, and I was not feeling it.

"Sky, what are you doing here?" Tierra asked.

"I should be asking you this? How do y'all know each other? Is it well enough for you to know Kyrie was her fucking husband? Cause if so, you failed to fucking mention that shit to me when you told me to go at him. Tierra, you whack as shit for that, and I should have known not to fucking trust you with my love life when you were all too busy setting the man you supposedly love up." She exposed.

"You did what!" I willfully misunderstood.

"I did not, and it wasn't my business to tell." Tierra finally acknowledges what was said.

"Wasn't your business to tell. Bitch, I oughta reach across this table and sleep your ass. I knew you was foul, but I ain't been shit but good to you. I knew your ass would get me back for fucking with Kyrie, but I thought you woulda just kept trying to fuck him. Then I thought by now you gave up, it's been years Tierra. You gone put ya cousin on to him though, and then listen to me cry about him having another child, and you never once said you knew her." I had to hold in my tears.

I wasn't sure if I wanted to cry because of all the hurt I was feeling or the fact that the baby she was holding and my daughter resembled each other so much, only reminding me more of my husband's infidelity.

"Yeah. I'm still hurt by that. That was supposed to be my husband and my baby. You knew how much I liked him. Then I had to watch from the sidelines. He wouldn't even fuck me or even let me taste his dick, and trust me. I've tried multiple times. It's not fair how you just get to have him. You ruined my plans had you not helped him that day we wouldn't be going through this. And Sky, I'm sorry I placed you in the situation, but since I couldn't have him and hurt Zailah, I used you to do it for me. You weren't supposed to have his baby though." Tierra spat

And just like that, I was across the table punching Tierra in the face. I swung as hard as I could, making sure to connect each one to her face. This bitch had caused my family pain in all sorts of ways. My father died behind her setups, my brother was at war because of it. My marriage was over, and my family was ruined.

"Zailah, stop, please stop. You going to go to jail." I heard Sky yelling.

I must have blanked out because I didn't know how I got on top of Tierra. I also didn't know when I started to slam her head on to the floor. Maliyah pulled me up off of her, and we made a dash for the door. I made a mental note to get Sky's number out of Kyrie's phone and have her come over so we could have this sit down. I also needed to get in touch with my lawyer just in case anything was to happen.

Getting inside Maliyah's car, I sat back and thought long and hard.

"Yo, you fucked her up. I ain't seen you that mad in years. Sis, you went in, then Sky was looking like she wanted to get in and help you. I can't believe she set her own cousin up like that." Maliyah laughed.

"That shit not funny, I'm real life hurt bout that. Out of all the things she could do. To play in my face like I meant nothing. I was there for that girl, I always had her back. I knew she liked a boy a lot, but she ain't even know his name at first. Once, she told me it was already too late because Kyrie and I were already attached to each other. It's crazy because you can really consider someone as family, hold on to some of their darkest secrets, and they will still do you dirty. I shared clothes with that girl, food, everything I looked at her like a sister. The whole time she was stabbing me in the back." I got out.

I couldn't fight my tears any longer, and I broke down again. This wasn't supposed to hurt like this because I knew how she was and what she was capable of.

CHAPTER 33

Kyrie

"Zailah, open the fucking door." I banged.

I wasn't understanding why the fuck she would change the locks on me. I let her have her space when she decided she wanted to move out but now she was taking things too far. Then she came back home and after we had that little argument I gave her a little space since that's what she was asking for. I didn't know giving her time alone and watching the baby while she supposedly went out on her little girl outings was gone have her on the next nigga.

"Kyrie, you need to leave before you wake my baby up. I don't want you here, and you're not here for her because it's three in the damn morning." She yelled from the door.

All I wanted to do was hold her, and the only thing in between us was this fucking glass screen door. Maurice had told me how he saw her around the way with this new nigga, and I wasn't feeling it. She was mines and rightfully mines. She was still my wife, and for her to be stepping off on me was something that didn't sit well with me. I didn't give a fuck what I did.

"Zai, I just want to talk to you. I miss you, I ain't trying to lose you, you feel me? I fucked up, I fucked up bad too, but we can work past that shit like we always do." I admitted.

"No, the fuck we can't. Sign the damn divorce papers, and then we can be friends; that's all I want from you. That will fix everything." She sighed.

"Fuck you mean? What you think you gone go be with another nigga? Have him raising my daughter? Fucking my pussy, loving my bitch? And I just sit back and watch? You everything to me, you all I know it's been you, and I fuck anything else." I reminded her.

How can she not see that I loved her, I loved her so much that it was turning me crazy. I couldn't eat, shit I could barely function, and she wanted me to let her go that easy. I guess she ain't understand when I told her only way out was in a box that I meant just that. Neither one of us was dead, so she would remain my wife.

"Kyrie, just leave me alone. I get that it's been you and me, but that shit was NEVER enough for you. Shit, you just want me to accept the fact you birth a baby with another bitch? That ain't love, let me go have a baby by another muthafucka, then we can discuss this marriage and work on it. See how that shit makes you feel to know I created a life while we married. You did that shit while I was pregnant, Ky, you hurt me in the worst ways possible. Still, I loved you, I held you down bid after bid. You fucked up, so count your losses, baby." She stated boldly.

"Fuck another nigga if you want." I heard everything she said, but that stood out the most.

"Please leave, I can tell you was popping those damn pills again. That's another thing, I dealt with that shit when we were younger and them pills have you on some other shit. I ain't about to deal with it now, and don't come here high off them and want to be with your daughter." She said.

Zailah, knew that pills were the only high that made me get in my bag. We would fight and fuck for hours when we were younger. She always told me she hated it when I took them, but I loved the high it gave me. I could feel my anger rising, and it could have all been avoided had she opened the door.

"Zailah, open the fucking door. What you got a nigga in here or something?" I questioned her.

Why did I ask that? It put something in my head now I believed that's why she wouldn't open the door. I was determined more now than ever to get her to open the door. I had to see for myself that she wasn't done yet.

"If I did, it would be none of your business, but I don't. Listen married or not, I'm going to move on." She let me know.

That was all it took for me to pull my gun from my hip and smash that muthafucka against the glass. It came shattering down all over the booth of us. Zailah stepped back with shock all over her face. That gave me enough room to step in and close the front door behind us. Placing my gun on the table at the door, I grabbed her by her neck.

"You not fucking leaving me," I yelled in her face.

"Kyrie, get the fuck off of me and leave," she screamed.

Maurice had to be right. The only time Zailah got like this is when she started to talk to another nigga. Of course, she never let the relationship go far because we would fix things. However, this had to had gone too far if she wasn't jumping at us fixing our marriage.

"You fucking this nigga that had you smiling all in the market ?" I asked her.

She didn't answer. Instead, she looked at me with tear-filled eyes.

"Answer me, tell me you ain't give up on me. I fucking need you. Zailah, how you gonna disrespect me like that?" I questioned.

"Kyrie, Get off me." She mumbled.

The more she didn't answer me and let me know what was going on, the more I got mad. Letting her go, I turned around and stormed up the steps into our bedroom. Snatching her phone off the charger, I quickly unlocked it and went to her text messages. Every contact was someone I knew. The name that stood out the most was Dejuan. I never heard of this nigga, and I knew he wasn't any long lost family member. Just as I went to click on their message, she snatched the phone from my hand.

"What you hiding? You really messing with somebody else. You need somebody to lose they life behind this shit." I threatened.

"You forget you did all this shit you in here screaming about? Kyrie, I ain't fighting with you no more. You the one who fucked this up now you want to come here high off of those pills and in your feelings?" Zailah frowned.

"I know what the fuck I did, that don't mean you go and do the same shit. You out here being a hoe, you just had my fucking daughter how you go jump on the next person dick that fast." I fumed.

"Stop disrespecting me." She laughed.

"You think this shit funny," I asked her.

She shrugged her shoulders just as her phone began to ring. She quickly clicked the silence button the feeling that shot through my stomach let me know that it was that nigga.

"Pick up the phone if you ain't fucking him." I threw out.

"No." She stated simply.

I leaped across the bed and grabbed the phone. She held onto it and wouldn't let go. We tussled for a while over the phone. Had I not been high, I would have been had the phone from her.

"You really fucking drawling right now." She huffed.

I didn't care about what she was saying. I dialed the nigga number back and placed the phone on speaker.

"Yo, baby." He answered

"Baby? This nigga call you baby?" I spat.

"So this must be the husband. You finally made it home to wifey." He antagonized

"Fuck is that baby boy? You telling this nigga my business. Listen, I ain't no Jody, and you ain't no Rodney. We gone keep this shit real simple, lose her number willingly, or I'm gonna make you." I told him.

"I'll lose the number when Zailah tells me too." Dejuan laughed before hanging up.

Tossing the phone on the bed, I contemplated my next move.

"Kyrie, listen, he was somebody to talk to when there was no one to talk to. I don't have to explain myself to you, but I'm going to anyway. I see that look on your face, and I swear to God I ain't fuck him." Zailah spoke.

Letting out a deep breath, I had to chuckle. I was beyond pissed. The more she talked, or I looked at her, the more I wanted to hurt her. Standing up, I went to leave. What stopped me was the message of this niggas dick popping up on the screen.

WHAP

I slapped the shit out of her before I could even think about what I was doing. Zailah held her face for a second before she charged at me. She grabbed at my face while I held on to her throat. Slinging her around, I tossed her onto the bed. Climbing on top of her, I looked her dead in her face.

"You not fucking him, but he sending you dick pics. Y'all talked about fucking? Zailah, I told you for years it was no leaving me. I'm not divorcing you. The only way out this marriage is if one of us dies. And I ain't dead, growing up, you thought me saying that was cute, but I meant it I still do." I growled in her face.

"That's gonna be your last time putting your hands on me. When I say I'm done, I mean it, don't contact me unless it's about your daughter. I don't want shit to do with you at this point." Zailah yelled back.

I climbed off of her and let her words sink in. Did I mean to hit her no? I was just upset and angry my emotions were all over the place and only she could make me feel that way. Which was why I was scared to lose her, but my actions continued to show her otherwise.

Walking out of the room, I slowly crept in my daughter's room. She was sleeping peacefully through it all. I kissed her cheek then walked out. I was going to give Zailah what she wanted. Seeing my daughter made me realize I wasn't the man to her mother that I wanted her to end up with. It wouldn't be easy letting go, but I had to at least try.

CHAPTER 34

 ailah

I WOKE UP WITH A HEADACHE, and Honesty screaming didn't make it any better. Kyrie had completely lost his mind, and I was hoping he found it and soon.

Climbing out of bed I went inside her room and picked her up out of her crib.

"Mommy's baby is wet." I cooed

Placing her down on the changing table, I quickly changed her then popped my boob in her mouth. As Honesty ate, I scrolled through my phone. Dejuan has texted and called me a few times, over the last few days. I didn't have the power to text him back nor pick up a call because I was completely embarrassed.

I was wishing that Kyrie's handprint would disappear like he did. The only communication we had was when he would text me every night to check on Honesty. When he wanted to see her, he would have Maliyah come pick her up.

Once Honesty finished eating, I placed my boob back into my shirt and burped her. Getting her dressed was super easy. However, keeping her clothes clean wasn't. For some reason, every time I changed her, she would throw up.

Today was the day Sky, and I would have a sit-down. There were a lot of things I wanted to address, and none were concerning my fucked up marriage at this point. Walking down the hall, I talked to Honesty and kissed all over her face gaining little smiles from her.

"YouTube, stinky momma. I love you so much, beautiful," I tickled her tummy.

She kicked her little legs and smiled brightly at me. Laying her down on her pillow in the middle of my bed, I cut Mickey Mouse Clubhouse on. Knowing her, she would fall asleep while I was in the shower.

Once I was sure she wouldn't fall over or get her face stuck in the pillow, I ran into the bathroom to take a quick shower and handle all of my hygiene.

I finished up as fast as I could, not wanting to leave my baby unattended for too long. Wrapping a towel around my body, I went into my room to get dressed. Just as I expected, Honesty was fast asleep. How she slept that much was beyond me.

Lotioning my body, I put on the same colors as my baby. I was rocking a pair of light blue distressed jeans and a pink off the shoulder shirt. I slid my feet into a pair of rose gold 990s by New Balance.

Since my weave was long gone I threw a few curls in my head with my wand curler and then ran my fingers through it. When I was satisfied with my look. I went and packed my baby diaper bag.

"Come on, my sleepy baby, let's go see what your brother and his mom talking bout," I spoke to Honesty while placing her in her car seat.

She moved around a little but went right back to sleep.

Grabbing her, the baby bag, and my bag was always hard work. Making it down to the front door, I realized I left my phone on my bed. I gently sat everything down and ran up the steps to retrieve my phone. I ran back down and noticed I was out of breath.

"I need to work out and bad, god damn I got lazy." I talked to myself.

Grabbing Honesty and everything else, I made my way to my car. Once I had everything inside and Honesty seat strapped in, I got in and pulled off. We decided to meet at del friscos. Pulling up to the place, I said a silent prayer that everything went well, and we could come to some kind of agreement as to where the kids would be around each other and know each other.

I texted her phone only for her to say she would be pulling up in the next five minutes. Deciding to just go ahead inside, I went in and got us a table. Sitting down, I waited for her before I placed my order for a drink or anything. By the time I got myself and Honesty situated, she came strutting in.

I looked her over from head to toe and really took her in. We were completely opposite, while I came casual and cute, she came dressed to impress. Her hair was in a cute bun on top of her head. The way the Once piece romper set hugged her waist and thighs, I could tell from here her ass was big. Just like me, she carried a diaper bag and a car seat. However, instead of a bag, she wore a fanny pack around her waist. While I wore sneakers she had on heels, her makeup was flawless.

"Hey, girl." She spoke once she reached the table.

"Hey, you need any help?" I questioned as she sat the car seat down. However, the diaper bag somehow got twisted with the car seat.

"No, thank you. Did you order yet?" She kindly declined my offer.

When she got herself together, I replied to her question.

"Was waiting for you."

She sent me a small smile, before reaching in the car seat and picking up a wide awoke Truth. I knew once our kids got older, they would look alike except Truth was darker than Honesty and held some really deep dimples.

"Aww, he so handsome. He looks just like his dad's baby pictures." I smiled.

"He does, is Honesty asleep?" She asked.

"Yeah, that little baby sleeps all day. So I wanted to sit down to formally introduce myself as well as speak on how we would make sure our babies stayed in each other's lives without going through Kyrie all the time. My problems are with him not with you, and as much as I thought they would be, they aren't. I do not want to raise my daughter as if she doesn't have a brother, and she does. At the end of the day, this can go one of two ways, and I hope it's a good way." I started.

"Understandable, I don't want any problems. I'm grown, and with working in a law firm, I refuse to lose my job to anything that can be avoided. I have been wanting to talk to you because I wanted you to know that had I known about you, I would have never slept with Kyrie, and once I found out about you, Kyrie and I's relationship is strictly based around Truth. Just like you said, I want Truth to be a part of his sister's life. I was going to enroll him in your daycare since I heard you had one. I figured you would let Honesty go there as well. I do want to be able to contact you directly, and even if you just need a break, I would come and get her vice versa. You know, like if I couldn't pick him up, I would be hoping you could and the same with me. I would never want to cause any harm to you or Honesty. I want the best for her just like I want for Truth." She replied.

"Girl, yes. I'm glad he ain't pick a girl that was on some bull shit like your cousin. And yeah, I'm down with that. Our kids can both have a bonus mom. The one thing I ask is that you don't allow your cousin around my child. I don't plan on ever speaking to that girl again. I'm hoping my brother doesn't either, but if he does, it has nothing to do with me. Have you had a chance to tell Kyrie because I haven't." I questioned.

Honesty began to cry, and I picked her up and bounced her on my shoulder. I wasn't big on pacifiers, so I didn't give her one. She did her thumb, which Kyrie hated.

"Look, Honesty, you see you brother," I said when she stopped fussing.

We turned the babies to each other as if they would bust out talking. All they did was look at each other. However I knew in that moment I would never separate them. Even though I didn't accept his daddy, I wholeheartedly accepted Truth and vowed in my head to protect and love him just like I would my own child.

"Nope, I didn't, and I don't want to talk to her either I can't stand the bitch. What she did was fucked up, but I'm okay. I'm glad she did because I have a son and now a beautiful bonus daughter. I don't even want to speak on that hoe but tell ya brother stay far away from her. We have to go shopping together and get them matching outfits and all that stuff. I'm a shopaholic, so I hope you don't mind if I buy her stuff when I buy for Truth." Sky let off.

"Girl no, cause I'll be doing the same shit. So keep me updated with son son size. I also want to do playdates every week. Maybe on a day we're both off because I'm going back to work tomorrow. Whichever day you off, I'll take off from the daycare." I told her.

"Cool, so I'm off on Saturdays and Sundays, other than that I'm in the office intern to become an attorney for family court. Can you let me know your prices? I'll need him there from eight until about four at the latest. I get off at three, but I need time to get there."

"Don't play, just come fill out paperwork in the morning, and he can start then. I do need you to bring his shot record and stuff like that from the doctors. Take ya time with that, and you'll get the job." I said.

We sat and talked for a while, and I could tell she was everything I thought she wasn't. And even though I lost a friend, I gained a baby mom that was on the same type of time I was.

"Now that we cool, can you tell Maliyah to ease up off me now. She said we cool, but her loyalty lies with you, so we ain't that cool. Something wrong with her." Sky laughed.

"That's my baby, and I sure will." I let her know.

Just like that, a family was born, and I was happy that I didn't have to worry about going through hell to get our kids to know each other. I was also glad that I didn't have to go through Kyrie to do so.

yrie

"Zailah, or Sky, ain't tell you how Zai fucked Tierra up. I'm talking bout she had to get three stitches in the back of her head and her shit closed." Bentley laughed.

"She what? Fuck she do that for I know Tierra had to do some shit cause I always would ask Zailah to fuck her up and she wouldn't." I doubted she had fucked her up.

"Sky and Tierra are cousins and Tee set that shit up that night when y'all met. I told her what club we were going to that night because she kept questioning me. On top of that, she the reason my pops got killed. She told them, niggas, what I would be doing, but she ain't know where I would switch the cars at so they thought they had me." Bentley said, hopping on top of his car.

"Damn, so what you gonna do about her?" I wondered.

"Real shit, I want to kill the bitch, but I love her. It puts me in a fucked up place because even though she put niggas on to me.

The love I got for her won't let me kill the bitch. I was thinking about making her leave Philly. Like go get a new start somewhere, change her life around. However, if she came back and stay longer, then I think is enough time to visit her people, Ima off her." Bentley voiced.

"Sounds like that could work. You just gotta make sure she understands you're serious. Let's pull up on her, and you gotta go in there with that crazy shit you be on. Snatch her up, shit smack her around a few times, pull ya gun on her make her real scared. I'll go with you so I can act like I'm talking sense into you, so it's real believable that you bout to kill her. That will make her want to leave. If not, I'll take the bitch out for you. I'll even have Maine come busting through the house like he ready to kill her too." I announced.

"Bet it. Yo, am I tripping, or is that car coming slow as shit." Bentley questioned.

I turned my head and saw the blue car cruising. It wasn't going at a fast pace like most cars that flew through the block. However, it wasn't going extremely slow, either.

"Come up off that car. We gone play it cool like we still talking and don't see it. We bout to walk to the house just so we got a better chance of being covered. Once we get to the house, go on the other side, and by then, if them niggas gone shoot, we gone be ready to bust back." I got out as quickly as I could.

Bentley hopped down, and I turned to walk, at that point we both had our guns in our hands but tucked to our side. I heard the car pick up, and shots rang out, so instead of walking, I ran to the side of the house. Turning around, I began to bust my gun back.

Wasn't no way in hell I was gone, not shoot back. Bentley was squeezing his trigger and ducked off on the side of the steps his ass ain't even make it to the side of the house. Windows were shattered, and I could hear the bullets hitting the walls. My heart was racing.

Click Click

"Fuckkk, bro. I ain't got shit left in either of my clips." Bentley yelled over the crossfire.

"Just get low and get covered." I hollered back.

I wasn't them one of niggas read about in books or seen on movies, so I wasn't about to run out there guns blazing. I was a real nigga, and I stayed my ass on the side of the house. Just like Bentley, both my guns were empty. I quickly switched clips just In case I needed it if someone thought they would just run down on me. Seconds after we stopped shooting back, the car peeled off.

"Yo, I was just scared as shit. That was Saps people's that car was his." Bentley stated.

"Man, I don't give a fuck who car that was all them niggas got to go. I ain't sparing a nigga on that team." I replied.

I was heated, a nigga ain't shoot at me in years so for someone to ever feel like they could disrespect me on my shit was gone have to see me. Jumping in my car I peeled off. It was time for me to get into rare form.

"Bent, call a meeting." I told him tossing him my business phone.

"For when?" He asked.

"Right now, send it to every contact. I want everybody there so tell em meet us at the warehouse." I seethed.

Whoever wasn't going to agree with what I said today was getting smoked. It wasn't nothing else to be said or done. I was letting nobody walk away or anything.

"It's done." He said.

I headed to the warehouse, and Maine came through seconds later.

"What the fuck is going on, and why I hear bout some fucking shooting on Alden?" Maine asked.

"Shit just happened. That's why I called this fucking meeting. All of them niggas in Sap's squad got to go. The only way you not is if you ain't participate in any of the activities that took place." Grabbing a water out of the mini-fridge I took a sip.

While we are waiting for everyone to come inside, I smoked and loaded the guns I decided to use. Maine sat a few knives on the table as well. I decided to cut the hands off any person who felt the need to shoot at me. After an hour or so, people began to pour in. I was pleased to see that each crew had made it.

"Welcome, now I know this meeting was called on short notice, so thank you to everyone who showed up. I'm gone give y'all a few minutes to get seated and for a few more people to show up. Just like a job once fifteen minutes pass, I'm locking us in." Maine began.

"Look, fifteen minutes is up, lock the doors," I called.

After I heard the locks click, I began my speech.

"I just called the meeting, so it ain't no speech written down or no shit like that. Basically, I ain't been having no problems, no shorts from anybody or anything like that. I have recently encountered a problem between my west crew and my uptown crew. Which are both here, I would have thought y'all was smart enough to not come at me. Seeing as though I cut y'all checks. Any nigga that ever went to war with me ain't here to tell the story. I don't do disrespect. With that being said, if you a part of Sap's crew, step up." I said.

About ten people stepped up, and I looked at them all. I remembered a few faces and some I didn't. I was prepared to kill all of them if need be.

"Aye look, I'm no bitch, and if I had to go at you, I would. My little brother, cousin, and I ain't got shit to do with that. We have been playing the blocks, and that's it." One of the boys spoke up.

"What makes you think I believe that?" I questioned.

"Ask ya man, Maine. I talked to him about this shit already. Told him I ain't want no parts. That's why he let us continue to make our money." He said matter of factly.

I looked over ain't Maine, and he gave me a head nod letting me know what the boy said was true.

"Cool. You and your people can have a seat. Oh, and all the uptown blocks that Sap ran is y'all a now if you want it. Don't fuck it up or my money." I warned.

"Bet," he said, he and two other boys went and had a seat in the back.

"Now there's seven. Which of you took place in that little shoot out today and don't bitch up now cause then I'll just kill all y'all." I shrugged, taking a pull from my weed.

"That was them. We knew about it, but we ain't going, shit y'all came and shot up our spot, making it hot and causing us to lose out on some money." One of the guys pointed out.

I looked at the four he pointed and smirked. I motioned for them to stand on the other side and allowed Maine to send a shot into all the others' heads silencing them forever.

"I feel like I should handle y'all four personally because y'all swore y'all was about to kill me. So each of you can take a seat." I smiled.

Two of them sat down, but you know it always had to be a tough guy.

"Fuck that if y'all niggas gone kill us, kill us now. We ain't bout to answer no questions or none of that. All you gone get from me is yeah we did that shit y'all killed ours, so we was gone take y'all." The smaller one spat.

Smacking him over the head with my gun, I made him fall into the chair the other one went to run up, but Bentley aimed his gun as his head.

"I wouldn't do that if I was you," Bentley told him.

Throwing his hands up, he sat down. I tied them each to the chair. I took my knife and went through them one by one, slicing their fingers off. They screamed in pain, some begging me to just kill them, and eventually, I would. Taking my ax, I slammed it down on one of their heads causing half of his head to land on the person next to him lap.

"Ohh, what the fuck." A person yelled.

Moving to the next one, I riddled his body with bullets from my gun until I left him slouched over. Two down two to go. The next person I grabbed my torch for and placed the fire on his lips. This was the one with all the mouth. I then grabbed his fingerless hand and placed the torch on his nubs. His ass was screaming and squirming. When I felt like I had enough, I sent a shot into the last two heads.

"This is what happens when you cross me or fuck up anything that belongs to me. I hope we don't have to meet like this again. Meeting over if you need anything see Maine. Come on, Bent." I said like nothing happened.

We had a clean-up crew already waiting, so I didn't need to call one. Our clean-up crew was also trained killers who are dismissed from the military and couldn't find jobs. So I wasn't worried about anybody trying Maine while he was by himself. Maine already knew where to come once he was finished at the warehouse. So I didn't need to tell him.

Getting in the car, we drove across town to Tierra's small apartment. The lights were all on, and you could hear her singing from outside. Bentley used his key to open the door. She was in the middle of the living room in a T-shirt cleaning.

"Hey, baby." She greeted Bent.

"You in here singing like shit all good. You really gonna do me like that. Then have the nerve to be excited to see me like you wasn't trying to get a nigga killed. I should fucking kill you, bitch." Bentley barked.

"You always talking that kill me shit. Relax ain't nobody doing none of that you talkin bout." She laughed nervously.

"Now just think I'm a joke. You think I'm playing bitch," Bentley screamed in one swift motion he pulled his gun from his hip and cocked it.

"Come on Bent, let her live." I acted as if I was stopping him.

"Nah, bro, she got me messed up. I will really kill you here, man. I loved your no good ass. You fucked up." Bentley began to cry.

I wasn't sure if that part was acting or real, but it looked real to me. Which was why I was glad Maine had told me he just pulled up.

"Where the bitch at I know Bent wasn't gone kill her. But I sure the fuck will." Maine said, coming through the door.

I looked at the door and almost laughed. I told the nigga to bust through the door, which was why I had left it unlocked, not kick the shit in.

"Oh my god. Okay, I'm sorry, Bentley. Please don't let his crazy ass kill me with that big ass gun. What do you want me to do, I'll do whatever you want." Tierra cried with piss running down her leg.

"Leave town. You have a few days to say your final goodbyes and don't come back or we will kill you. If you do come back contact me first and you can't stay longer than two days. I'll have someone watching you when you come and up until you leave. Don't make me regret this." Bentley spoke.

"Okay." She sighed a breath of relief.

"Come on, you gone come with that big ass gun." I laughed at Maine.

"Hell yeah, I should've shot the bitch in the ass." Maine joked as we left out.

Now that business was handled, I was ready to go home to my wife, however, I knew that wasn't an option, so I took my lonely ass to my baby mother's couch.

CHAPTER 36

 ailah

WALKING into Love To Learn Day Care, had me super excited. I was back at the place I had always wanted since I could remember. How I got convinced to step back and let someone else run my business for me was something I would never understand. In my head, I was making time for my family, especially since I had a baby on the way, and Kyrie hadn't been playing the block for years.

I loved the flow of the money; however, it seemed as if I had no job, and even though my husband's money started this I built it by myself. Everybody that was anybody sent their kids to me. I did after-care and even helped moms who worked overnight. This place was my baby and I would never leave it again.

"Dang, look who finally blessed us with their presence. I forgot you even owned the place. You just neglected us." Miss Pat my favorite worker said.

"You better leave me alone. I had things to deal with and I knew you would handle this for me." I replied honestly.

"That doesn't mean anything Zailah, this is your place. Nobody not gonna run it like you, and no man should have ever been allowed to stop you from even checking in. It's been two years since you stepped in this place. I loved the pay that I was receiving and would do it again for you if I had too. However, I'm forty-three years old, and I spend every day here like I built this place. I don't have any time for my family because it's all here. That's not fair to me, you let that man not only make you step back from your place but completely forget about it. You need to get your shit together." Miss Pat stressed.

"I apologize, Miss Pat. I will be here every day but one day out of the week, which I will take off for family. Now that I have one, I understand how important it is. I would like to give you a two week paid vacation. Yes, I allowed him to take me into stepping back but as for not coming in at all that was all on me. I've been going through a whole lot in my marriage to the point I'm ready for a divorce." I confessed with my head down.

Miss Pat had me feeling like shit, and I should. I was working her entirely too much, and that wasn't fair on my behalf. I hadn't even thought about how much stress it could have been on her dealing with everything.

"Everything will be fine honey, when God has a plan for you then it's what he has. Now let me see this little baby you've been keeping me away from. Oh and a lady by the name of Skylar stopped by and filled out paperwork. She said to give it directly to you." She said, handing me Truth's application.

"Yeah, that's Truth's mom." I smiled.

"Truth? Truth who?" She asked.

"Kyrie has a son a few weeks older then Honesty. At first, I wasn't sure about the baby, but now I'm completely sure that I'll be the best bonus mom ever. He is so handsome." I beamed.

"Oh, okay. That's something we will discuss whenever you're

ready. Tell that damn Kyrie Mama Pat is looking for his ass. He needs to be smacked upside the head." She warned.

"Heard you. Now is there anything new? Any people I should be concerned about. How are the teachers and assistants are they doing what we hired them to do?" I questioned.

"Yes, for the most part. I did just hire a new girl Nina. She's wonderful with the kids. Her son attends, as well. However, Naomi doesn't like her too much because she came in and did her job. I told them to stay away from each other and remember this is no place for any kind of violence. There are a few bad kids I don't have to name them. You'll see for yourself as they come in. When the mothers come in, you can see exactly why them kids need their ass whooped too." She laughed.

"Okay. I know who Nina is I told her to come apply, and Naomi will get over it especially now that I'm back." Honesty woke up so I picked her up and handed her over to Miss Pat.

"She so small and adorable. I cannot wait until my vacation is over. I'm just gonna love all over this little one. Ma Ma Pat gone have you spoiled." She told Honesty.

All the kids in the daycare called her Ma Ma Pat. Shit even I did sometimes. Miss Pat was special, and I was glad she decided to work for me. I had known her since I was younger. She used to babysit Maliyah and was known around the hood. Miss Pat was someone everyone respected and loved. She was as real as they come. She came off mean, but had a heart of gold. On top of that, she never bite her tongue. She let you know how she felt or what she thought and didn't care not one bit if you liked it.

"Good morning MaMa Pat, morning sis, glad to finally meet the owner." Nina jokes.

"Don't get fired on my first day back, bitch." I laughed.

"Language ladies." Miss Pat said, pointing at Honesty.

"Sorry, how you like it here?" I went on.

"Love it, my kids are so sweet. Well, minus two of them overall, it's amazing. MaMa Pat is doing great with this place. I can't wait to see what you have planned. There's this little pumpkin place I want to take the kids too in October, and I want to do some pumpkin paintings and those things as a reward for all their good work in October." Nina happily stated.

"I was looking into trips for October, so yeah, we can do that. I'll also be printing out the work and homework for your class as well as Naomi class. I'm also thinking of maybe a back to school cookout. We can give back and just have a fun day for the kids. So Maliyah will be in these next few weeks for planning." I explained.

"Cool, I have to get to my class. Could you get that work for me fast? We are working on the letter F, today, and the number five." Nina let me know as she bent down to tickle Honesty then made her way out the door.

I looked after her before drifting off into my own thoughts. I hope I was a better parent than my parents. Then again, how could I be a great provider and teach her about work if I wasn't even consistent with my business? I wanted Honesty to grow and be the best she could be at whatever she decided to be. I would let her make her own decisions because my parents not letting me make my own is what caused a rift in us.

"You're going to be an amazing mom and business owner. You just have to be committed and speak it into existence. Pray baby, God can't give you what you not asking him for." Miss Pat shared.

I nodded my head in agreement. While she played and talked to Honesty, I printed out the work Nina needed. Naomi has come and gone so I decided to give her the same work I made for Nina class.

I walked around the school, checking in on each class and letting everyone know I was back for good. I loved how they kept everything clean, and each class still followed the rules I had created. The kids were to come in each morning to have breakfast and then brush their teeth. Afterward, they would do the Math and focus on numbers. Once they completed that, they did music and worked on letters. We had lunch and went out to play, then once we came back, it was bathroom then Storytime. I had everybody lay on their cots and take a nap until their parents came.

When I was done with the older kids, I went and checked on all the babies. I was surprised to see that each baby was attended too. Some were asleep in the cribs, and others were either having tummy time or on the potty. I was falling in love with the place all over again and made a vow to keep this thing running so it could be passed down to Honesty. I made it back to my office to see that Kyrie was there being cursed out by Ma Ma Pat.

"Hey, I came to get Honesty. I'm about to take her and Truth shopping." He said.

"Okay, let me go pump right fast, so she has milk and be careful," I told him.

Sitting down, I grabbed my breast pump and filled two bottles and a half. I placed the caps on them and put them inside her little bag with her ice pack from out of my small fridge.

"Stop looking at me," I told Kyrie.

He laughed and took the bag from me. I kissed Honesty and allowed him to take her. Once I was alone in my office, I locked the door and got down on my knees.

"God, if you hear me, then I'm coming to you with everything I have on my shoulders. I know I barely pray. Most of the time, I don't pray at all, but I'm asking you to forgive me for that. God, if you listening, please help me. I'm coming to you in a time of need as well as to thank you. I want to first thank you for my baby and Truth too. I thank you for blessing them and me as well. Thank you for allowing my business to continue to run smoothly, and thank you for everyone around being in good health. I asked that you protect my family, my loved ones, and myself. Help me get through this time in my marriage,, and if divorce is what I need, then allow me to get through that process without any trouble. I ask that you protect Kyrie and Bentley keep them safe. Allow me to be the best me, that I can be and not the best someone wants me to be. I know you got something good in store for me;, it's just not my time yet. God,, please let me be the mom I know I can be. I'm honestly scared and need all the help I can get. Allow me to be a better mom than the one I had. Allow me to be patient and understanding with her. Allow me to be able to forgive Kyrie, God please take the pain from my heart and the hurt from my body. God, please help me. Thank you, amen." By the time I was finished, I was in tears. Why I was crying, I didn't know, but I felt like God heard me. I would do my part to be everything I wanted and allow him to handle what I couldn't.

CHAPTER 37

 yrie

NOW THAT ALL THE drama was over with work, I needed to focus on fixing home. Each passing day I found myself in my feelings more and more. I was grateful that Sky and Zailah were able to start building an amazing relationship. However, I wanted Zailah to fix things with me.

I was glad she was back at work, and seeing her happy was something I didn't want to interrupt. I almost felt bad; I asked her to stay at home and be a wife instead of allowing her to do what she loved. That was one of the arguments that caused a drift between us.

"You my wife now and we just found out you gone have my baby. I'm not hugging the blocks no more, and we both financially set, fuck you need to be there every day for? I want you home taking care of my child and the house." I tried to convince her to be a stay at home mom.

"No. You want me to become my mother? Stay at home doing nothing while you run the streets doing whatever. You heard what the

235

doctor said unless I have a high-risk pregnancy, I'm cleared to work until further notice. I want to work, I don't want to stay at home. I've always made my own money and worked since you met me, why do I have to stop now?" She challenged.

"Because that's what a wife does. That's how it was done back in the day. I refuse to have you working while you carrying my baby. Then after you have him or her, what you gone get a nanny and allow someone else to be with our child every day while you work?" I questioned.

"I own a damn daycare so why wouldn't my child be with me. You sound stupid as hell. How bout I take more days off." Zailah tried to compromise.

"No, I want what I want. I make sure you have everything it's not like you missing out on no money. At least try it, and then once the baby is one, if you don't like it, you go back." I said with hope.

"Okay." She forced a smile.

I could tell that was not something she really wanted, but I was content with knowing she would give it a try.

That was the first time she was pregnant, she lost the baby a few weeks after that and just didn't go back because she was depressed. It took us a lot of work and therapy sessions to get her to where she was now, and before we knew it, she was pregnant with Honesty.

At that time, before she got pregnant, she blamed everything on me as if I didn't already blame myself. It hurt me worse, hearing exactly what I thought from someone else. Often times, I wanted to remind her of why I stepped out. If I could go back to that day and change it now that I think back on it, I wouldn't. Imagine how I felt when she decided to dog me out in front of some out of town niggas who was trying to fuck her. Of course I was mad that she was all in their faces but when she shouted everything was my fault, it killed me and my only thought was to get even.

I never brought up how she made me feel because I would

have to bring up the baby we lost, and that was a sore spot for her still. I wasn't very considerate of her feelings, but for the most part, I protected them.

Grabbing the bottle of my new found love D'usse, I took a swig of it. The drink seemed to put me out of my feelings and have me ready to go and find a nasty hoe. Since Zailah wouldn't even touch me or talk to me unless it was about Honesty, I found myself not able to fuck anyone else. Just In case she decided to forgive me.

The more I thought about it, the more I figured that's why she was hurt because had she not been so stressed out about me, she would have given birth to my first child.

"Yo, I collected about three hundred thousand today. On some real shit you gone need to pull your shit together." Nina tossed the paper bag on my lap.

Yeah, I had her working for me, she made great money with my wife, but she felt like it wasn't enough. At least that's what she told Maine. He was the one to actually put her on. I was more of the laid back one. When Zailah told me she wanted me out, I completely stepped back and let Maine do everything. I just saw over it and still collected the money.

"Bet, did you go by Maine first and allow him to give you your cut and take his?" I asked.

"Yeah, that's yours. I'm about to go by Zailah, we bout to go out." She smirked.

"Man gone, head." I shrugged.

She laughed and strutted off. I continued to drink until my face felt numb. Pulling out my phone, the shit looked blurry. Wiping my hand over my face, I took a swig from my water bottle and tracked Zailah's location. I drove to her location and got out of the car.

Walking into the small dinner, I saw her sitting with Nina, Sky, and Maliyah talking and laughing. Her smile was beautiful, and my kids were with them.

"Let me holla at you right fast," I said to her.

She looked around and then let her eyes stop on Sky as if that's who I was talking to.

"Zailah. I'm talking to you man," I said, twisting my wedding band on my finger. Yeah, I still wore it.

"No, thank you." She stated simply.

"Don't make me snatch you the fuck up. My kids right here, so I'm not trying to trip in front of them, but you gone talk to me. And why y'all got them out like it ain't seven something. It's almost too late to have them outside." I snapped.

"We're having dinner, and I can see your drunk. I'll talk to you another time, but right now, I won't." She said.

"Fuck, you mean," I questioned.

Maliyah was holding Honesty, and Sky was sitting next to her with Truth in his car seat that was facing the table. Zailah dug her fork into her food, ignoring me. She was seated at the end of the table, so I knocked her food off the table, causing it to spill all over her and the floor.

"Now you done eating let's go talk." Snatching her up, I pulled her towards the door.

"You are acting crazy right now." Sky chimes in.

"Mind your fucking business and make sure my son don't fall out that car seat. Maliyah keep an eye on Honesty." I said in one breath.

Pulling Zailah out the door and into the parking lot, I pushed her against the wall. I looked at her for a second, and she had a frown attached to her face.

"You gone have to talk to me. I love you, and I want you bad. I miss you, I miss my pussy and all." I growled.

"You may love me and miss me, but that's not gonna change nothing. I love you and always will, but I've been thinking, and I think it's time we let each other go. I want a divorce for real this time. I already have the papers." She hesitated to say.

"You went and did what? I'm not divorcing you. You gone

put all this shit on me? You don't know what the fuck I go through man. So just fuck me. So you ready to die right" I yelled.

Wrapping my hands around her throat, I squeezed tightly. She didn't even fight me back; she just allowed me to choke her. Letting her go, I pulled my gun from my waist. Cocking it, I placed it to my head.

"I ain't bout to watch you love someone else." I cried.

"Please stop, you have kids to look up to you. Kyrie, you are not perfect for me, but you are perfect for them. You love them remember they need you." She knocked my hand down.

I allowed her to grab the gun from my hand and place it on her waist. I fell down to my knees and cried she didn't want me anymore, and I could feel it. I grabbed on to her waist and begged her to stay with me. Instead of answering me, she just looked at me and allowed me to cry in her stomach.

I whispered over and over again, how sorry I was and for her to at least allow me in her life even if it was just as a friend. I knew me, and I knew I would try and get back with her or have sex with her. However, I would wait until we got better.

CHAPTER 38

 ailah

"I JUST WANTED to stop by to apologize. I now know everything I did was wrong, and I could have handled things better. I will not be in your life anymore, nor will you ever see me again. I'll be leaving Philly and starting life over in Canada. I hope that you can forgive me for my actions." she offered a small smile with her apology.

Looking at Tierra inside my job offering an apology was something I couldn't imagine in a million years doing, but she was here, and I wasn't pleased. I heard her apology loud and clear and was willing to accept it, but I was cool off of any friendship with her ever again.

"I accept your apology and wish you well in life," I admitted.

At one point in time, Tierra was my best friend, and we did a lot with each other. We fought together, laughed together, cried, and even did stakeouts on our boyfriends. Which is why I found it hard to believe she would cause me pain.

"I was wondering if we could just sit down and talk about all the times we shared one last time. The wild and crazy things we did will be a memory I always hold on to." She asked.

"Yeah, of course. Member that time when you were messing with that boy, and we had to fight his girlfriend and her old ass mom." I laughed, thinking back to the day.

I was sitting on the couch, waiting for Tierra to come back down the steps. I knew I should have just taken my ass to school, but I decided to cut so this bitch could get some. Charles has an ugly ass friend over by the name of Brick, and he looked just like he was smacked in the face with one. His front tooth was missing, and his breath smelled like he had a really bad tooth in his mouth.

Him being in my face had me questioning myself. As if I looked like the type of person to fuck with him. I kept popping Trident gum in my mouth hoping he would ask for a piece.

"Baby girl, you just gone sit all the way over there." He asked me.

"This is the only place to sit, and your breath smells really bad. Would you like a piece of gum, or would you rather us set you up and appointment to the dentist? I'm pretty sure that smell coming from a bad tooth." I replied.

"Fuck you, bitch, my breath don't stink." He spat.

I was dipping and moving around, hoping a piece of that spit flying from his mouth didn't land on me. How could he be so upset at me for telling him his shit was humming. He lit up a cigarette, and I knew that, and having bad hygiene was the cause of that shit smell flowing from his mouth.

"You need to bounce, you ain't come to fuck, so ain't no need for you to be here. Ole stuck up ass bird ass bitch." He shot.

"Whatever you say. Just please close your mouth. And I'm not leaving until my friend finished." I shrugged.

Just as I finished my sentenced, the door came open, and two females walked in. One being young and the other being old.

"Who the fuck is this, Brick?" The older of the two asked.

Brick looked like a deer caught in headlights, and in that moment,

I knew some shit was about to go down. Sliding my blackberry phone into my bag, I prepared for a fight mentally, but on the outside, I remained calm.

"Where the fuck is Charles ass?" The younger girl questioned.

Why she asks that Charles' ass must have been laying mad dick on my friend because her ass got to screaming and the girls took off, so I followed behind them.

"You gone fuck this bitch in my momma house." The girl asked, busting in the door.

Tierra's ass was in the air, and the room reeked of sex. Plus it was hot as hell in there, they should have turned the air on.

"Sheen, what the hell are you doing home?" He questioned as if he didn't still have his dick in Tierra.

Tierra jumped up and went to grab her clothes, but the girl snatched her ass forward and started hitting her. Tierra gained her footing and pushed the girl back, causing her to fall into the bed. I'm sure she landed right in Tierra juices. At that point, Tierra had the upper hand and began to rain punches on the girl who held onto Tierra's hair.

"Oh, no bitch, get off my daughter." The mom pulled her taser out of her bra.

Before she had a chance to use it, I punched her in the back of the head causing her to drop it. She spun around and grabbed hold of my hair. I latched on to hers as well with one hand and began to swing with my other hand. Somehow the mother ended up on the floor begging Charles to get me off of her.

Charles and shit mouth pulled us off of them. They stayed out while Tierra got her clothes on and we left out the house laughing.

"You was really in there but ass naked fucking that girl up. Had I not come, her mom would have tased the shit out of you." I laughed.

"How bout that time when you had us out all fucking night because Kyrie ass ain't come home. No member that time the

girl got smart with Bentley, and we had that big ass free for all."
She pointed out.

"Hell yeah. That fight was crazy." I replied.

"Zailah, them bitches up the street outside." Bentley called up the steps to me.

Jumping up off my bed from doing my homework, I flew down the steps.

"What bitches? Fuck that come on Zailah, we gone go out there together. It's only you, and I be damn if the gone jump my baby." My mom slung the door open.

It was about six or seven girls and a bunch of niggas with them all outside yelling in the middle of the street. I could see Tierra and Maliyah running up the street.

"What the fuck y'all in front of my door for?" My momma called.

"Tell Bentley to come out now my brothers here." A dark skin girl yelled out.

"What he want to rumble? Bent, go fuck him up. And if anyone of you bitches touch my son it's on." My mom threatened.

As always I was the quiet one. However when my brother stepped off the porch I went with him. Bentley and a heavy set boy stepped in the middle of Everyone and squared up. Heavy set through the first punch and Bentley dipped it. Bentley swung a left hand and connected to the boy jaw. The guy rushed into Bentley and grabbed a hold of him.

"Get the fuck off my brother." I yelled my defensive side kicked in and I swung punching the boy in his face.

"Bitch." I heard and was punched in the face by probably the sister.

I swung back on her, and we began to go at it. We ended up on the ground with someone holding on to my hair from behind.

"Fuck that." My mom yelled, and I felt whoever had my hair come up off me.

I quickly stood up and kicked the girl in her face. When I looked around, Maliyah and Tierra were fighting, and so was my mom. Out of nowhere, Kyrie and Maine pulled up. Kyrie slapped the shit out of one of the boys. Maine had punched another one, and we went right to sleep. Kyrie snatched his gun from his waist, causing then everyone to begin to scatter like roaches.

" Nah. Don't fucking run. Who bought this shit to my chick crib, huh? Who was that fucking stupid." Kyrie yelled, chasing them down.

"Go get that damn man so he can calm down." Maine laughed.

Jogging, I made my way to Kyrie and told him I was okay. He looked at me, scanning my entire body causally turning my head to check for any marks before he kissed me.

"I'm glad you cool, next time call me before you go out there. We would have beat the hoe ass together on everything." He smiled.

"That shit was cool. Your parties were always the best. I'm not gonna lie, I'm gone miss your shit-talking ass, but you really hurt me. I know that you hurt Bentley even more though. How he feel about you leaving?" I wondered.

"He's actually the reason I'm leaving. He told me if I didn't, he would kill me. I believe him, they even had Maine's crazy-ass kick my door in with this big ass gun I never seen before. I'm scared for my life staying here they have someone watching my every move. Anywhere I go, there is someone following me. I swear they even took my phone so I have no way of contacting anybody. And I refuse to go get another one because once I leave here, I'm leaving everyone and everything behind me." She said as tears began to spill from her eyes.

"It'll all be okay, just pray and have a safe flight. I would love to get to chat some more, but my boobs are leaking, so I need to go get Honesty and feed her," I told her.

Tierra stood up and pulled me into a hug she cried on my shoulder for a second then pulled away.

"I love you, don't you ever forget that. You'll always be my best friend even though I wasn't the best friend to you." She smiled softly, then made her exit.

Making my way to get Honesty so that I could feed her, I checked on Truth, who was in a crib sleep. Picking up Honesty, I walked to the rocking chair and placed my boob in her mouth.

I was happy that I got to see Tierra before she left and happy that that chapter in both of our lives was closed. I genuinely hoped she made it to her destination and did well. I knew she had a lot of money saved from her grandmom's passing when we were younger as well as money from niggas and Bentley.

I felt like God had somewhat heard my prayers and was starting to allow me to have some pieces in my life. I watched Honesty eat, and she looked at me with a big toothless smile before latching back on to me.

"You wanna play stinky momma?" I asked.

She smiled again and kicked her feet as if she understood me. My baby had some pretty brown eyes. They were the exact same eyes my father passed down to Bentley and I. Looking into them, I wished for the thousandth time that he had gotten a chance to meet her. I knew that he had to be with her because she always smiled really big while she was asleep. My mother always said when babies smiled in their sleep, they were playing with Angels, so my dad had to be with her. A chill flew through my body and I felt like that was a sign that he was indeed with her.

"I hope you forgive me daddy," I whispered.

I was asking for forgiveness for being a disobedient child and for not making more of an effort to fix things while I had the chance. He was the reason I made amends with everybody even if we were on bad terms because I never knew when it would be mines or their time to go. Which meant I needed to work harder on at least allowing Honesty to have a relationship with my mother.

CHAPTER 39

K yrie

"KYRIE, get up off my couch. You not gone come here every night in the middle of the night, fucked up." Sky yelled.

"Chill." I groaned; my head was hurting badly.

"No, you come in here crying about Zailah, and I get what you going through. Shit, I like her ass too, but you fucked up. You can't be mad or upset with nobody but yourself. You did that." Sky reminded me.

" I know what I did, and I tried to fix it. How she gone throw all these years away. A whole fucking marriage. I ain't ever gonna love another bitch again." I whined.

"You are acting like a bitch. Got my living room smelling like a fucking bar." She frowned her face at me.

"My bad man, this is the only place I know I can sleep, and nobody knows where to find me besides my house. And I can't go there. Plus I ain't gonna lie I don't wanna be alone." I admitted.

"Well, you gone have to find something out because this ain't it. You come here for your son, and that's it. Eventually, my man gonna want to start coming over, and that can't happen if your ass passed out on my couch. I ain't gone feel right bouncing on dick while you here." She laughed.

"Come on, nobody wants to hear that. Just make sure if you have a nigga up in here with my son, he the right one for you. I don't need you just having any muthafucka up here." I told her.

Who was I to say she couldn't fuck with somebody or bring him around my son. I trusted her judgment and knew she wouldn't place my son in harm's way. If it were up to me, she would find the perfect man to love her because she deserved it. Her couch was comfortable as hell, but I guess I had to start staying home so she could have her privacy.

"Thank you for making that easy. Try talking to Zailah, maybe a break is what you two really need. And not a few weeks and still fucking break. One that lets you go out in the world get to know new people and experience different shit. She may need to see if you are really it for her. If so, y'all will end up back together, and if not, that just means it wasn't meant to be. It also doesn't mean to give up on love." Sky said.

"You right." I nodded.

Even though I agreed with her, that didn't mean that's what I wanted to do. I had to really put my mind to letting her go. I wouldn't allow myself to keep sitting outside in front of the house just watching. I would even fall asleep in the car and then knock on the door in the morning like I just pulled up.

Getting up off the couch, I took me a shower and played with my son until it was time for him to go to daycare. Sky had a rule that when she left, I had to leave too. So I made my way to the block to check on Bentley.

"Aye, Maurice, come here," I called my neighborhood watch.

"What's up!" He asked.

"What's been going on 'round here, any news for me?"

"Nah. Ain't shit, things been quiet. It's been hot around here though they said it's been too many shootings, so they been out." He responded.

"That's what's up. Have you seen my wife around?" I was looking at him, ready for him to answer.

"No, only see her when I walk past they daycare. I seen the nigga she was talking to that night I told you about with another bitch looking all happy. Bentley's chick been by here too. I heard she's moving." He answered.

"Oh, word that's good for her and him." I acted like I didn't know about Tierra'.

"Good looking." I dismissed him.

I pulled my hood on my head and kicked my feet up on the porch. I lit my weed and began to smoke it. I had everything in order, and I was almost content with it. For some reason, Zailah kept popping up in my mind, and I just wanted to make sure she was okay. So I sent her a text telling her I wanted to talk and not on no angry shit.

I was almost scared to look at my phone because she had finally replied to me and it was a fast reply. She said okay and that was it. I left the message open and just stared at it. I couldn't think of anything I wanted to say to her, but I would get it together by the time I saw her.

"Yo, what you doing out here, it's been a while since I saw you." One of the local crackheads said.

"Lester, my guy, what's up. What you selling today?" Standing up, I looked down at all the stuff he was carrying.

"I got soap and laundry detergent for the low. I'll give you all this shit for forty dollars." He smiled his grill was fucked up.

"Aight, let me get it all," I told him, peeling a crisp fifty-dollar bill of my wad of cash.

"Thank you." He handed me the stuff and took off running.

I know his ass was about to go get his next fix, and even though I didn't keep none of the stuff I bought for him, I would go down and give it to the homeless shelter or a homeless person I saw with a few extra dollars to go wash their clothes. Sitting back down, I smoked the rest of my weed while deep in my thoughts. I had to figure some shit out and fast so that I kept everyone around me and even myself happy. We all deserve that, and if it were up to me, we would all have it.

CHAPTER 40

ailah

"YOU JUST KEEP TRYING to come back in my life. I keep telling you I don't need you. I'm better off by myself. Honesty cool, she gone always be straight. All I want you to do is to do right by her. That's all that matters Kyrie. You don't want to give me the divorce fine. Have it your way, the only title you gone have that I agree on is that I'm your child's mother." I yelled at Kyrie.

For some reason he was not understanding that I didn't want to be with him anymore and that our love had run its course.

"I'm the fucking KING OF PHILLY. Any bitch would be happy to have the title of being my wife." He snapped.

"Any bitch but me, so can you go give it to another bitch. I'm tired of your shit, I dealt with you for the last fucking sixteen years of my life, and I don't want you no more. Fuck you and who you think you are. I know the real you and you maybe the king of the streets but that's all. And don't forget I helped you get that title. I put that work in to, yet I would rather you keep all that shit and just give me my sanity." I pleaded.

Yes he was the King of Philly I wouldn't deny him of that. Yet, being married to him wasn't all that it was caped up to be. I would rather a regular nigga from Philly then him. At some point I was dumb for him, I fell for everything he told me. I looked pass the signs that told me to leave and kept the mentality of I helped him build what he has and I didn't want nobody else to reap the benefits.

Now that I had a child, I didn't want her to grow up watching her mother settle for anything and thinking she had to do the same or that, that's what life was about. What I wanted for her was to have the best in life and if she had to see me with a man. He would treat me how a wife or significant other should have been treated. I also didn't want her to grow up having to split holidays and everything else in half. However, if that was what we had to do to make co-parenting easy for one another we would.

I gave half my life to a man I thought would be mine forever and would always give me as much love as I gave him. Yet what I realized was that I have and was willing to give up everything that kept me grounded to make things work with a man who couldn't even remain faithful enough to not bring home babies and even after that fateful enough to keep our marriage together. I would have probably forgiven him, yet, his hands became a big problem in our lives, and whooping my ass for things that weren't true was unforgivable. We fought all the time, but when it turned into me not fighting back and fearing for my life, especially him doing it in front of Demi was a different story.

"I'm gone go." He stood up and kissed Demi's forehead.

"So now, you don't want to spend time with your daughter because I don't want to be with you? Kyrie, if this is how things are going to be, let me know now. I would rather raise her alone then you to be inconsistent in her life over problems that we have." I sighed.

"It's not what I want, I love my daughter. How I'm supposed to look at her though? She looks exactly like the very woman I failed. She looks just like you, I fucked up, and I fucked up her life. What was supposed to be so perfect. I'd give up anything to just right my wrongs. Now it's too late, you don't even look at me the same, so if you feel like us separating is best for you, I'll give you that. I love you enough too want to see you happy." He cried.

It was fucked up because his tears didn't mean nothing to me this time. I feel for his shit over and over and had he had this change of hearts before he started putting his hands on me, or even when I found out about the baby then maybe just maybe things would have been different. As of now I was regretting every part of being married to a street king. Because of him, my daughter would never get the chance to meet her grandmother, and I would never get to settle things with my father.

My mother felt like it was my fault that her husband was gone when, in all actuality, it had nothing to do with me. I had to live with the results of him and my brother being in the streets and the people they choose to deal with. I know that with marriage, it was for better or for worse. However, or worse wasn't fixable, and we couldn't come back from this. I had done everything I could to change him and I couldn't. I had to teach myself it was okay to be alone. And it was okay to outgrow love. Maybe love was out there waiting for me, but right now, I don't want it or what came with it.

"I hear all that, but you caused this Kyrie, and if you want to fix things, start by making it work with your daughter that relationship y'all can build will mean the world to me. I chose you over my father, and he late died, so our bond was cut short. Don't have that with Dem. You know what hurts though, it hurts too look yourself in the mirror wondering why you're not good enough, or what you did wrong. It hurts to feel insecure about yourself when your really beautiful, and it hurts to watch the person you love create memories and give the things that should only be yours to another. It hurts to get your ass whipped for even thinking about moving on. I have been nothing but good to you, and you dogged me in every way possible." With that said, I left him standing there with his daughter.

Making my way up my steps, I let my tears fall. I refused to cry in front of him anymore. I cried not for him but for my sanity. Sitting down on my floor, I prayed that God would help me out of this situation. That God would help the man, I once loved and allow him to build an everlasting relationship with his daughter. I prayed that he sent me a man who would love us unconditionally as well as a woman who could do the same for Kyrie. However, if he didnt I would be fine with that.

In the end, when it's all said and done, maybe loving him wasn't what I needed at the moment, and that was alright. When the time came, I was pretty sure the right person would come scoop me off my feet. I had given all I could in this relationship, and it wasn't enough. There was no way in hell; I could give him more than I had to offer. I would not dim down to be the person he needed me to be when he wouldn't be the man I needed him to be. Maybe his all wasn't what I wanted, and maybe my all wasn't enough. That didn't mean I didn't love him; it just meant that our love had run its course, and it was okay for me to love myself more.

I was happy with my ending and knowing that the love I needed the most came from myself. At some point I learned that everyone's love story didnt have a happy ending, nor does it have too be bad. Sometime you're story ends right when it needs too.This was my ending and though it wasnt like most I was happy for it.

Made in the USA
Middletown, DE
24 April 2023

29053093R00154